Kathleen McGurl lives near the sea in Bournemouth, UK, with her husband and elderly tabby cat. She has two sons who are now grown-up and have left home. She began her writing career creating short stories, and sold dozens to women's magazines in the UK and Australia. Then she got sidetracked onto family history research – which led eventually to writing novels with genealogy themes. She has always been fascinated by the past, and the ways in which the past can influence the present, and enjoys exploring these links in her novels.

When not writing or working at her full-time job in IT, she likes to go out running or swimming, both of which she does rather slowly. She is definitely quicker at writing, even though the cat tries to disrupt the writing process by insisting on sharing Kathleen's lap with the laptop.

You can find out more at her website:
http://kathleenmcgurl.com/, or follow her on
Twitter: @KathMcGurl

Also available from

KATHLEEN McGURL

The Emerald Comb

The Pearl Locket

The Daughters of Red Hill Hall

The Girl *from* Ballymor

KATHLEEN MCGURL

ONE PLACE. MANY STORIES

This novel is entirely a work of fiction. The names, characters and incidents portrayed in it are the work of the author's imagination. Any resemblance to actual persons, living or dead, events or localities is entirely coincidental.

HQ
An imprint of HarperCollins *Publishers* Ltd.
1 London Bridge Street
London SE1 9GF

This edition 2017

1
First published in Great Britain by
HQ, an imprint of HarperCollinsPublishers Ltd. 2017

Kathleen McGurl asserts the moral right to be identified as the author of this work.
A catalogue record for this book is available from the British Library.

ISBN: 9781848457058

Printed and bound by
CPI Group (UK) Ltd, Croydon, CRO 4YY

Our policy is to use papers that are natural, renewable and recyclable products and made from wood grown in sustainable forests. The logging and manufacturing processes conform to the legal environmental regulations of the country of origin.

Dedication

For my sons, Fionn and Connor McGurl

CHAPTER 1

Maria, present day

There was something about Ireland that made it look and feel completely different to England as I drove through it in my hire car, on the way from Dublin airport south-west towards Ballymor. I mean, the motorways were much the same except that the road signs showed place names in Irish as well as English, and the distances were given in kilometres. And the fields and woods either side of the motorway were green and lush, as they would be back home during a rainy summer. But there was something foreign about it all that I could not quite put my finger on.

Perhaps it was to do with the way houses were dotted randomly across the landscape, whereas in England they'd all be grouped into villages, apart from the odd farmhouse. Or was it the ubiquitous whitewash of the cottages, or the colourful shopfronts and lack of chain stores in the small towns I passed through once I'd left the motorway and headed deep into County Cork.

I found myself pondering all this as I drove onwards. Anything to take my mind off the last conversation I'd had with my boyfriend Dan, just before I'd left for the airport that morning. I wanted to blot the memory of his expression of disappointment and hurt from my mind. And there was the other thing I wanted to forget all about as well, during this trip. I'd deal with it all when I went back home. This week was to be purely about me-time.

After all, it wasn't as though Dan hadn't had fair warning I would be going on this trip. I'd been talking about the possibility of doing it for ages. I'd originally suggested that he might come along as well, but he'd said no, he couldn't take that amount of time off from his job. I was disappointed at first that I'd be on my own, but after what had happened I was relieved. It'd be good to have the time and space on my own to get my head straight.

Anyway, it'd be easier to concentrate on my research into my ancestor Michael McCarthy without Dan around.

*

It was late afternoon, the weather overcast but thankfully not raining, when I finally drove into the pretty little town of Ballymor in west Cork. My online research had described it as a typical small town in the south-west of Ireland, nestled amongst bleak moorlands and craggy hills, about ten miles from the coast. I easily found O'Sullivan's pub and guest house, where I had booked a room for the next ten days. It was the nearest accommodation to Michael McCarthy's place of birth I'd been able to find. The pub was situated in the middle of town, opposite an old, grey-stone church, just off the central square. Next door was a bookmaker's, then a gift shop, both with brightly painted shopfronts, then a small branch of Dunnes Stores in a more modern building. There were a couple of parking spaces in front of O'Sullivan's. One was free so I pulled into it and heaved my luggage out of the boot. The pub had two bow-fronted windows with leaded glass, with a door to the side and an Irish tricolour hanging from a pole mounted between the first floor windows. I looked upwards, wondering if one of those windows would be my room. It was clearly a very old building, with warped windows and a wonky roof line, but it looked welcoming and comfortable – just what I needed right now. Maybe Michael McCarthy would even have drunk a pint or two here, in his time.

Inside, the pub was dark, with low ceilings and a long polished bar set against the back wall. Mismatched wooden tables and chairs were dotted around on a stone-flagged floor. A huge fireplace dominated one wall, but being midsummer it was not lit. I imagined it would be very cosy in here on a winter's night, perhaps with a few musicians sitting in the corner, playing tin whistle, *bodhrán*, fiddle and accordion, sipping pints of Guinness between sets. Clichéd west-of-Ireland image I know, but, to be honest, that's exactly what I was hoping to find. Something a million miles away from my usual life in London with Dan.

Today, the bar was deserted apart from one whiskery old man, wearing a worn black suit over a frayed sweater, who was sitting on a bar stool. He glanced in my direction, looked me up and down and took in my luggage, then without saying a word shuffled off his stool and disappeared through a door beside the bar. A moment later, he reappeared and climbed back onto his bar stool. He nodded at me and took a deep pull of his pint. Guinness, I was pleased to see. A youngish woman of about my own age followed him and came straight over to me, her hand stretched out.

'Welcome, welcome! You must be Maria McCarthy, here to stay with us, so you are. I'm Aoife, the landlady here. I'm sorry there was no one here when you arrived. Did you have a long journey?'

I smiled. She seemed nice, her curly brown hair bouncing around as she shook my hand, her Iron Maiden t-shirt with its screaming skeletal figure at odds with her friendly, open expression. 'Yes, pretty long. I flew from London to Dublin and drove from there.'

'Ah, it's a tidy way from Dublin, sure it is. You'll be wanting a cup of tea, now. Or something stronger? What can I get you?' She bustled behind the bar ready to get whatever drink I requested.

'Tea, for the moment, please,' I said.

'Tea, that's grand,' she replied, and went through to the back, presumably the kitchen, to make it.

I sat down at a small table by one of the windows, and put my bags on a chair. The old fellow at the bar watched in silence, taking occasional sips of his pint. I smiled at him, wondering how to start a conversation. I was still pondering this when the door opened and a young man entered. He was tall, sandy haired, wearing an open-necked shirt and jeans.

'Paulie! How're ye? Aoife about, is she? I'm parched.' He clapped a hand on the old man's shoulder. The old fellow – Paulie, I guessed – raised a bushy eyebrow in my direction and the newcomer turned, seeing me for the first time. He smiled, and approached the table. 'Hello! Ah, looks like you are a new guest here, staying in O'Sullivans? Is anyone looking after you?'

'Yes, someone's fetching me a cup of tea,' I replied.

'That'll be where Aoife's got herself to, then. Sure and I'll have to wait for my pint. Declan Murphy,' he said with a smile, holding out his hand to shake.

I took it. His grasp was firm, and now he was close, I could see he had startlingly blue eyes and a smattering of freckles across his face. 'Maria McCarthy. Nice to meet you.' His warmth and geniality reminded me with a pang of Dan, back home in London. My lovely Dan, who I'd left behind.

'McCarthy – now that's a local name, but you don't sound at all local, sure you don't.'

'No, I'm visiting from England. But my ancestors were from here. Well, near here, anyway.'

His eyes lit up with interest. 'Oh, really? Are you researching them?'

At that moment Aoife arrived with my tea, and a selection of cakes, which she put on the table in front of me. 'Now. You'll be needing more than tea after your long drive. When you've eaten that I'll show you up to your room. No hurry. There's never any hurry here, you'll be discovering that. Declan, what can I get for you?'

'At last!' He grinned. 'Thought you'd never ask. I'll have a pint of the black stuff, please, and another for Paulie while you're about it.'

Paulie nodded his thanks. I was beginning to wonder if he was mute, as he'd said not a word since I arrived. Declan came back over to my table. 'Mind if I join you?'

'Not at all,' I replied, through a mouthful of a delicious fruit cake. 'And feel free to help me out with these cakes.'

'Thank you,' he said, taking a small scone. 'So, where is it your ancestors are from?'

'A small village, somewhere near here. I couldn't find it on Google maps. Kildoolin, it's called.'

'Ah, Kildoolin.' He nodded.

'You know it?'

'Sure, and it's not too far away. A pleasant afternoon's walk.'

'Can't I drive there?' I didn't mind a walk, but would rather save my energy to walk around the village rather than to it.

He shook his head. 'There are no roads. None suitable for cars, that is. Just a track, for horse riders or walkers. And a few mountain bikers.'

I was confused. 'What about the people in the village? How do they come to town?'

Paulie, at the bar, sniggered into his pint. Declan shot a frown in his direction then turned back to me. 'Pay no mind to old Paulie, there. He'll soften when he gets to know you. Always a bit shy around strangers. Don't you know about Kildoolin?'

'It's just listed as the place of birth of one of my ancestors, on some censuses. Like I said, I couldn't find it on Google maps. But one census said "Kildoolin, Ballymor, Ireland" so I thought I should start here.'

'That was a good plan, all right. Kildoolin's a deserted village. No one lives there any more. It was abandoned during the famine years, in the 1840s. Everyone either died or moved to the towns, and probably many of them emigrated. It's just a collection of ruins today. Quite evocative, so it is. As I said, it's an easy walk up there so you'll be able to see for yourself. There's a path leading up from the end of Church Street, just as you leave the town. You can park there or it'd only take five minutes more to walk it from here. It's signposted –"The Deserted Village". You can't miss it.'

A famine village! I felt stupid that I hadn't realised that. I'd never actually researched Michael McCarthy's birthplace in detail. He was a Victorian portrait painter, and my great-great-grandfather. I had one of his pictures hanging above my bed back home – *our* bed, I should say, mine and Dan's – and I'd come here to research more about him, as well as work out my personal problems along the way. Find my ancestors; find myself. Something like that, anyway. I felt a shiver of anticipation as I imagined walking around the ruins of a village abandoned over a hundred and fifty years ago. Michael and his family must have been among the last inhabitants of it.

'Thanks, Declan, I'll definitely go there. Probably tomorrow if the weather allows it.' I glanced out of the window. It had begun to rain, just a light drizzle, but not the sort of weather you'd want for undertaking a hike across the moors.

'You might have to put up with a bit of rain if you're staying here in Ballymor,' Declan said. 'Anyway, that's not proper rain, is it, Paulie?'

The old man shook his head and cleared his throat. 'Ah no, 'tis a grand soft day,' he pronounced. His voice was surprisingly soft for such a grizzled old man, with a beautiful west-of-Ireland sing-song lilt.

Soft. Not the adjective I'd use for the rain which was now beginning to run down the window. I was glad I'd brought my luggage in already and only hoped I wouldn't need to move my car.

'So, who were your ancestors that lived above in Kildoolin?' Declan asked, with what looked like genuine interest.

'My great-great-grandfather was a man called Michael McCarthy. On the UK censuses he gave his place of birth as Kildoolin, though he spent the latter half of his life living in London. He was a Victorian artist, and I'm here to research him.'

'You must be very interested in genealogy, then?'

I smiled, suddenly feeling shy. 'Yes, but I'm also interested in art history. I did a degree in it, and my final-year thesis was on the work of Michael McCarthy. Now I'd like to research him a bit more, find out about his life as well as his work, and write a book on him. I know he was born here, had a spell in America where he first became noticed as an artist, then settled in London, although he continued to travel for his work. He mostly took commissions – he painted portraits of the rich for money.'

'That's fantastic, so it is, to write a book about him. Are you an artist yourself?'

'Sort of.' I told him about my job teaching art at adult education classes. There was something about Declan that made him easy to talk to. He was a good listener, and managed to ask questions that drew me out without him seeming nosy. I liked him instantly.

'You're here on your own?' he asked, at one point.

'It'll be easier to get on with the research on my own. Dan would have distracted me, and I'd have spent half the time worrying he was feeling like he was wasting his holiday. So, yes, just me.'

'Dan's your partner?'

'Yes.' I poured myself another cup of tea, keeping my eyes down.

He frowned slightly, as if my short answer had raised questions in his mind, but seemed to realise

I was not going to elaborate on mine and Dan's relationship. Although he was easy to talk to I didn't feel I could tell him all my relationship problems within five minutes of meeting him. He took the hint and returned to asking about Michael McCarthy, a safer topic. 'Your artist ancestor, should I have heard of him?'

'Not really. He's quite well known in academic circles, I suppose – if you were studying Victorian art you'd come across him. But he's not well known to the general public. There are a few of his paintings in museums, and the National Portrait Gallery in London holds several but doesn't often display them. I had to make special arrangements to see them when I did my degree. And I'll need to do the same again for the book, I guess. There's a little bit of a mystery surrounding him, actually.'

Declan raised an eyebrow. 'Really? Go on.'

I grinned. I loved telling people this story. 'Many of Michael McCarthy's portraits are of the same beautiful red-haired woman, in different settings. Some in Ireland, some in England, New York, Paris, all over.'

'Someone he loved?'

'They were all entitled "Kitty". That was his mother's name. The rumour is that she disappeared, and he spent much of his adult life searching for her but he never found her. Instead, he painted her from memory, wherever he travelled.'

He gazed at me wistfully. 'That's a lovely mystery. Are you hoping that maybe you can find out what happened to Kitty while you're here?'

I nodded. 'That's my dream. She was my great-great-great-grandmother. She was stunning – at least, if Michael's paintings are at all accurate.'

'He must have really loved his mother to keep searching for her.'

'Yes, he must have.' I couldn't imagine feeling like that about your mother. My own mother and I had very little to do with each other these days. If she went missing I'm not sure I'd spend that long looking for her. I'm not sure she'd want me to.

Declan smiled. 'I think it's grand that you're writing a book. Really interesting. The kind of thing I'd love to do myself if I wasn't . . . so busy. Well now, if I can help at all in any way while you're here, you've only to ask. I come in here most days, to keep an eye on old Paulie, there. Isn't that right now, Paulie?'

The old man grunted and raised his pint in Declan's direction.

'Ah well, I should leave you now. Your tea's drunk, cake's eaten and you'll be wanting to take your things to your room. So, have a good day tomorrow exploring Kildoolin. There's an ancient stone circle up there too, not far from the old village, but if you go off the tracks and across the moors watch out for the abandoned copper mines. There are a few mine entrances ought to be better protected than they are. They're not a danger if you're sensible, mind, and keep to the paths. So, will I see you in here tomorrow evening, perhaps? There'll be some music later on, if you like that kind of thing. Aoife prefers heavy metal herself, but she tolerates traditional Irish music in the bar for the sake of the tourists. It's good *craic*, anyways. You can tell me how you got on up at the old village.'

'Sure. I'll probably have my dinner in here tomorrow evening, catch you then.' I grinned as Declan raised an imaginary hat to me and took his pint over to the bar to sit beside Paulie.

Aoife came to clear away the tea and cakes. 'Come on, I'll show you up, now.' She led me through the door beside the bar then up a narrow staircase panelled in dark wood. My room was at the top, surprisingly light and spacious after the dark bar and staircase. It had windows front and back, an uneven stripped wood floor, dark oak furniture and bright white bedlinen with lacy trim. Over the bed was a picture of Christ, his arms outstretched, his heart depicted exposed and shining. The room smelt of beeswax polish. The rain had stopped and weak sunshine was shining in at the back window. I put my bags down and smiled. It felt like the kind of room where you could really relax and sort yourself out – just what I needed. It had been a very difficult few days.

'This is perfect, thanks. What time's breakfast?'

'Any time you want it, love. You're my only guest this week so I can work around you. You'll fit in nicely, I can see. You've already met two of my regulars, Declan and Paulie.'

'Declan's nice.'

She chuckled. 'Yes and he is that, to be sure, but don't be getting ideas. You'll not get far with that one.' She laughed again, and left the room, closing the door behind her.

I spent an hour or so unpacking, sorting out my room, and setting up my laptop on the dressing table. The pub had Wi-Fi and the signal was pretty strong, so I then began some Googling to find out more about Kildoolin. Should have done that before coming over, I suppose, rather than appearing an idiot in front of the locals for not realising it was a derelict famine village! Well anyway, now I knew, and was excited at the prospect of a walk up there tomorrow. The weather forecast online showed a bright day with just a chance of a few showers in the afternoon. If I got up and out early, perhaps I'd be able to avoid them.

It'd be the perfect way to start my holiday and my research. But first, I thought I had better call Dan and let him know I had arrived safely. I took a deep breath before picking up my mobile. It might not be an easy call, given what had happened last night.

He answered straight away.

'Hi, Dan,' I said. 'Just letting you know I got here OK.'

'That's good.' He sounded deflated, and I felt a pang of guilt. What had I done to him?

'So, um, the pub where I'm staying seems nice.'

'Great.'

'You OK?'

He sighed. 'What do you think, Maria?'

'I'm sorry.' I sounded lame, even to myself. I realised there was no point trying to discuss things right now. It was too soon. We – or at least I – needed some time before we could talk. 'Look, I'll call you again soon, OK?'

'OK.'

'Bye then. Love you.' I realised he'd already hung up.

I did love Dan. I wasn't just saying that from habit. I knew I'd hurt him, and I was sorry for it. It's just . . . there was stuff I needed to think about, stuff to get my head around. Things he didn't know about. Things I should have told him long before now.

The mind is a funny thing. Something really big and important can be happening in your life, and yet if you don't want to face it, you can sometimes simply let yourself forget all about it. For a while, at least, until it becomes too big to ignore. I knew I was in denial, but I didn't care, and wasn't ready to face it all head on. Not yet, anyway.

Hopefully here in Ireland, immersed in my research into Michael McCarthy and his mother Kitty, I'd find the time and headspace to work it all out, and sort things out with Dan, one way or another.

CHAPTER 2

Kitty, 1848

The potatoes were all gone. There was not a single one left. Kitty climbed down from the storage area set into the rafters of her tiny cottage and sighed. She'd crawled right into the corners, hoping against hope that there might be a few stray potatoes that had rolled right to the back. Anything to allow her to cook a meal of some sort for the children and herself tonight. Anything to hold off starvation for one more day.

She dropped to her knees on the cold stone floor. 'Please God let there be something today for the children. I'll be all right going without, sure I will, but young Michael needs to eat if he's to work, and little Gracie is fading away, Lord bless her soul.' The prayer was said in a whisper, for fear of waking her daughter who was curled up in a corner of the room. She was thankful Gracie slept, for all the time the child was sleeping she was not feeling the clawing pangs of hunger.

Kitty hauled herself upright again and crossed herself, feeling slightly dizzy. She had not eaten anything that day. The little family was reduced to a single meal each day now. She shook her head sadly, wondering what, if anything, she'd be able to give them this evening. Perhaps if Michael was paid what he was owed today, she could walk to Ballymor with his wages and buy some cornmeal. Or could she knock on doors and see if anyone could spare a potato or two? It was rumoured that Martin O'Shaughnessy still had a good stock. Probably blighted, like those she and the children had been living off these last months, but nevertheless they were just about edible and better than nothing. Could she bring herself to ask him for help? Old Martin wasn't the friendliest of neighbours. His children had grown and left – two sons to America, a daughter wed in Limerick and another in Dublin. His wife had died of the consumption a couple of years ago, and he'd become a bit of a hermit since then. Kitty had helped nurse Niamh O'Shaughnessy at the end of her life, despite Martin telling her he could cope and she wasn't needed. Now Martin was fast becoming Kitty's only neighbour. The village was almost deserted. As the famine entered its third year, people had moved away in search of work and food. Or gone to be with God, like Kitty's other children. She felt a wave of sadness wash over her as she remembered Little Pat and the three babies she'd lost. For a moment she could barely move or breathe, paralysed by grief, but she pulled herself together. She still had two children living, and they needed her to be strong.

She crossed the floor of her single-room cottage, to the rough straw mattress and pile of blankets that served as a bed for herself and Grace. She sat down and laid a hand on her daughter's forehead.

'Well now, Gracie. Have you slept well? Will I get you a sip of water?'

Grace's huge dark eyes stared up at her, and a sweet smile came to her lips.

'Bless you, child. Your smile lights up the cottage, so it does.' Kitty scooped some water from a bucket into a pottery mug, and held it to Grace's lips. The girl managed a few sips before lying back down on the blankets.

'Mammy, will Michael catch a rabbit today?' she asked.

Kitty closed her eyes as she remembered that glorious day, three weeks ago now, when Michael had come home with a rabbit he'd caught in a trap. They'd still had some potatoes then, from the meagre summer crop, and the stew she'd made that night with the rabbit meat had been a feast. There'd been some for the day after as well. But Michael wasn't the only one in the community setting traps for rabbits, and he'd had no luck since that day. 'Ah, sure rabbit stew would be lovely, wouldn't it?' she said to Grace, who nodded and feebly licked her lips.

It was another hour or more before Michael would be home. He was working in the fields for Mr Waterman today. Digging, hoeing, planting, weeding, tending, reaping and harvesting – all food that they'd see none of. Mr Waterman's fields were planted with wheat and barley, all destined for export to England. Thomas Waterman, an Englishman, owned most of the land around here, and the villagers rented their cottages and small, private patches for growing potatoes from him, as well as working for him.

At the thought of Waterman, Kitty stopped stroking Grace's hair and sat still, staring at nothing. There was another avenue, if she could bring herself to ask for charity. Thomas Waterman did not have a reputation for kindness. On the contrary, he was like his father before him – aloof and arrogant, seemingly immune to the poverty and suffering of those who worked for him. As with so many other English landowners in Ireland, he was often absent, and if he was on his Irish estates he'd keep to his big house and close his eyes to the effects of the famine. But he might make an exception for Kitty, if she asked him in the right way. They had history, a shared past. But could she do it? She silently shook her head. No. Not Thomas Waterman. She despised him with every breath of her body. She hadn't run to him last winter when the famine carried off her three youngest. Neither had she when her boy Pat had succumbed of a fever, made worse she was sure by the hunger, the previous autumn. And she wouldn't go to him now.

She would try Martin O'Shaughnessy. In her experience, the poor were more generous than the rich.

With a burst of resolve, she stood up from the bed, took her shawl down from its hook and knotted it around her shoulders. 'Gracie, I'll be going out for a little while, now. Have yourself another little sleep,' she said softly, and Grace murmured something in reply.

She pushed open the wooden door of the cottage and went out, remembering the long-gone days when the lean-to pigpen beside the cottage had always housed a pig nursing her piglets, and with a goat tied up beside it providing them with milk each day. When the potato crops first failed in the autumn of 1845, she'd had to sell the goat. She'd had to sell the pig the year before, after her husband Patrick had died in the terrible mining accident. In Thomas Waterman's copper mine, she thought, pressing her lips together hard.

It was a fine day. Cold, but with no rain or drizzle. If you had the time to stand and stare, there was a grand view from the village across the heather moorlands towards the coast. On a good day you could see a ribbon of silver that was the sea. Kitty had been there once, when she was courting Patrick and old Mother Heaney had looked after Michael, then aged just three, for the day. She had gazed in awe at the vastness of the ocean. 'Somewhere over there's America,' Patrick had said. 'We'll go, when I've made enough money working in the mines. You, me and Michael. We'll make our fortune there.'

She'd kissed him deeply then, loving his optimism for the future, loving that he was taking on her child that was not his own and not judging her for it, loving his strong arms and broad shoulders which she'd thought would protect her and her children for ever.

But that was not how things had turned out. She cast aside the memory. There were more important things to think about today – such as how she was going to feed her remaining children.

Martin O'Shaughnessy's house was at the top end of the village, past a dozen empty cottages, some of which were already falling into ruin. She remembered when the village had been vibrant, buzzing with life, children running up and down in front of the cottages, goats and pigs tied up outside most homes, women hanging washing out to dry, men repairing thatch or hauling sacks of healthy potatoes inside to store in their roof-spaces. Strange to think that was only a couple of years ago, before the blight came, before the repeated failures of the potato crop.

She passed the Brennans' cottage. When Seamus Brennan had died Mary Brennan and her five young children had gone into the workhouse, there being no one left in the family able to work. Kitty had been luckier, having Michael old enough to earn while she looked after the children. But it was a hard life for a young lad to have to provide for his mother and siblings. Sibling, she corrected herself. Only Gracie left now, of all of them. Her beautiful babies, all gone, buried in a single plot in the Ballymor churchyard. Beyond the Brennans' cottage was the Delaneys' old place. Two dead, one gone to Dublin in search of employment, and one seeking his fortune in America. And so it continued up the row of cottages. Everyone gone; either died or emigrated or in the workhouse. No one left. Finally, she reached the end cottage. Smoke curled from its chimney, and a scrawny tethered goat scrambled to its feet as she approached. She smiled and scratched its head. It was a little reminder of how things used to be.

She rapped on Martin's door. 'Mr O'Shaughnessy? It's me, Kitty McCarthy. Are you at home?'

The door opened, and Martin, a grizzled-looking man with the beginnings of a hunchback, came out. 'Welcome, neighbour. Is it your little girl?'

Kitty was momentarily taken aback, then realised he was assuming someone had died. To be sure, that had been the usual reason for knocking on doors these last two years. 'No, no. She's sickly, but still with us, God be praised,' she replied.

'Well, that's something. Such a bonny little thing, she is, with her copper hair and her sunny smile,' Martin said. He looked at her expectantly.

Kitty suddenly felt uneasy, now that she was here on Martin's doorstep. How could she ask him for charity? It wasn't in her nature – she was too proud. But if she didn't, they'd go hungry tonight, and tomorrow, and the next day. An image of Grace's big, trusting eyes came to her. She couldn't fail her little girl, her only remaining daughter. 'Mr O'Shaughnessy, it pains me so to ask, but I have no choice. Could you see your way to sparing a few potatoes for us? We're completely running out. It's not for myself I'm asking, you understand. It's for the children. For Gracie.'

She stopped talking and stood quietly, watching him, waiting for him to reply. She had a sudden intuition that their fortunes depended on his response. If he turned her away that would be the beginning of the end for all of them. They'd be joining Patrick and the children in the life beyond. 'Mr O'Shaughnessy, as soon as Michael is paid I can repay you, buy you some corn perhaps.'

But he was shaking his head. 'No, no. I won't be taking young Michael's wages. Wait here.' He went inside his cottage and reappeared a moment later hauling a bulging sack. 'Here. Take these. I have enough.'

Kitty couldn't believe it. He was giving her a whole sack of potatoes! Enough to last, if she was careful, a month or more. She peeked in the top. They didn't look to be blighted, either. 'I can't take so many, Mr O'Shaughnessy. You'll need them. It's a long while till the next harvest.' She tried to push the sack back to him, but he refused.

'You'll take it, Kitty McCarthy. Your need is the greater – you and those bairns of yours. I haven't forgotten your kindness when my Niamh was dying.' He coughed, a harsh, rasping rattle that came from deep in his chest. 'I still have enough to last the winter, though I think the good Lord will be wanting my company before next harvest. When I'm gone, you can take all that's left. For your little colleen.'

'Ah, thank you, thank you, Mr O'Shaughnessy. God will spare you for your kind heart. If there is anything I can do for you, you must ask me.'

He shook his head. 'There's nothing. Maybe I'll need a spot of nursing at the end, but until then, I'm grand. Away with you, now, back to your little girl who needs you.'

He made a shooing action with his hands, and closed the door.

Kitty offered up a silent prayer of thanks for good neighbours, and resolved to check on him every day. If he was as sick as he thought he was then certainly she would nurse him and make his last days as comfortable as possible. It was the least she could do for him. She hauled the sack back to her own cottage, and stored most of the potatoes, unblighted, fat and white, in the loft space, while little Gracie slept on in the corner.

She kept out three large potatoes, and put them in the pot ready to cook. There'd be a meal awaiting Grace when she woke, and ready for Michael when he returned from work. The sky outside was beginning to darken; he'd be home soon.

*

But Michael did not return until an hour after dark, when Kitty was just beginning to worry about what might have happened to him. He was carrying something wrapped in a piece of sackcloth, which he put down upon the scarred table in the middle of the room.

'What's that?' Kitty asked, her curiosity greater than her wish to tell him of Mr O'Shaughnessy's kindness.

'A duck,' Michael said, with pride.

Kitty looked at him with equal pride. He was tall and strong, too thin of course, but handsome, with his black hair and blue eyes. So unlike her own copper hair and milky freckled skin, which Grace had inherited. 'Where from?'

'Waterman's ornamental pond,' he replied, with a sideways look at her. 'So we will eat well tonight.'

He was aware, she knew, that she objected to poaching, even from Thomas Waterman, who had more than enough. 'Ah, Michael,' she said, shaking her head but unable to stop the beginnings of a smile at the corners of her mouth. 'What if you were caught? What if the steward saw you? If you get taken away and locked up for thievery that'll be the end of us, so it will.'

But Michael wasn't listening. He'd crossed the room to the pile of straw and blankets, and was kneeling beside Gracie, stroking her hair and whispering. Kitty went closer to hear what he was saying.

'You'll eat like a princess tonight, Gracie. Duck breast, fried with a little rosemary and sage, cut into succulent thick slices. And duck broth tomorrow. Meat, Gracie! Meat such as Mr Waterman has every day. And when this duck has gone, I know where I can get more. We'll have duck every week, so we will. Awake now. We'll be eating in an hour or less.'

'There's potatoes as well. Good ones. Enough for a month,' Kitty said.

Michael turned to her with wide eyes as she told him how she'd come by the sack of potatoes. 'He's a good man and a true friend,' he said. 'I'll take him a leg of this duck, will I, in return?'

'But he will ask where it came from,' Kitty said, frowning. She wanted to repay Martin's kindness but feared what would happen if people heard Michael was poaching from Waterman.

'Sure, and I'll make him up a story. He'll guess the truth but he won't tell, sure he won't.' Michael unwrapped the duck and pulled out his knife. He swiftly removed a leg, including the thigh, and wrapped that in a smaller cloth. 'I'll be back in a minute, Mammy. Get that duck and some potatoes in the pot!'

CHAPTER 3

Maria

I woke up early the next morning, with the sun streaming in through the thin white curtains of my room at O'Sullivan's. For a moment I wondered where I was, and why Dan was not beside me, and then I remembered with not a little guilt my sudden decision, the early start on my travels and the way I'd left Dan with barely a chance to say goodbye. I sighed. I would put this right – I had to. But I also had to sort myself out, and half the point of this trip was to do just that.

I pulled back the curtain and looked out of the window, across the town square towards the church. The sky was azure, with just a few fluffy white clouds scudding across it. The perfect day for my expedition to the ruins of Kildoolin, and after the long day of travel the thought of a good walk to stretch my legs and clear the cobwebs was very appealing. I glanced at my watch and saw that it was just seven thirty. Aoife had said I could have breakfast at any time, but was this too early to expect a pub landlady to be up and about? I decided to take a leisurely shower, have a cup of tea in my room and generally potter about until eight o'clock which seemed a more reasonable hour.

I shouldn't have worried. By the time I went downstairs, Aoife was already busy behind the bar, unloading the glass washer, polishing the optics, restocking the beer mats.

'Good morning! Did you sleep? Will I get you the full Irish breakfast?'

I grinned at the hearty welcome. 'Slept like a log, and the full breakfast would be lovely, thank you.'

She nodded and went through to the kitchen. While I waited, wondering whether a full Irish breakfast was the same as a full English breakfast, I wandered around the bar, peering at the various pictures on the walls. The pub had been too crowded yesterday evening to be able to look at them. There was a fine miscellany of pictures – black and white photographs of Ballymor; framed newspaper cuttings about the pub, its food and music; signed photos of traditional musicians sitting in the bay window playing their instruments. I recognised one or two of the musicians from last night. They'd started playing around nine o'clock, with no announcement, no microphones. Just a clutch of middle-aged men, who'd pulled instruments out of pockets and cases, and played jigs and reels and ballads and old Dubliners numbers for a couple of hours until Aoife had called time. I'd meant to get an early night, tired after the long drive, but the music had made me smile and tap my foot, and I'd stayed till the end, making an experimental half-pint of Guinness last most of the evening. The music had helped me forget, and that was good.

When breakfast came it was huge, just like a full English including bacon, sausage, fried potatoes, mushrooms, toast and fried tomatoes but with the addition of a huge hunk of black pudding – the real thing from Clonakilty, just up the road, so Aoife informed me. I wouldn't need lunch, that was for certain. It smelt divine.

With that lot inside me, I went back to my room, stuffed a lightweight fleece, fold-up mac and bottle of water in my small day sack and set off for my walk. First stop was the tourist information office to pick up a map of the town, but they weren't open till nine o'clock and I wasn't prepared to wait. Declan had said the path began at the end of Church Street so I found that and followed it out of town. Sure enough, as the last housing estate petered out, there was a rutted track leading off to the left signposted 'To the Deserted Village'. I turned off on the track, enjoying the exercise, relishing the sun on my back, thinking about Michael, my ancestry, the past, and most definitely not about the future.

The track climbed steadily, weaving its way between fields of ripening wheat which eventually gave way to open moorland, covered with magnificent purple heather. To my right was a range of hills; far over to the left I could just make out the sea, shimmering in the morning sun. There was a light breeze keeping the temperature just right, and I was accompanied by constant birdsong – a skylark was up there somewhere. All in all, it was a pretty perfect day. I was working up a bit of a sweat on the hill, and stopped to admire the scenery and have a swig of water.

Just over the brow of the hill, the remains of the village came into sight. I stopped and took in the view. It was more of a hamlet than a village – a single row of cottages alongside the track, with their backs to the hill and their fronts facing the view over the moors towards the sea. It would have been a beautiful place to live on a day like today, with the sun shining and only a light breeze, but I could imagine life would have been tough here when the weather was bad. Although it rarely snowed here in the south-west of Ireland, it could be pretty stormy at times, and the village was high on the moors and exposed.

I continued walking along the track towards the village. There was a worn-out sign for tourists, showing a plan of the village and with a brief summary of the famine, but it was faded and almost unreadable. The cottages were all ruined – very few had any kind of a roof left and none had doors. I imagined the roofs would have originally been thatched. The walls were made of a greyish stone, like the church in Ballymor. Some walls were more or less intact, and others had long since toppled, leaving mossy piles of rubble.

As I approached I could see the layout of the cottages – they were all tiny, single-roomed, with a fireplace at one end and a door in the middle of the side facing the track, looking across the moors to the sea. Most had two small windows, one on each side of the door. I guessed the windows would not have been glazed but perhaps originally had wooden shutters. The first cottage I reached was one of the more intact ones, although its roof was gone, so I ducked in through the low doorway to have a look inside.

The heather had found its way in, along with a few ash saplings, some gorse and plenty of bracken, and there was a burned-out circle on the ground – evidence that someone had lit a campfire. The cottage was tiny. I tried to imagine a whole family living here – where would their beds have been? Their table and chairs? I wondered what possessions people would have had, before the famine. Maybe Declan would know more. I smiled with pleasure at the idea of sitting in a corner of O'Sullivan's quizzing him on it. Now that I knew Michael McCarthy's home had been abandoned during the famine years when he was just a teenager, I realised I'd need to properly research that part of Ireland's history. I made a mental note to get hold of some books about the famine so I could fully understand what had happened. It had obviously impacted Michael's life – how could you not be affected by something like that happening around you? And maybe that's what had become of his mother, Kitty. Perhaps she had been a victim of the famine. But if that was true, why then had he continued to paint her, and why the rumours that he had searched for her all his adult life?

I went out of the first cottage and into the next. This had one collapsed wall and a skull of a sheep in the remains of the fireplace, with a foxglove growing up through it.

The village was an eerie place, even on a glorious summer's day. To think that once it would have been full of people going about their business – children playing, women cooking, men repairing thatch or tending to vegetable plots – and then the potato crops failed, people starved or moved away, leaving the entire village to crumble. Some walls looked pretty unstable, listing at precarious angles as though the next gust of wind would blow them over.

I pulled out my water bottle and took a long swig from it. It had been a hot, tough walk up here. Without meaning to, I found myself thinking of Dan, the way I'd hurt him, the secrets I was still keeping from him. I knew I wasn't being fair to him. I walked further up through the village, going in and out of every ruined cottage, in an effort to put it all out of my head, for a little longer anyway. A stream ran down the hillside behind the cottages, and crossed the track between two cottages about halfway along the row. There were slippery stepping stones to enable walkers to cross the stream. I guessed this had been the villagers' water supply.

There was someone else up here – someone sitting on a tumbledown wall that had once been part of the cottage at the far end of the village. A man, who was staring out across the moors towards the sea. As I approached I realised it was Declan. He hadn't spotted me – he seemed lost in his thoughts the way I'd been lost in mine a few minutes ago. I coughed a bit and deliberately kicked a few stones to make a bit of noise. It worked.

'Well, hello there, Maria! You found it, so.' He stood to greet me, smiling, the sun making his hair look more blond than it had appeared in the pub.

'Yes, thanks, great directions. We could have walked up together if I'd known you were coming.' As soon as I said the words I wished I could claw them back. That sounded like a come-on. I racked my brains – had I mentioned Dan last night at all? Declan was lovely, and I certainly felt attracted to him to an extent, but I wasn't available. I didn't need any more confusion in my life. Dan was my man, despite everything.

'Ah, it was a spur of the moment decision this morning. I often come up here, to sit and meditate, and just soak up the glory of God's creation. On a day like today it was irresistible.'

'It's amazing.' I stood beside him and took in the view. The heather was in full flower, giving the moorlands a deep purple hue. Here and there stunted ash trees grew, their leaves a vibrant green in contrast to the dark heather. There was gorse too – its time for flowering was mostly over but here and there were splashes of bright yellow bloom. The sea on the distant horizon glinted gold and silver as the sun, now high overhead, reflected off it. The air was scented with summer. It was hard to believe that this place had seen tragedy.

'So, I wonder which cottage your ancestor lived in?' Declan said, shielding his eyes with a hand across his forehead, as he turned to face me.

I shook my head. 'No idea, and I don't see how I could find out. Were all the cottages abandoned at the time of the famine?'

'I believe so, yes. Not everyone would have died, though. Some probably went abroad, to England or America. Perhaps others went to try to find work in the cities – Limerick or Cork, or even Dublin. Public works schemes had been set up – building roads and suchlike – so people could earn money to buy food to offset the loss of the potato crop. But there weren't enough places on them, or they were badly managed, or they weren't running in the areas where the poorest people lived. The people here, like so many across Ireland, depended on their potato crops. They failed several years in a row in the late 1840s, with the blight making the few potatoes that could be salvaged almost inedible. And without the potato crops the people had nothing.'

'What I don't understand is, why did they only grow potatoes? Surely if they'd grown other crops and not been so reliant on potatoes, the blight wouldn't have affected them so badly?' I felt a bit like a schoolkid on an educational visit, but I'd need to understand this properly for my book.

'The farm workers only rented a tiny patch of poor land from the big landowners – it's all they were allowed to have, to grow their own food. You can still see evidence of cultivated land where the Kildoolin inhabitants grew their potatoes – halfway down the track on the right you can just make out lines and ridges in the heather. Potatoes are a high-yield crop; they'll grow in the poorest soils and are very nutritious. There aren't many vegetables you can live on if you're not eating much else, but potatoes you can. On the big farms, plenty of other crops were grown – wheat, barley, maize – and cattle were reared. The great tragedy is that Ireland was producing enough food to feed itself, right through the famine years. But the majority of it was exported, mostly to England, and sold to make money for the English landowners.'

I felt guilty, as if I should apologise on behalf of all English people. 'Did the landowners not realise what was going on, or how bad it was?'

He gave a small shrug. 'Some did, some didn't. Many were absentee landlords who hardly ever set foot on their Irish estates. Others were well aware of what was happening. To be fair, some tried to help by donating food. But some people were too proud to accept charity, preferring to work for their money. And there was the option of workhouses, but those of course were the last resort.'

I shook my head. 'You'd think if your children were starving you'd do anything to save them.' As I said it I wondered if that would be true for me – would I do anything to save my child? Was I capable of self-sacrifice? To be perfectly honest, I wasn't sure. It was presumably something that came with maternal instincts, and I did not believe I had those. I wondered if my own mother had ever considered this question. I could not imagine her sacrificing herself to save me. She'd never really given up anything for me.

Declan was looking at me oddly. 'Are you all right there, Maria? You look as though you're fretting about something. If you want to talk . . .'

'No, it's all right. I was just thinking about these poor people, what they had to go through. You're very knowledgeable on it, Declan. Thank you for explaining things; it's very helpful.'

'Ah, to be sure we're all taught about the famine in history lessons in Ireland. It's one of the big events that defines our nation. That and the 1916 uprising and fight for independence.'

I made a mental note to buy myself a book on the history of Ireland. It'd all be good background information for my biography of Michael McCarthy. From my thesis I knew plenty about his painting techniques, his style and his subjects, and his later life in London, but so little about his early life and the land of his birth.

We sat and chatted a while longer, then walked back to Ballymor together. He pointed out where the potato fields would have been, part-way down the hill, beside the track. I must admit I could not see much evidence, but maybe the heather was kind of growing in rows, following the lines of old potato ridges.

Declan left me in the centre of town. I wanted to start making some notes for my book, and had a long list of questions to research on the internet. Declan had told me about a good bookshop in the town, where I might find some local history books, and the prospect of a light lunch in a coffee shop followed by an hour or so browsing the bookshop felt like a good plan for the rest of the day.

I found a pleasant-looking café which overlooked the town square and ordered a sandwich and a pot of tea, then pulled out my phone. There was a text from Dan, which I opened nervously. ***Any decision yet? I still love you. xxx***

Tears pricked at my eyes as I read the text. I'd been such a rubbish girlfriend to him and felt so guilty. As I ate my lunch, I recalled the events of last Sunday night, two days before I'd left for Ireland and one day before I'd booked my tickets.

Dan had surprised me by taking me out to eat at a swanky restaurant. It wasn't one we often went to – only on very special occasions. He'd even reserved us one of the best tables – by the window, overlooking the river. At this time of year, it would be light till almost ten o'clock, so we'd be able to watch the sunset over the water as we lingered over our meal.

I'd made an effort and put on a floaty summer dress, some strappy sandals and a bit of make-up. It made a change from my usual jeans and paint-spattered t-shirt combinations that I wore when teaching art.

'You look gorgeous,' Dan said, as I came downstairs ready to go out to the restaurant. 'Really pretty.'

'Thank you,' I said, giving him a kiss.

We walked to the restaurant – it was only about twenty minutes away and the evening was warm and still. Dan insisted on holding my hand the whole time. I felt as though we were teenagers on our first date. There was a slight tenseness about him which was unusual. He was normally so easy-going and relaxed. I wondered if he had problems at work. He worked in IT, and I knew he was under pressure to bring forward delivery dates on his current project.

But it wasn't that at all that was making him tense and preoccupied during our walk to the restaurant. As we were shown to our table, and took our seats each facing the window at an angle, he ordered two glasses of champagne. The waiter brought them, along with the menus, almost immediately.

It wasn't really what I wanted to drink – I'd have preferred a refreshing glass of sparkling water – but I lifted my glass to clink against his anyway. 'Champagne, how lovely! Well, cheers then!'

He shook his head gently. 'Not yet, Maria. There's something I need to ask you first.' He put his hand into his pocket and pulled out a small box. Inside was a ring – white gold, diamond and ruby. Delicate, pretty, modern, and perfect. Exactly what I would have picked myself. He knew me so well. 'Marry me?' he said.

I was lost for words, and gaped for a moment.

His nervousness made him fill the empty silence. 'Registry office or church. Or hotel. I honestly don't mind – whatever you want. All *I* want is you.' He smiled and reached for my hand.

I found myself blinking at him while a thousand images raced through my mind – us standing at an altar exchanging vows while my mother, Jackie, watched disapprovingly (she disapproved of everything I did); Dan and I pushing a pram through a park together with another dozen children hanging off our arms; us aged ninety sitting opposite each other with nothing to say, in an old people's home. Was this my future flashing before me? Was it the future I wanted? I loved Dan, with all my heart, but the whole marriage and children thing felt far too terrifyingly grown-up for me to contemplate. I loved him, no question, but could I agree to all this, right now, just like that?

I must have looked unsure, because his face fell and he removed his hand from mine. 'You don't need to answer now, Maria. But don't say no straight out – think about it, please.'

I nodded mutely. I could promise him to think about it at least. I felt so sorry for him. My reaction surely had not been what he'd have hoped and dreamed for, but it was at least an honest one. Finally, I managed to squeeze some words out. 'Dan, darling, I love you, you know that. This has been a bit of a shock. We've never before talked of getting married. Of course I promise you I'll think about it.' I took his hand again, and stroked it with my thumb.

'I know we've never spoken about it,' he said. 'But we've been together five years now, we're so good together, and I suppose I always assumed we would marry, like it was some kind of unspoken agreement. Sorry to spring it on you.'

'I guess I've never really thought much about the future. I'm just a bit scared of change, that's all.' There was more change going on than he knew about, but now was not the time to tell him. Or maybe it was the right time, and I was just being weak and feeble by not feeling able to do it.

He smiled, with relief that I hadn't said no, but disappointment that I'd felt unable to say yes. My heart broke for him. What a rubbish girlfriend I was.

'I love the ring, by the way,' I said, by way of consolation. 'You got that right.'

'It's yours, whenever you're ready for it,' he whispered. He snapped the ring box shut again and put it in his pocket, as though to signal the subject closed, for now.

And indeed it wasn't mentioned again for the rest of the meal. Our conversation was a little stilted and awkward. I could see I'd upset Dan by not giving him the answer he wanted. But how could I say yes if I felt unsure and unready for such a big step? It was such a huge commitment. I needed time to think about his proposal. I needed space. I needed to get away. There was so much happening and I couldn't cope with it all. I found myself switching off from his conversation and thinking instead about my planned book on Michael McCarthy.

The very next day I'd made a snap decision to go to Ireland, a trip I'd talked about for ages but not got around to planning. While Dan was at work, I'd booked flights and the room at O'Sullivan's, but then Dan was out in the evening at a work colleague's leaving do, and I was in bed by the time he returned, and somehow I didn't get the chance to tell him about the trip until I was leaving for the airport the next morning. He'd been, understandably I supposed, pretty miffed.

'You're running away,' he'd said, as I finished my hurried packing. 'Getting as far away from me as you can so you don't have to answer my question. I thought you loved me, and were happy with me?'

'I do, and I am,' I said. 'But it's all so sudden. So many changes . . .'

'Not that big a change really. Just a couple of rings, to symbolise our commitment to each other.' He pressed his hands to his temples and shook his head, sadly.

But he didn't yet know the extent of the changes. And still I couldn't tell him. 'Dan, I'm so sorry. I just need some time alone. Please, give me that.'

That was when he'd given me that look of deep hurt and disappointment. I'd turned away, zipped up my suitcase and hooked my handbag strap over my shoulder.

'So. I'll see you when you get back, I suppose,' he'd said, as he left for work, not catching my eye.

'Yes. See you, then.'

And that was it. We'd parted, so much unsaid and unresolved, and now here I was, sitting alone in a coffee shop in a small town in the south-west of Ireland, wiping away a tear that had trickled down the side of my nose, trying to smile reassuringly at the waitress who'd given me a look of concern, and no nearer to being able to give him an answer, or be as honest with him as I ought to be.

CHAPTER 4

Kitty

The duck stew had lasted three days, and the sack of potatoes from Martin O'Shaughnessy would last a few weeks yet. And Michael had been paid, which meant Kitty had been able to walk to Ballymor and buy flour to make bread and a laying chicken which provided one or sometimes two eggs each day. She and the children had had full bellies for days. Grace had improved, and was able to get up and spend part of the day helping Kitty with chores. They had fended off starvation for a little longer. The weather had been mild too, and despite everything, Kitty was hopeful that this year's early potatoes might be harvested blight-free. That early harvest was still three months away, however, and it'd be a struggle to find enough food to last until then. She prayed daily that somehow she'd manage, and that the potato harvest would be a good one.

She had baked two loaves of soda bread, and wrapped one in a cloth to take to Martin. He'd been so kind. Giving him small gifts whenever she had something to share was the only way she could repay him.

'Grace, love, will you take this along to Mr O'Shaughnessy. He'll like to see your bonny smile. Away with you, girl.'

Grace took the bread and skipped out of the door and up the street. Kitty smiled to see her go. She was a different child to how she'd been a week ago, when Kitty had feared she was near death. She was still horribly thin – they all were – but she had some life and energy in her. It was good to see, and gave Kitty hope for the future. Maybe they were through the worst.

If only her dear Patrick was still here. He'd have been another pair of hands to work. He'd been a trained copper miner, and although the mines were gradually closing, being unprofitable, he'd surely still have been able to get work. That would have brought in money, and perhaps they'd have been able to afford food when the potatoes went bad. Perhaps the little ones, Nuala, Jimmy and tiny Éamonn, might have survived those terrible winters with no food. She sighed as she remembered her beloved husband. Her thoughts began to run on that awful day when she'd heard the news of his accident, but not now, she did not want to dwell on that now. Instead, she forced herself to bring to mind the happy times. Their first meeting.

*

It had been at the Ballymor midsummer fair that Kitty saw Patrick for the first time. She was then nineteen years old, and old Mother Heaney had taken Michael for the afternoon, so that Kitty could go to the fair. If her own mother had been alive, she'd no doubt have helped out with little Michael, but then again, she'd have been mortified at the idea of her daughter having a child out of wedlock. No matter what the origins of that child. But dear old Mother Heaney, who'd brought her up, helped out with Michael and Kitty was eternally grateful for it.

Kitty had longed to go to the fair that year. She had not been since she was fifteen, before Michael was born. The year when she was sixteen she'd been big with Michael; indeed, he was born just two days after it. The following two years she'd wanted to hide away from people, and had kept at home, raising Michael and tending their potato patch. But Mother Heaney had been nagging at her to get out more, meet people, find herself a husband, for she would need someone to provide for her and the bairn in the long term.

And so it was that on the day of the fair, which dawned bright and clear, a hot sun in a glorious blue sky, Kitty left Michael with Mother Heaney and set off along the road to Ballymor. The fair was held in a field on the other side of town and, as she got near, she caught up with crowds of excited people, all heading the same way. As she walked, occasionally skipping with the sheer joy of being alive on such a day, she found herself alongside a tall and well-built young man with sandy hair and a wide smile, who kept looking sideways at her and grinning. She liked the look of him, and couldn't stop herself from smiling back.

'Will you be entering the Queen of the Fair competition?' he asked, blushing to the roots of his hair.

'No, I will not!' she replied.

'Ah, but there you're wrong. You'd win, for sure, with your beautiful red hair and your lovely smile. I think you should enter. I'll cheer you on, so I will.'

Now it was Kitty's turn to blush. 'Away with you! I'd never win. I'd no more win that than fly to the moon.' Still, she was flattered that he thought she might, and couldn't help but smile. She wondered what his name was and where he was from, but was too shy to ask. If he would ask her name, she could ask his in return. But he seemed too shy as well, and they walked in silence until they reached the fair and he was swallowed up in the crowds.

Kitty took her time wandering around the fair, looking at the horses being traded by gypsies, the pens of sheep and cattle on show, the stalls selling pies, hot potatoes and flagons of stout, the sideshows where magicians made handkerchiefs and pennies disappear or fortune-tellers told your future. At the far side of the field, a number of young women were gathered, and a man in a bright red jacket was pinning numbered badges to their dresses. As she watched, he beckoned to her.

'Ah, now there's a pretty thing! Come here, bonny colleen, and let me pin a number to you. You'll stand a good chance of winning the Queen of the Fair, so you will.'

The other girls scowled at her, except for one who smiled and nodded. 'He's right, you're prettier than any of us. There's a good prize for the winner. You might as well.'

Well why not? Kitty thought. That was three people now who thought she could win. She didn't so much as own a mirror, but if they all thought she was pretty then perhaps she was. Only one person had praised her looks before, and that was Thomas Waterman and she did not want to think about him.

She stepped forward. 'All right, I'll enter. What do I need to do?'

'Good girl!' the man in the red jacket said. 'Let me give you a number and write down your name. You have to walk around the arena, and the girl who gets the loudest cheer and is thought the bonniest by our judge will win the prize. We start in half an hour, so wait here with the others till then.'

It was a nerve-racking half-hour, but Kitty made friends with the girl who'd spoken to her, and the time passed reasonably quickly. She worried no one would cheer for her. The others all seemed to have friends and relatives at the show to support them, but she had no one. But when it was her turn, and she was walking round the fenced-off ring in the centre of the field, a huge cheer went up from people on the left of the arena. Looking over, she saw the sandy-haired boy she'd met on the way to the fair. He was encouraging everyone around him to cheer for her, and it made her smile with delight, her confidence boosted. She resolved to look for him afterwards and thank him. He'd never be interested in her, of course, shackled as she was with a small child.

As she turned at the end of the arena to walk back, she saw a man sitting on horseback, watching the parade. Her stomach lurched. She hadn't thought for a moment that Thomas Waterman might be here. She'd assumed he'd be in England. Surely he was too high and mighty to attend the fair? He was watching her closely, then he leaned down to say something to the man in the red jacket who stood beside him. Kitty was shaken to the core. It was the first time she'd set eyes on Waterman since that terrible day, nearly four years ago. She hurried through the last of her walk, and ducked underneath the ropes on the opposite side from Waterman. The sandy-haired boy ran round to meet her.

'You were the prettiest by far, and got the loudest cheer – I made sure of that! You'll win, wait and see!'

'Ah, but it depends on what the judge thinks. And I don't even know who is the judge,' she replied.

''Tis Mr Thomas Waterman, of course,' the boy said, pointing him out on his huge bay horse. 'Old William Waterman usually does it, but they say he is sick this year so the duty has fallen to his son.'

Kitty did not turn to look. She felt as though Waterman was still watching her, his eyes burning a hole in her back. If he was the judge she wouldn't win, that was for sure. And if by some strange twist he did pick her, she would not accept her prize, not if it meant approaching him. She tore the number from her dress and walked away from the arena. It was time she left the fair and went home.

'Wait! Don't you want to see if you've won?' the boy called, as he ran to catch up with her.

'No. I shouldn't have entered. I want to go home now,' she said.

'Let me walk you home,' he said, falling into step alongside him.

She smiled in response. She still didn't know his name. 'I'm Kitty Tooley,' she blurted out, before she could stop herself.

'And I'm Patrick McCarthy.' He grinned at her, his cheeks dimpling deeply.

'Pleased to meet you, Patrick, and thank you for getting people to cheer for me.'

'You are welcome. I still think you are the winner. You're the winner for me, anyways.'

He walked all the way home with her that day, and by the time they reached her home they were firm friends. He'd told her of his job working in the copper mines and his home in the hills above Ballymor, in a small miners' village called Kildoolin. She knew all about his family – his mother who'd died some years back, his aged father, his older brother in Limerick, his younger brothers who'd moved into the town, his sisters all married and moved away. She'd told him too of her parents, who'd both died when she was a child, and her mother's aunt, Mother Heaney, who'd brought her up, and whom she still lived with although these days Kitty looked after her rather than the other way around: Ma Heaney being lame after a broken leg set badly some years before.

'Is it just you and your great-aunt in your cottage?' he asked.

She took a deep breath. Now was the time she needed to tell him about Michael, and that would mean he would lose interest, leave her to walk the rest of the way alone, and never want to see her again. But she could not lie to him, this kind, sweet boy with his dimpled cheeks and twinkling eyes. 'There's Mother Heaney, me and little Michael,' she said.

'Michael? Is he your brother, or cousin?'

'He's only three. And, well, no he's not my brother or cousin. He's my son.' There. She'd said it. He'd turn tail now, sure he would. She was only too used to being judged harshly for having had a child out of wedlock.

'What happened to his father?' he asked, tentatively.

'Michael doesn't have a father,' she replied, the same reply she'd always given to anyone who asked that question.

He nodded, as if that explained everything, and they walked in silence for a time. All the while Kitty expected Patrick to make his excuses and leave. But instead, suddenly and unexpectedly, he said, 'I'd love to meet your little fellow. Will you let me meet him, some day?'

'I will, that,' she had said, grinning broadly.

*

It was a good memory. Kitty smiled as she picked up the water bucket. She then climbed the hill behind her cottage, to a pool in the stream where the villagers fetched water. She could recall every second of that day when she had met her wonderful husband, her saviour and best friend.

But, as she dunked the bucket in the stream to fill it, she sighed sadly. When Patrick was lost she had cursed her bad fortune, railed against God who had punished her so, and for why? She had not thought anything so bad could happen to her again. But then, the year after Patrick's death was the first winter that the potato crop failed. They had struggled through it, but the crop failed again the next autumn. Eleven-year old Little Pat had collapsed from exhaustion in the fields, and never recovered. She had felt his loss like a limb being torn from her body. It had left a scar that would never heal. In the second winter of the famine – a terribly cold and harsh one, which only added to their suffering – the three babies had died of malnourishment and fever, despite her going without to allow her to fill their plates. One after the other Nuala, Jimmy and Éamonn had weakened and died, each death dealing a blow to her soul, each burial feeling as though she buried another part of her being. There were only Gracie and Michael left. Kitty had wondered, many times, if the children might have survived if she'd taken them and gone into the workhouse. But she would have been separated from them. And she'd heard such terrible stories of what happened to children in workhouses. There would have been no way back for them. People only came out of the workhouse in wooden boxes.

She hauled the bucket out of the stream and set off back down to her cottage. For now, at least, they had food, and she'd saved Gracie from going the way of her brothers and sister.

Grace was back from delivering the bread to Mr O'Shaughnessy, and almost as soon as Kitty entered the cottage she heard Michael's familiar whistle as he came up the track from Thomas Waterman's fields.

'Look!' he said, excitedly, as soon as he reached her. 'I saw Mr O'Dowell in town and he's after giving me a whole book for drawing in, and a box of pencils!'

Kitty smiled to see what Michael was holding out. A week ago she might have cursed, wondering what was the use of paper and pencils when they were starving, but now they had food in their bellies and more food stored in the cottage they could enjoy life a little, for a while. Michael had always been good at drawing, ever since he was a small boy attending the National School down in Ballymor; but since Patrick had died of course there had been no money to spare for non-essential things like artist's materials.

'That was kind of Mr O'Dowell,' she said. Patrick's old foreman had done what he could, over the years, to help them out a little. Giving Michael drawing materials was a lovely gesture, something the boy would really appreciate. He'd had to grow up so fast after Patrick died, and he'd become the main earner in the family. And the deaths of Little Pat and the babies had hit him hard. It would do him good to have something to do, other than work.

'I've drawn some pictures already,' Michael said, flipping open the book to show her. He'd sketched James O'Dowell, showing him leaning against the outside wall of O'Sullivan's, pipe in one hand, pint in the other. It was a good likeness.

Kitty nodded appreciatively, and Michael turned to the following page, which showed a man on horseback, his back straight, his expression haughty. He held a horsewhip in one hand, raised as though he was about to use it.

'Mr Waterman came to the fields today,' Michael explained. 'He stopped near me while I was eating my lunch, and I quickly drew him, so I did.'

Kitty pursed her lips. Again, it was a good likeness, but not a face she wanted to see in her son's sketchbook. That man had done her family enough damage. Wasn't it in his mines Patrick had perished?

'Is it good, Mammy? Would you recognise him?'

'It's like him, to be sure,' she said, then flicked the page to see what was next. But it was the last drawing. She turned back to the one of O'Dowell. 'You're a fine artist. Perhaps you should give Mr O'Dowell this picture as a thank you.'

'Sure, and I'll do that,' Michael said. 'Where's Gracie? I want to show her. And then I'll draw a picture of her, before the light fades.'

'She's inside,' Kitty replied. She remained standing outside the cottage while Michael went in. That picture of Thomas Waterman had disturbed her. Michael had captured the essence of the man – his aloofness, his cruelty, his tyrannical nature – as well as his appearance and stance. She hated Thomas Waterman with every inch of her being. She had not set eyes on him for many years – thankfully he spent most of each year in England – but he owned the land, he owned the mines, he owned the cottage she lived in and the ground in which she grew her potatoes. Their lives were entirely dependent on him, and she knew, more than anyone else, that he was not at all a good man.

CHAPTER 5

Maria

The next day was overcast and threatened rain, so I decided to drive into Cork city to visit the art galleries and museums there. I hoped I'd find a few Michael McCarthy portraits in one of them, and maybe even a 'Kitty'. I had a leaflet from Ballymor tourist information office – a Cork city tourist guide with a list of galleries – and, having parked the car not far from the small but beautiful university campus, I set off on foot with my trusty rain-mac to visit as many galleries as possible. Disappointingly most of the galleries were dedicated to modern art so did not detain me long. I mean, it's nice enough, but not what I was looking for. Mid-morning, in need of refreshment, I ducked into the nearest café and was delighted to find it specialised in chocolate. I wanted to drown in the glorious deep warm aromas. I could have sampled everything on the menu but made do with a hot chocolate and a slice of chocolate brownie. Heaven.

Heading away from the town centre and along a riverside walk, I eventually came to the Cork city museum. Perhaps this would be more likely to have some McCarthy pictures. He was, after all, a local artist. The museum is an impressive Georgian building set in pleasant grounds. I went in, mooched around various displays related to Youghal lace, Irish patriot Michael Collins and a history of copper mining in County Cork, then finally, tucked away in a corner, I found a section devoted to local artists. There, side by side with two other McCarthy portraits and a couple of sketches, was an unmistakable 'Kitty'. My heart beat faster as I stepped forward to examine it. It wasn't one I'd seen before in any books, and it was a beauty. The museum had labelled it 'Unknown Woman by Michael McCarthy' but, as I gazed at her long copper curls and startling green eyes, I knew it was her – my great-great-great-grandmother. In this portrait she was sitting on what looked like the deck of an ocean liner, with a glass of wine at her side and an open book on her lap. She was wearing a pale pink dress and a grey shawl, and I noticed the shawl was pinned with the same distinctive Celtic knot brooch she was wearing in my own Kitty portrait, back home. The brooch must have been a treasured possession, I thought, though it was hard to imagine that someone who lived in such a poor cottage as the ones I'd seen at Kildoolin yesterday would own anything of value. I stood for a while, staring into her eyes, trying to see beyond them into her mind. 'What happened to you, Kitty?' I whispered. 'Where did you go? Where did you end up?'

I took some notes and a couple of photos of the portrait (I knew I'd have to get permission from the museum and a professional picture of it if I was to include it in my book, but this would do for now), then looked at the other McCarthy works on display. One intrigued me – it was a rough pencil sketch of a haughty-looking man on a horse. Something about the expression of the man made the hairs on the back of my neck stand up. It was quite unnerving. It was unsigned but the museum label said it was attributed to Michael McCarthy and had hung for many years in Ballymor House. The style was odd – it looked almost amateur, juvenile, as though Michael had not yet refined his technique. I wondered who the man was, and whether Ballymor House still existed and who had lived there. More questions for poor Declan when I next saw him!

*

All in all, it was a pleasant day in Cork city, with the rain holding off for most of the day. I drove back to Ballymor full of chocolate and thoughts about the Kitty portrait and the sketch of the man on the horse.

Back at O'Sullivan's, I went up to my room to freshen up before dinner and an evening in the bar. I felt like dressing up a little after the last couple of days in my jeans, which were feeling a little tight on me these days, so I put on a loose summer dress and wedge sandals. I fancied wearing my Pandora bracelet to complete the outfit, and rummaged through my toiletries bag for it. Usually I put jewellery for a holiday into the side pocket of my toiletries bag, but it wasn't there. I upended the bag on the bed and rooted through – a pile of tangled necklaces but no bracelet.

'Shit. I'm sure I packed it,' I muttered, and tried my handbag. Perhaps I'd put it in there for some reason. But there was no sign of it. Oh God, I couldn't lose it – it was my most precious piece of jewellery, the last present my father had ever given me, the Christmas before he'd died of cancer. Dan had bought me a new charm for it every year that we'd been together.

I grabbed my phone and called Dan. I'd promised him we'd talk, but this call wasn't it. I just needed to know where the bracelet was. Maybe I'd failed to pack it. I had been in a bit of a rush, after all.

'Dan? Quick call, as I know you'll be having dinner and I need to go down and order something soon. I can't find my Pandora bracelet. Can you have a look for me?'

'Hi, Maria. Sorry, love, I'm not at home at the moment.'

I registered sounds of a busy pub in the background. 'Where are you?'

'Crown and Sceptre, with a couple of lads from the office. Drowning my sorrows and all that, ha ha. I'll look for your bracelet when I get home and will text you. Where's it likely to be?'

I thought hard. 'Top drawer in my bedside cabinet, probably. Or the next drawer down. Sorry to be the cause of your sorrows.' I felt that all-too-familiar band of guilt tightening across my chest. But he didn't sound as hurt as he'd been during our last phone call. Just businesslike, as though he wanted to get me off the phone as soon as possible. Well, he *was* on a night out.

'OK. I'll have a look. Two Peronis and a Stella please, thanks, mate.'

'You what?'

'Sorry, Maria, it's my round. Just ordering. Cheers, mate, no, that's the lot. Here's a twenty. Maria, I've got to go, love you. Still waiting for an answer . . .'

'I know. I love you too.'

'And that's why we should marry. What's to stop us?' He blew a kiss down the phone and hung up.

*

I'd had Aoife's Irish stew on the day I arrived and it was so delicious I decided to have it again. My favourite table by the window was free so I sat there, nodding and smiling at the family who occupied a larger table in the corner. I hadn't seen them before and something about them suggested they were tourists. The parents looked to be around forty, with a frazzled-but-happy-to-be-on-holiday air about them. There was a girl in her mid-teens, with plaited blonde hair, a slightly sullen expression and a surgically attached phone, a boy of about thirteen with gelled black hair wearing an assortment of leather wristbands and another boy of perhaps five with a sweet freckled face and a grubby stuffed elephant toy under one arm. Their food arrived before mine, while I was flicking through the photos I'd taken so far on my phone.

'Come on, Sammy. You asked for chicken nuggets and now you've eaten none of them,' the mother was saying, in an exasperated tone. Her accent was from the south of England, which confirmed my suspicions they were holidaymakers.

'I have. I've eaten two.' Sammy had seated his elephant beside his plate and, as he spoke, it fell over, trunk first, onto his plate. The older boy laughed and looked expectantly at his parents for their reaction to this tragedy.

'What have we said about keeping Nellie off the table at mealtimes?' the mum said, snatching the offending toy and placing it on the bench seat between her and Sammy.

'That thing's disgusting,' said the teenage girl, wrinkling her nose. 'I wouldn't eat his dinner now that smelly toy's been in it.'

'That's enough, Kaz,' said the father, glaring at her.

But the damage was done. Little Sammy pouted and pushed away his plate decisively. I tried hard not to smirk but even I as a non-parent could see that he would eat no more of his dinner on principle. Perhaps if they bought him cake or ice cream as dessert he'd be tempted, but that was it for the chicken nuggets, chips and beans.

The mother rolled her eyes. 'For goodness sake, Kaz, now see what you've done. Sam, there'll be no dessert for you and when we go back to the caravan you'll go straight to bed, no playing, if you don't eat at least half of what's on your plate. Come on, it's what you asked for. It's perfectly all right. Nellie didn't make it dirty.'

Sammy picked up his toy and inspected its trunk. 'Nellie's dirty though.' He showed it to his mother. There were beans all over it.

'Give it here, I'll lick them off,' the older boy said, trying to snatch the toy, but Sammy hugged it tightly to him, neatly transferring the beans to the front of his t-shirt.

The mum caught me watching, and gave a wry smile. 'Kids, eh? Who'd have 'em?'

I chuckled politely in return. Who indeed? I thought. It always looked like a nightmare to me. All parents seemed to have moments like this when they snapped at their kids and wondered why on earth they'd ever had any. Surely if you had a child you should love it unconditionally, no matter how infuriating it was? You shouldn't be saying to complete strangers, 'Who'd have 'em?' especially not in front of them. My mother had done that to me all my life. She'd told me many times she'd never wanted children. She wouldn't even let me call her 'Mum' – I always had to call her by her first name, Jackie. She'd reluctantly attended parents' evenings at my schools, and spent ages telling my teachers how she'd never intended to have a child and how life would have been so much easier without me. 'Surely though,' my Art teacher had said during one of Jackie's worst anti-Maria rants, 'now that you've got her you're proud of what she's achieving?' Jackie had shaken her head. 'No, not really. Just daubs of paint, isn't it, and when she does it at home she makes a mess of her homework desk.' My teacher had looked at me with sympathy and I'd had to turn my head away before I started blubbing. It was always like that.

I didn't think this mum was as bad. She was just having a moment, making a joke. No one could be as bad a parent as Jackie. Thankfully, Dad had been a great parent, making up for Jackie as best he could.

'Why doesn't she love me?' I'd asked him a hundred times.

'She does, in her way, sweetie. She just finds it hard to show it,' he'd always replied.

My own dinner arrived as I was pondering this, and I ate it in silence, occasionally tuning in to the banter and bickering at the next table. Eventually, Aoife, who was wearing a My Chemical Romance t-shirt today along with heavy black eyeliner, came to clear my plate, and, as she did so, she spoke to the family.

'Really sorry, but the musicians will be here soon and they always take this table. Would you mind moving for me?'

'Not at all,' said the father. 'Come on, Sammy, bring Nellie. Nathan, Kaz, come on, we need to find another table.'

The pub had filled up while I'd been eating and, as I glanced around, I realised the only spare seats were at my own table. I'd been kind of hoping Declan would come in and join me, but it looked like I'd have the company of this family.

'Is it OK if we sit here?' the mother asked.

'Yes, that's fine, I'm on my own,' I replied, and they sat down gratefully, dragging one stool over from their previous table for little Sammy to sit on.

'Hi. I'm Sharon, this is my husband Dave, Kaz, Nathan and Sam,' the mum said, smiling, indicating her family. She had an open, likeable face and I warmed to her instantly.

'Good to meet you. I'm Maria,' I replied. 'Are you on holiday here?'

'Yes, camping just outside town,' Sharon said. 'Well, in a static caravan, so hardly camping but enough to manage with three kids.'

'Where's the campsite?' I asked, just for something to say, really. Sammy was making his elephant walk around the table. I snatched up my glass of J2O before it got knocked over by Nellie's bum.

'You go out of town on Church Street for about a mile then turn right,' answered Dave. 'It's a good site – in the grounds of an old ruined country house. The laundry and campers' toilets and showers are built into the old stable block. The house itself is still there but in ruins, thankfully fenced off or the kids would be roaming wild in there no doubt.'

'Ballymor House?' I asked, remembering the caption under the sketch in the museum.

Dave shrugged. 'Don't know what the house was called but it could have been that, given its location. Campsite's called "Clear View Campsite".'

'Huh.' Kaz looked up from her texting. 'There's no view. The trees are too tall.'

'I think there's a view from the pitches at the top of the site, Kaz,' Sharon said, as Kaz rolled her eyes and returned her attention to her phone.

'Put that away. It's very rude when we're with other people,' Sharon muttered to her. I wondered whether to say, *No, it's all right, Kaz, I don't mind*, but decided against it. The girl sighed theatrically and slipped her phone into the back pocket of her ripped jeans, then folded her arms across her chest. A moment later, a faint buzz alerted her to an incoming text and, with a defiant glare at her mother, she pulled the phone out again.

'So, what brings you here, Maria?' Dave asked. 'You're not local, I can tell that much!'

'Ha, no, I'm not. Though if you go back far enough my family were from around here. That's what I'm doing, actually – researching my ancestors.' I didn't want to tell them about the book just yet. It was too easy to sound arty-farty and pretentious if you started talking about writing books on obscure Victorian artists.

'Wow, I've always wanted to do that,' Sharon said. 'Must be great to know the names of all those people who had to exist so that you could exist. I'd never have the time to do the research though, not with this lot consuming all my energy and my job and everything.'

'Yes, it does take time.' I took a sip from my glass. Was she really interested or was I in danger of boring her senseless if I said any more about my family history?

'So did your ancestors live in Ballymor then? In the big house at the campsite?' Nathan asked. He ran his fingers through his hair to smooth it into place across his forehead.

'Not in the big house, no. But in the abandoned village. Have you been there?'

Dave answered. 'Not yet. We only arrived yesterday and the weather didn't look good enough for a walk today. Little one, there, needs a bit of encouragement. Actually, so do the others.' Kaz and Nathan both scowled at him for this, while Sammy cuddled Nellie tighter. I saw his hand creep towards his mouth, before he pulled it away and tucked it around the toy. If I had to guess, I'd say he was being trained out of a thumb-sucking habit.

'It's worth a visit,' I said. I turned to Nathan, who'd shown the most interest. 'You can explore all the cottages, try and imagine what it would have been like to live there.'

'Cool.' He shrugged, then tried to look over Kaz's shoulder at her phone. She punched his arm to stop him, earning herself a telling-off from Dave.

We chatted for a while longer, until the musicians arrived. I told them about Michael McCarthy, but not about my book. I kept looking round to see if Declan was in the bar as I had a number of questions for him, but there was no sign of him all evening, which left me feeling strangely disappointed. Paulie, however, was in his usual place at the end of the bar, steadily working his way through a number of pints of Guinness, and exchanging a few words with other local regulars. It was my third night in the pub and I was beginning to feel quite at home here.

When the musicians had got themselves set up, Sharon leaned over to Dave. 'We should go before they start. Sam's looking tired.'

Dave looked disappointed, as did the older kids. 'Aw. I was hoping to hear a bit of traditional Irish music.'

'Yeah, me too,' said Kaz. 'It'll probably be crap but I'd like to hear some while we're here.'

'Language, Kaz,' Sharon said, with a frown. 'Maybe we could stay for one or two tunes, then, but not too late, or Sammy will be overtired. And you know what he's like then.'

Sam's hand crept towards his mouth again, and I couldn't help but think if he curled up against his mum with his thumb in his mouth he'd probably stay happily for the entire musical set.

But, after the first two tunes – 'The Rose of Tralee', then 'The Fields of Athenry', which Dave clearly recognised as a rugby song, as he hummed along happily to it – Sharon stood and gathered up their belongings. 'Come on. I'm driving and I'm leaving now. So you either come with me or you're walking.'

The rest of her family pouted but got up and followed her out, waving at me as they left. I went to sit on a bar stool for the rest of the evening, rather than take up a table by myself when there were people standing. As I perched beside Paulie, he acknowledged me with a slight tilt of his head. I smiled to myself. It was probably as near as I'd get to being accepted in this community by the old fellow. I wondered whether Dan had found my bracelet. Hopefully he'd text me later and say he had it.

CHAPTER 6

Kitty

The rain was heavy, turning the lane in front of the cottages into a muddy stream. Kitty slipped several times as she picked her way up through the village to Martin O'Shaughnessy's cottage. She hadn't much to give him on this occasion – only a sketch Michael had made of the view across the valley, which might cheer him a little. Nothing to eat. She knew Martin still had some potatoes, and if he was unwell she could stay and boil some for him. She could milk the goat as well. Her gift today was her time and her labour.

She pulled her shawl tighter around her shoulders in an attempt to keep the worst of the rain off. The sketch was rolled up and tucked into her skirt. Martin was ailing and it was her neighbourly duty to go to him every day.

As she approached the end cottage, she stopped a moment and patted the goat, tied by a frayed rope to a post beside the door and huddled under the eaves out of the rain. It clambered to its feet and nosed around her skirts. 'I've nothing for you today, girl,' she said. 'Maybe next time.'

But something was wrong. There was no plume of smoke from Martin's chimney. He always kept a turf fire alight, but today there was nothing. The cold hand of dread clutched at her heart as she tapped on the door.

'Mr O'Shaughnessy? Martin? Are you there?' There was no answer, so she pushed open the wooden door and peered into the gloomy interior of the cottage.

A rasping cough came from the corner, and with relief she saw that the old man was lying there – sick, but alive.

'Has your fire gone out, Martin? Will I light it for you?' Kitty didn't wait for an answer but set about immediately raking out the ashes, laying turf, kindling and a few sticks of wood in the fireplace and lighting it with her own tinderbox and flint.

It wasn't long before she had the fire going again. Martin had coughed piteously throughout. When she turned back to him, she could see by the firelight that he had weakened considerably since the previous day. 'Ah, Martin, let me clean you up a little. Have you had anything to eat today?'

'No, Kitty, and there's nothing I want to eat. Just a sip of water, if you would . . .' His voice was weak and rasping.

She fetched him a cup, filled it from his bucket which she'd replenished from the stream the day before, and held it to his lips. He could barely lift his head to sip it. It wouldn't be long now, she knew. But for once it wasn't the hunger ending a life. Martin still had potatoes, and the goat.

'Will I milk the goat? Perhaps a sip of fresh warm milk will perk you up a little. Or a hot drink? The fire's burning nicely now,' she said.

'No, Kitty, nothing more. You've done enough for me. Milk the goat if you like, but take the milk for yourself. Now away back to your own home and your children. How's your young Michael doing, anyway?'

'Ah, he's grand. He's strong, and is getting plenty of work. That reminds me—' she pulled out the picture Michael had drawn and handed it to Martin '—he said to give you this. To cheer you up, like. 'Tis the view from in front of our cottage, across the valley. Look, you can see the hills, dropping away there to the sea.'

Martin peered at the drawing. 'He's a talented fella, your Michael. He deserves better than this life. He should get himself to Dublin, find a sponsor, have his pictures shown in a proper gallery. People would pay money for them, so they would.'

Kitty sighed. 'He should. But how can he? He's not got the money to get himself to Dublin and set himself up. I've no way of helping him.' And, if he goes, it's the workhouse for sure, for me and Grace, she thought but didn't say.

'Poverty is the tragedy of the Irish,' Martin said, then succumbed to a coughing fit. Kitty stayed with him, mopping his brow, helping him sip from the cup of water, until he was settled, and drifting off to sleep. She resolved to call in again before nightfall. Poor Martin. She hoped the end would be painless for him.

The rain had stopped when she left Martin's cottage, and the sun was trying to break its way through the clouds. Good. She needed to walk to Ballymor and see if she could buy a little cornmeal. She had a few pennies left from Michael's last wages, and they were short of food again.

The walk along the lane, down the hill and into town was pleasant enough as the sun came out, drying her hair and shawl. As she entered the town and passed the church, she decided to go inside and sit for a minute, to pray for Martin O'Shaughnessy. She had no money to spare to light a candle for him. Her silent prayers would have to do.

The church was dark and cool inside. There was a stained glass window, depicting St Michael, at the far end above the altar. She slipped into a pew and smiled, remembering how she had gazed up at that window on the day she'd brought her Michael here to be christened.

*

Finding out she was pregnant had been devastating. She'd been not yet sixteen and terrified. Part of her had wanted to hide it for as long as possible, refuse to acknowledge what was happening to her body. If she ignored it for long enough maybe it would all go away, maybe it wouldn't be happening to her, maybe things would be as they had been, before. But the more rational part of her realised that she could not hide this, and neither could she handle it alone. If it was God's will that she should have a child then she would have one, and would do her very best for that child, regardless. She'd steeled herself, and told Mother Heaney about the pregnancy early on, before the old lady suspected anything herself.

'How did this happen, child? Who is the father?' Ma Heaney spoke with repressed emotion. Kitty had the impression she wanted to scream and shout, but knew that would not help matters. She told her then how the pregnancy had begun, and Ma Heaney grabbed the mug she'd been drinking from and flung it across the cottage smashing it into the fireplace. Kitty flinched in fear, but the old lady's rage abated as quickly as it had arisen, and she'd slumped in her chair. 'I'm not after blaming you, Kitty. That monster! Well, what's done is done, and I will help you with this child as far as I am able to.'

Kitty had knelt on the cottage floor at her feet and laid her head in Mother Heaney's lap. 'Thank you. I'm after thinking I'll need all the help I can get.'

She'd been sixteen by the time Michael was born. He had torn his way out of her as though he couldn't stand another minute inside, and had emerged red-faced and shouting, leaving her drained and exhausted, although the labour had been mercifully short. Old Mother Heaney had wrapped him deftly and passed him to her. Kitty gazed into his deep blue eyes and ran a finger across his furrowed forehead.

'Whisht, there, little man. Hush, now.'

And he had stopped crying and looked back at her with eyes full of suspicion and confusion, an old soul in the youngest of bodies.

'I'm your mammy, so I am,' she told him. 'I hope we're going to be friends, now.' The baby regarded her as though making up his mind about this, then turned his face towards her, mouth open.

'He's looking to suckle,' Mother Heaney said, and helped her get him latched on. He sucked at her strongly and greedily, and fell asleep immediately after.

'I think you and I are going to get along very well,' she told him, smiling. She hadn't known how she would feel about this baby, when he finally made an appearance. But, as he suckled, and she felt the warm weight of him in her arms, she knew that she loved this child. He was a part of her and always would be, no matter how he'd been conceived.

'What are you after naming him?' Mother Heaney asked.

Kitty had not given any thought to what she'd name her baby. She'd spent the first few months of her pregnancy ignoring the signs, praying it wasn't happening. And then the latter part had been all about fending off the taunts and jibes of the townsfolk, disgusted at her for having a baby out of wedlock. As if it was her fault! 'There she goes, the slattern!' women had called after her, spitting as she passed, while men had looked at her with a disconcerting mixture of disgust and desire written in their eyes. She'd done her best to keep working: looking after Mother Heaney who'd put her foot in a rabbit hole and broken a bone, and tending their potato plot. She'd barely paused to consider the idea of actually holding a baby, her own baby, in her arms, and being required to give him a name.

'Well, girl? Father John will be asking. He can hardly baptise a baby that has no name, can he?'

'I'll decide later,' she said, 'but don't worry, I'll have a name ready for his baptism.'

''Tis Sunday tomorrow. You can take him for baptism then, at the end of Mass.' Mother Heaney bustled about the cottage, tidying up, putting water on to boil to make tea.

She was a good woman, Kitty thought. What Kitty would have done without her these last few years since her parents died she did not know. Mother Heaney had taken her in, brought her up, shared her cottage and potato plot and been like a parent to her. She was a distant relative – an aunt of her mother's – but it had been out of kindness that she'd given a home to Kitty. 'Well, if you call it kindness to let someone share your work and look after you in your old age,' she'd said with an amused snort, whenever Kitty had thanked her for it.

Kitty spent her first night as a mother curled on her straw mattress, with the baby tucked in beside her. Even as she slept deeply, exhausted from the birth, she felt herself still aware of the warm little body pressed up against her. Once or twice she woke, helped him to latch on, and lay quietly, savouring the delicious scent of his soft head, as he fed. He was only hours old but already she felt the deepest, most profound love for this tiny being that she could ever have imagined. Despite the way he'd come into the world, she knew that she would do anything for him, anything at all.

The next day Kitty rose, washed and dressed, fed the baby and left with him wrapped in a shawl to go to Mass with Mother Heaney. Some of the town women who'd spat at her while she was pregnant came now to look upon the baby. 'No one can resist a newborn,' Ma Heaney whispered, 'not even one that has no father.' Kitty still had not decided upon a name. On entering the church, she gazed up at the stained glass window above the altar. It depicted St Michael the archangel, defeater of Satan, guardian of the Church, the angel who attended souls at their moment of death, to ease their passage into the next life.

'Michael,' she said.

'What's that you're after saying?' Mother Heaney asked.

''Tis what I'll name the baby,' Kitty replied.

The old lady nodded her approval, and an hour later, at the end of the service, Father John anointed him with oil of chrism and poured holy water over his head, welcoming him into the Catholic Church. Kitty swelled with pride as she watched. Michael kept his eyes open and fixed upon the priest throughout, as though he understood the seriousness of the occasion.

When Father John handed him back to Kitty, her eyes had filled with tears. Michael had been born fatherless, but now he had God as his father. He would live a long, good life, she'd been certain of it. And she'd known then that she would do everything in her power to ensure it.

*

Now, so many years later, with that tiny baby almost a grown man, she left the church feeling calmed and uplifted. Remembering those good times – the early days with Michael when she'd learned what it was to be a mother, the support and love of dear Mother Heaney – had eased her soul. Outside, the clouds had cleared and the sun was fully out. There was beauty and peace to be found, even if there was poverty, starvation and death all around. She resolved to try to hold on to that thought, no matter what happened.

She paid a visit to the churchyard, laying her hand on the simple wooden cross that marked where her children were buried. 'May God rest your souls,' she whispered. And may Gracie and Michael never need join you here, she thought.

The food stores were further up the high street, past O'Sullivan's pub, where a few men were standing outside, enjoying the sunshine as they supped their pints. Time was when Patrick would have been one of them, enjoying a pint once a week after work. She nodded to the men and continued to the grain store. There was a crowd outside it. She joined the edge of the crowd and asked the woman standing next to her what was happening.

'There's no corn. 'Tis all down at the docks in Cork still. They've not been able to distribute it to the towns where it's needed. Disgusting state of affairs. What are we to do? How are we to feed our children?' The woman shook her head sadly. Around her, the crowd was becoming angry. Two men at the front began beating on the doors of the store with sticks.

'If there's no corn, why are they hammering on the door? If there's none to be bought there's nothing to be done,' Kitty said to her neighbour.

'They don't believe the warehouseman. They think he has sacks out the back that he's keeping for himself. I'm waiting here to see if they're right. If they're not, and I can't get any, there's nothing for us to eat today. And me with seven mouths to feed. Where will it all end, I ask you?'

'Where indeed?' Kitty replied, wishing she had something to give the woman. At least she only had three mouths to feed now. She felt a rush of pain as she remembered that only a year ago, she'd had seven mouths to feed too. Poor Nuala, Jimmy, Éamonn and Little Pat. All taken at such a young age to sit at Jesus's feet.

There was no point her staying in town. The crowd might turn violent, and she wanted no part of it. Her earlier tranquil mood had vanished, and now she wanted only to be home, in the cottage with Gracie and Michael. The chicken had laid an egg that morning. She still had a few of the potatoes Martin O'Shaughnessy had given her. And perhaps if he didn't want his goat's milk, he'd let her have it. They wouldn't go hungry tonight. She patted her companion on the arm in a gesture of sympathy and support, and set off back to Kildoolin, her basket as empty as it had been on her way to town.

On the way home, she paused for just a few minutes to gather some sprigs of wild rosemary and golden broom. Some for herself, and some for Martin, to brighten and scent his cottage. If he was now unable to leave his bed and see the beauty of the day for himself, she would bring a tiny piece of it inside to him.

*

That evening, after Michael had returned and they had eaten their meagre meal, Kitty once more walked up the village track to Martin O'Shaughnessy's cottage. She had a cold cooked potato, wrapped in a piece of muslin, to try to tempt him to eat. If he did not want it she would share it between Grace and Michael. She also carried the little posy she'd picked earlier. The sun was just dipping down behind the hill, but it would be light enough for another hour, for her to make sure he was settled for the night.

She tapped on the door, called out, and went straight in without waiting for an answer. No need for him to struggle to catch his breath to reply. The fire had gone out again, though the ashes were still hot, so she quickly banked it up and got it roaring again. She put the flowers in a mug of water on the table. Then she turned her attention to the bed in the corner, and the rasping, irregular breaths that were coming from it.

'Well now, Martin, are you feeling any better?' She knew the answer already, but it was as well to be cheerful. She knew Martin was dying, and he knew it too.

'No, Kitty, I can't say that I am,' he said, his voice barely a whisper, and his words followed by a coughing fit.

'Hush now, Martin. Don't speak if it hurts you so.' She fetched a cloth, wet it and used it to clean the dried spittle from around his mouth. His lips were dry and cracked. She held the cup of water for him to sip from, but he wasn't able to lift his head. Instead, she found a second cloth, a clean one, wet it and let the water trickle into his mouth from its corner. He sucked at it like a newborn baby. It was better than nothing.

'Not long now,' he croaked. 'Not long.'

'Should I fetch Father John for you?' It was a long walk back to Ballymor this late at night, but she'd do it, if Martin wanted it. Or she'd send Michael who'd be much quicker. She cursed herself for not having spoken to Father John about Martin while she was in town earlier, but to fetch the priest to administer the last rites was an admission that death was imminent, and she had not wanted to frighten Martin or hasten his end.

He was shaking his head. 'No, I've no need of Father John.' He reached out a crabbed hand, and she took it. It was cold and thin, but he squeezed her hand with surprising strength. 'Sit with me, Kitty. It won't be long. Sit with me, till the end. I don't want to go alone.'

Her eyes filled with tears as she nodded. 'Of course, Martin. I'll stay, and I'll do what I can for you.'

He squeezed her hand, and closed his eyes, letting out a rasping sigh.

She settled herself into a chair pulled up beside his bed, keeping her hand in his. It might be a long night. She was thankful she had banked up the fire so much when she first arrived. But if this was all she could do for her kind neighbour then it is what she would do. No one should be alone at the time of their passing.

Kitty watched the light slowly turn to dusk and then dark through the small window. The moon rose, its silvery light slipping into the cottage, caressing everything it touched. She listened to Martin's laboured breathing, stroked his head and moistened his lips, but otherwise allowed her mind to swim deep into her thoughts.

An hour or so after she'd arrived, Michael tapped on the door and entered.

'Mammy? We wondered where you were. Grace is in bed. Is there anything I can do? Is Mr O'Shaughnessy . . . is he . . . ?'

'It won't be long,' she whispered. 'There's nothing you can do, except – milk the goat. Take the milk back for Gracie. I'll be staying here.'

He squeezed her shoulder, and she leaned into his arm, drawing strength for the night ahead from his presence. And then he was gone, leaving her once more watching the life slowly leave Martin O'Shaughnessy.

The old man woke once more, and mumbled a few words, gasping between them. She had to lean close, and strain to make them out. 'Take the . . . goat, Kitty. Don't let . . . Waterman . . . have it. Look after . . . young Grace . . . and Michael. Write to my sons, tell them . . . And . . . thank you.'

After another hour, or was it two, perhaps three, his breathing became irregular, with long gaps between each one. Each time she wondered whether it would be his last. And then finally, one last breath, a gurgle in his chest, and stillness, apart from a twitching muscle near his eye. A minute later that stopped too. Kitty released her hand from his, placed his hands on his chest, crossed herself, and murmured the Lord's Prayer.

She sat quietly for a few minutes more. So now there was only herself, Michael and Gracie left in the village. In the morning she would go to Father John, and arrange for Martin's body to be collected, and buried. She didn't know whether Martin had any money – if she could find any she would make sure he had a proper burial in the churchyard. If not, he would be put in the mass grave along with the latest famine victims. It was not something she could bear to think on, while she still sat with his mortal remains.

'Bless you, Martin. May you be at peace now,' she said, and hauled herself stiffly to her feet. It was time to go.

Outside, the full moon shimmered across the landscape, oblivious to the events inside the cottage. Kitty raised her face to it and breathed in deeply. The air was fresh and clean, damp with the night's dew but refreshing and cleansing.

The goat had scrambled to its feet as she came out, and now Kitty untied her. 'Come on, girl. Come on and I'll see if I have some eggshells and potato scraps for you.'

It walked obediently beside her, down the lane back to her own cottage, as though it knew its master was dead. There would be goat's milk to drink in the morning, Kitty thought, but immediately chastised herself for thinking of her own family's fortune, when poor Martin lay dead not a hundred yards away.

CHAPTER 7

Maria

I stayed in the bar till closing time, sipping J2Os and mineral waters, enjoying the music and pondering Dan's question. We'd been together so long – five years, and had lived together for three. Why upset the status quo? What was marriage anyway, other than a piece of paper that made it 'official'? We loved each other, we were committed to each other – financially at least, since we had a joint mortgage on the house – what more would being married give us? I was scared of change, I knew that. Dan had spent ages talking me into buying a house with him. We'd originally rented a place together, and I'd liked the fact that if everything went wrong I could move out and give up the tenancy with only a month's notice. Buying a house was a much bigger commitment. But it had made financial sense, and I had been certain Dan was the person I wanted to spend the rest of my life with, even if I had never thought about marriage. I was still certain of that, although looking to the future was not something I was very good at. The future looked scary from here.

I was better at thinking about the past. Dan and I had met in a pub, much like this one but in Camden Town. It had been packed to the rafters and there was a live band playing – some kind of alternative rock band, clothed all in black with spiky neon-coloured hair and dragons on their shirts. Aoife would have loved them. I'd been at the bar, trying to buy drinks for myself and two mates who loved this music and had dragged me along, and I was being totally ignored by the bar staff. Probably, I'd thought at the time, because my looks weren't alternative enough. There was no gel in my hair, no rips in my jeans and no piercings in my nose. The bloke to my left at the bar – mouse-brown floppy hair, matching eyes, lovely smile – was also being ignored. He'd been waiting even longer than me. After a while the two of us began rolling our eyes, sighing with exasperation and then giggling.

'I guess we're not the kind of customers they want here,' he'd said to me. 'I'm Dan, by the way.'

'Maria. Nice to meet you,' I'd said, and instinctively put out my hand for him to shake. The formality of the gesture made us both giggle some more, and by the time we were both eventually served, we'd swapped phone numbers.

He texted me on and off during the evening until, when I could take no more of the thrashing guitars and screaming lyrics, I'd told my mates I was going home with a headache, texted Dan, and we met up outside the pub. He'd walked me home the long way, via the canal towpaths, and we'd had our first kiss at the door of the flat I was renting at the time. I think I'd known even then that this was a relationship that would last. Why then was I unable to say a simple yes to his proposal? Or was it just the other thing, that I hadn't told him, and that he should know before he had my answer? That he should have known before he asked the question?

O'Sullivan's band were now playing the Irish national anthem, and everyone in the pub stood up in respectful silence. Even Paulie shuffled off his bar stool and gazed into the middle distance, his eyes misty. I loved the patriotism of the Irish, but playing the national anthem signalled the end of the night, and indeed Aoife turned up the pub lights, the musicians packed up, and the pub slowly emptied of customers. Time for bed. No text from Dan about the bracelet yet.

It was when I was half undressed, pottering around my room in my underwear, that he called me.

'Hi, Maria. I found the bracelet.' His voice sounded strangely taut, as though he was trying to control his emotions.

'Great! Where was it?' I felt a huge wave of relief. That bracelet was so important to me. So many memories were bound up in it, starting with Dad waltzing me around the sitting room to Marianne Faithfull's 'Dreaming My Dreams' on the Christmas he'd given it to me, while Jackie watched, scowling, jealous of the attention I was getting from him.

'It was where you said it might be. In the top drawer of your bedside cabinet.' Dan took a deep breath. 'Maria, is there something you need to tell me?'

Oh God. I suddenly realised what else I had stuffed into that drawer, underneath shop receipts and packets of painkillers. I didn't know what to say, how to start the conversation we were clearly just about to have, that we *should* have had weeks ago. My mind raced, hunting for the right words.

'Maria, when did you take the test? Is it recent, or what? I mean, are you actually . . . right now . . . or . . .'

I sat down heavily on the bed. This was it. No more denying it. I had to tell him, and it would change everything. 'Two months ago.'

'Two months? And you're still . . . I mean, you haven't lost it, or . . . shit, t-terminated it?' His voice was shaking. 'Because I don't think I could handle . . .'

'No. I'm still pregnant.'

'Oh thank God! That's . . . that's bloody amazing! I'm sorry, Maria, but when I found it and saw the blue line, I was terrified it was an old one, and you'd . . . ended it, and never told me. Sorry, I don't know how could I even think that. You wouldn't do that. 'Course not. Sorry. Been drinking. Maybe I had a few too many. Oh wow! We're going to be parents!'

I *had* thought about a termination. God, I'd never admit that to him, but the fear of the future that had coursed through me when I did the test and that blue line appeared had been so profound that researching abortion clinics had been my first thought. It was very swiftly replaced with the knowledge that, whatever happened, I could not go through with that. I couldn't do it to Dan.

'Yes, we are,' I said. Parents. God, what a big, grown-up, terrifying word that was. I found myself crying again. Tears came so easily these days – hormones, I guessed.

'Wow! When? Do you know the due date? Have you been to see a doctor? How have you been feeling? And when . . . *when* were you going to tell me?'

'I'm about fifteen weeks. It's due in mid-January.'

'Fifteen weeks? Already? But how long have you known?'

'A few weeks. I was going to tell you soon . . . just hadn't quite found the right moment. I was . . . kind of in denial, I suppose. I'm scared.'

'Aw, but, Maria, you should be excited, not scared. Is everything OK? Are *you* OK?'

I was silent. Images of Jackie rushed through my mind: her berating the five-year-old me for tipping my crayons out over her polished oak floor, telling me to 'grow up and stop crying' when as a seven-year-old I'd fallen off my bike and cut my knee, sneering that 'even dead bodies float' when I'd come home proudly bearing a swimming certificate from Brownies. What if being a bad mother was an inherited trait, and I'd be as bad as she was?

'Maria? What's wrong? You've gone quiet. God, I wish I was there with you now.'

So did I. I took a huge breath, but even so my words came out as a sob. 'What if I'm no good as a mum? What if I'm like Jackie?'

'But what if you're like your dad? I never knew him, but from everything you've told me it sounds like he was a wonderful man and a fantastic parent.'

'He was.' He'd made up for Jackie. His death had driven Jackie and me even further apart, if that was even possible. I was seventeen when he'd died, and I moved out a week after his funeral, not wanting to spend any longer around Jackie than I had to without Dad there. We'd had a huge row. Jackie accused me of leaving when she needed me most, but couldn't she see that I'd needed a mum? A proper mum, with warm, welcoming arms, who would be proud of me no matter what. I couldn't cope with her coldness and distance once Dad was no longer there to act the go-between.

'So, there you are then. Half your genes come from him. You'll be great. I mean, this is a life-changing experience for both of us, and I won't deny it, I'm nervous too, but – I always wanted to be a dad. And although we may not be perfect, I'm sure we'll be *good enough*, and that's all that matters.'

He was so wise. And he was right, I knew it in my heart. But I still could not get my head round it all. Would I ever feel ready to get married and be a mum? An image of me standing at an altar, heavily pregnant in a scarlet wedding dress looking like an overripe tomato flashed through my mind. Is that how it would be? Is it what I wanted? I still needed time alone, to get myself straight. It was all happening so quickly.

'Dan, it's late. I should get to bed now.'

'I suppose you need to get a good amount of sleep, in your condition.'

'Please don't say that – "in your condition". Hate that phrase.'

'Sorry.' He was silent for a moment. 'Hey, weren't we always careful? How did you even get pregnant? Shit, Maria.' His excitement suddenly seemed to ebb away. 'Oh God. Am I making a fool of myself being excited about becoming a dad? It's not mine, is it? That's why you hadn't told me, and why you ran off to f-fucking Ireland when I proposed. You're pregnant with someone else's kid. Fuck, that's it, isn't it?' His words were beginning to slur. This was not the sort of conversation to have when he'd been drinking, but here we were, in the middle of it.

'Wait, no, let me explain . . .'

'Jesus, Maria. I can't take this right now. You said yourself, it's late. We'll talk again.'

'Dan, just let me—'

But he was gone. I tried to ring back immediately but he must have turned his phone off. I curled up foetus-like on the bed and hugged a pillow against my tummy. Whatever happened, I didn't want to damage my relationship with Dan. He was the best thing that had ever happened to me. And yet, I had damaged it by not telling him about the baby until now. I put a hand on the small but firm bump below my belly button. What if we split up over this? What if I ended up pregnant and alone, losing the best thing in my life? And how on earth was I ever going to cope with motherhood, whether we were together or not?

Maybe keeping it secret had been a bad idea, and I should tell people, talk it through and come to terms with it in that way. I instantly thought of Declan. He seemed like such a good listener, and that's what I needed right now. Someone to listen.

CHAPTER 8

Kitty

The village was a lonely place after the death of Martin O'Shaughnessy. Kitty wondered about moving, but where could they move to? They had no money. They could just manage to pay the rent on the cottage and their tiny potato patch, as long as Michael was able to get work. It was a precarious existence. Kitty often dreamed of a different life – one across the ocean in America, with Patrick, and the other children still alive and thriving. One where they had a two-storey house, a garden and regular income. With a park nearby where Patrick could teach the boys to play hurling. Where there were shops within a few minutes' walk – shops with fresh goods on the shelves, goods that she could afford to buy. A life where they were never hungry or cold. If only she and Patrick had taken the children and emigrated, before the accident, before the famine. If only they'd had the money for the passage, they'd have done it. It was the life they should have had. Not this one of poverty, starvation and death.

The last few months, since Martin's demise, had been a little easier. She'd taken the goat, milked her every morning and the family had welcomed the fresh goats' milk and cheese. The chicken had laid an egg, sometimes two, every day. They'd had enough potatoes between the remains of the sack Martin had given her and the others she'd found still tucked away in his cottage. She'd cleared his cottage, retaining anything of value or use to her, before Waterman's agent came to take it.

And it had been summer – bringing lighter days and warmer weather.

But now autumn was here. It was almost time for the potato harvest. The summer crop had been a disaster, but they'd been hopeful the main crop would have escaped the blight. Kitty had been ignoring the wilted stems and blackened leaves, praying that was caused by the damp, cold weather at the end of the summer and not by blight. They needed the autumn crop to be a good one, to provide enough potatoes to store, to last them through the rest of the autumn, the winter and spring. After these potatoes were lifted there would be no more produce from the ground until the early summer. Everything was resting on this crop being a success. It *had* to be a success. The alternative was unthinkable.

In Ballymor, as the potato harvest time approached, there was a palpable tension in the air. Men were discussing when they should lift the potatoes, but no one was mentioning the blight, or speculating on how good a harvest it would be. Last year they'd all thought the autumn harvest would be a bumper crop, and it had turned out to be disastrous. It was as if no one wanted to court fate by predicting either a good or bad harvest. It was, after all, a matter of life or death.

Another week, people were saying. Another week, and it'd be time. Kitty nodded and prayed daily that the harvest would be a good one, and the potatoes would be unblighted.

And then the rain came. For five days it rained solidly, so that the fields turned to quagmires and the roads to ravines. There would be no harvest until it stopped raining and dried out a little. Every day Kitty stood at the door of her cottage and looked to the west, hoping for signs of clear skies and better weather to come. But it was not to be.

Michael went off to work every morning regardless, coming home in the evening soaked through after a day labouring in the rain. Until the day he came home at lunchtime, with a worried expression on his face.

'Michael, why are you home so early?' Kitty asked. She'd been churning some goats' milk to make cheese.

He didn't answer immediately. He sat down heavily on a chair, and leaned over to dip a cup into the bucket of water. He drank it thirstily, wiped the back of his hand across his mouth and sighed.

'Waterman's laid me off,' he said. 'Well, not Waterman himself. His agent, William Smith, on Waterman's orders. They're economising. Wanting more work from fewer men, so they are.' He shook his head sadly. 'We were lined up and every second man sent home. I was one of the unlucky ones.'

'But just today, Michael? They'll be wanting you back again tomorrow, or next week at least?' Kitty twisted her apron in her hands. If Michael stopped earning money how would they pay their rent?

He raised his eyes to her and shook his head again. 'He said this was a permanent reduction. Waterman's saying his crops have failed too.'

'That's an outright lie,' Kitty said.

'I know. The grain harvest was grand, back in August. I should know – I brought half of it in. His beef cattle are fat and healthy. All that food, all being exported to England. And us with our few meagre potatoes. 'T'isn't right, Mammy. I'm glad not to work for him any more. I'll find another job. I'll find something. Don't you be worrying, now.'

She crossed the room to him, knelt beside him and hugged him. Grace, who had been sitting in the corner listening quietly, came over as well, and Kitty put an arm around her too. She didn't share Michael's optimism about him finding more work, but she wasn't going to say anything. With the chicken, the goat and the potatoes they had enough to eat, and the harvest would surely be a good one. Maybe Waterman would hold off from asking for the rent, now that his agent had put Michael out of a job.

*

Over the next couple of days, Kitty found herself appreciating having Michael around. He'd always worked so hard – gone from dawn to dusk – that she'd often felt she did not see enough of him. But now that he was out of work he was able to do some of the heavier jobs around the cottage that she'd been putting off. He repaired the roof where some thatch had come loose. He cut back the heather and gorse beside the track that was threatening to take over, now that there was no one else left in the village to keep it under control. He played with Gracie and sat for hours sketching her and Kitty.

Kitty knew it couldn't last, but while she had him at home, she made the most of him.

One day he was down at their little field, checking on the condition of the soil and deciding whether it was time to lift the potatoes yet. Kitty was finishing a few chores in the cottage and had planned to follow him there, when she saw two men on horseback coming up the track to the village. She laid aside the broom she'd been using, smoothed her hair and apron, and stood at the door to her cottage. As they approached, she realised with trepidation that it was Thomas Waterman and his agent, William Smith.

Waterman pulled his horse to a standstill a little way off, but Smith continued right up to her cottage and dismounted. Waterman did not. He was staring out across the moors towards the sea.

'Kitty McCarthy?' Smith said. 'Your rent's due.'

'Sir? Not till next week, I thought.' Kitty frowned in confusion. She had not got the date wrong, she was sure.

'It's gone up. You're in arrears for the last month. Pay that now, and then the next month's is due next week. Do you have the money?'

'No, sir, I don't. I will have the rent I'm expecting to pay next week though, as per the agreement I signed. I've had no notice of a rent increase.' She held her head high as she said this, but knew she would not win any argument with William Smith. The Englishman was known for his ruthlessness. Hadn't he just sacked Michael only three days before?

'I'm giving you your notice now, Mrs McCarthy. So if you've no money, I'll have to take something else in lieu of the rent. That goat, perhaps. She'll do.'

'No! Please, sir, not the goat. We need her milk, so we do.'

Smith sneered at her. 'Goats' milk? The peasants drink goats' milk, do they? I was thinking we'd carve her up as dog meat. The hunting hounds are hungry.'

Thomas Waterman turned to stare at her as Smith said this, and she felt cold shivers run through her body. She'd managed to keep away, out of his notice, for so many years, but now here he was, outside her cottage, his cold blue eyes on her. 'I know you, don't I? Ah ha, yes, I do know you. Pretty thing you were, when you were young.'

'Please, sir, leave us the goat. I'll have the money for you next week.' God only knew how she'd find the money, but somehow she'd have to.

Smith looked at his master, but Waterman said nothing, and continued staring at her.

Grace came out of the cottage at that moment, and stood behind Kitty. 'They're not taking Nana Goat, are they?' she whispered, using the nickname she'd given the animal.

'I think they might,' Kitty whispered back.

'You, child. Stand out here where I can see you,' Waterman commanded.

Grace took a step away from Kitty, and stood quaking before the great horse.

'Pretty, like your mother was.' Waterman was staring at her, an odd look in his eyes. He had no children of his own, Kitty knew. She'd heard rumours he had married in England, but then lost his wife in childbirth. The baby had not survived either.

'Grace, go back inside. Now.' Kitty was shaking with fear. She must keep Gracie away from this monster. He would not do to Grace what he had done to Kitty, all those years ago. She would not allow that, ever, no matter what it cost her.

Smith was untying the goat. 'Well, that's settled. Your rent's paid now, until next week. Make sure you have the cash.'

Kitty felt something snap inside. 'And how am I going to do that, now that you've sacked my Michael and taken my goat? Maybe I could have sold some goats' cheese. Or sold the goat herself. Will you give Michael a job? That's my only hope of being able to pay you next week. My only hope of keeping the hunger from the door, or that colleen in there won't live to grow up.' This last part she said quietly, for fear of Gracie hearing it.

Smith laughed, and Waterman sat impassive on his horse. Kitty shook her head. There was nothing she could say or do. They'd come up here today in the hope of harrying her out of her cottage, that was clear. She did not know why. But hers was the last inhabited cottage and perhaps Waterman had other plans for the village.

Smith remounted his horse, tying the goat to his saddle, and, without another word, the two men rode off back towards Ballymor House, with the goat bleating plaintively as it trotted along behind them. Waterman glanced once over his shoulder at her, his mouth open, as though there was something more he wanted to say. But he said nothing, and instead spurred his horse into a canter, ahead of Smith and the goat.

Kitty let out a roar of frustration, which brought Gracie running outside. The little girl put her arms around Kitty. 'It's all right, Mammy. It'll be all right. I didn't like those men, so I didn't, and I know it was one of them that's after taking away Michael's job. But they've gone now.'

'Ah, you're such a comfort, my love.' Kitty bent down and hugged her daughter. But she was wrong. They were not all right. In seven days' time they had the rent to pay, but no means of paying it. It'd be the workhouse for them, if Michael couldn't find a job, regardless of the state of the potato harvest.

She could not get the image of Waterman, aloof and uncaring, out of her head as she walked down the track towards their potato plot, to meet Michael. After all that she and her family had suffered at his hands, anyone would think he might have now taken pity on them, and left them the goat, waived the rent, and reinstated Michael in work. It was all within his power. Instead, he had allowed his agent Smith to ride roughshod over them. He was like his father had been – uncaring, harsh and callous. She ground her teeth as she remembered that it was Waterman's cost-cutting that led to the disaster in the copper mine which had taken her Patrick's life. And now his cost-cutting had put Michael out of a job and quite possibly would put them all in the workhouse.

*

When she was young she'd thought perhaps Thomas Waterman was different to his father. Perhaps he had some good in him – someone so handsome could not possibly be all bad. She'd been fifteen when she first saw him, working in the small plot of land leased to Mother Heaney. It was June, and she'd been bent double pulling up the early crop of new potatoes, shaking the soil off them, putting them into a basket, and throwing the stems onto a pile for composting. A man had come by on horseback, picking his way through the potato plots, occasionally stopping to speak to the labourers.

When she caught sight of him, she stood upright, arching her back to stretch her aching muscles.

He was tall, dark-haired, extremely handsome with dark eyes and a strong jaw, aged somewhere in his mid-twenties. A fine young man. She guessed he was Master Thomas, the son and heir of William Waterman, the English landowner to whom they paid rent for the cottage and potato plot, and for whom every able-bodied person in the area worked. William Waterman was usually absent, preferring to spend his time at his estate in England, leaving his Irish farms to be run by stewards, as long as they were making money for him. Kitty had only seen him once or twice, years before, and she had never set eyes on his son, although she'd heard tell of a good-looking, arrogant young man who one day would be their landlord and master. And here he was, sitting proud and aloof on a fine bay horse. She couldn't help but stare at him. She'd never seen a man quite so handsome before, and it made her insides feel funny, and her head feel light.

He was looking directly at her, she realised, and then he pulled his horse's head around and approached her, the animal's hooves trampling over two of her as yet unharvested potato ridges, containing the autumn crop. She could not believe that he had noticed her, and was coming her way. No matter that he was damaging the ridges – she could repair them when he'd gone. Hopefully none of the precious roots beneath the soil would be damaged.

'You're a pretty young thing. What's your name?' he said, his voice imperious, as though he was accustomed to being instantly obeyed.

'Kitty Tooley, sir,' she replied, dipping her head in a slight bow. She wondered if she should curtsey, but wasn't sure how.

'Loosen your hair, Kitty Tooley,' he commanded, smiling slightly at her.

She was confused. Her hair was tucked away under a headscarf, tied under her chin, as usual when she was working in the fields, to keep it out of her way. 'My hair, sir?' she said.

'Yes. Let it loose. I wish to see it hanging about your shoulders.'

She did as he asked, pulling the headscarf off and giving her head a shake, so that her long tresses swished over her shoulders. Despite his brusque manner there was something about Thomas that excited her. She should confess her feelings to the priest on Sunday – but as soon as that thought crossed her mind she dismissed it. The way she felt when looking up at Thomas on his horse was something she wanted to keep secret, even from the priest. Even from God. Even though she knew it was very wrong to feel like this.

He was watching her closely, then suddenly he slipped down, off his horse, and stepped over to her. She gasped as he reached for her, and clasped her chin in his hand. His fingers felt smooth on her face, as though he'd never done a day's manual labour in his life. He was squeezing her cheeks, not too hard, but tightly enough that she couldn't pull away, whether or not she'd wanted to. He was looking right into her eyes, and she gazed back, hoping it would not anger him. Close up he was even more handsome, and she felt a tingle of excitement. He had noticed *her*, of all the pretty young girls there must be on his estates!

'You're a pretty thing,' he said again. 'Yes, very pretty. Come to Ballymor House this evening at sundown. Wait for me behind the stables. I'll have a gift for you. Something nice for you to wear, perhaps.'

'Sir, is it right I should meet you? My great-aunt's after saying—'

He held up a hand. 'I don't give a fig what your great-aunt says. You're a grown girl. Do you want my gift or not?'

'Yes, sir, you're very kind, sir, but I—'

'Then come.' He smiled at her once more, and she smiled broadly back at him. This fine young man, heir to a huge fortune and all the land around, had singled her out and was paying her so much attention!

With that he let go of her, mounted his horse and spurred it into a canter, its hooves demolishing yet more of her potato ridges.

She set about repairing the damage with vigour, her thoughts on Thomas Waterman. He considered her to be pretty. He seemed to like her. What gift would he have for her? Her thoughts ran to fantasies in which he kissed her, proposed to her, scooped her up and onto his horse behind him, and galloped away across the moors to a castle where she would be mistress and never have to dig a potato plot again. Now those dreams really *should* be confessed on Sunday.

*

Kitty shook her head at the memory. How young and foolish she had been – a naive fifteen-year-old who'd known nothing of the ways of men, especially the ways of arrogant, rich landowners' sons. How different her life would have been if Waterman had never stopped to talk to her on that fateful day, or if she'd refused to go to meet him as he'd asked. She set off towards their potato plot, to tell Michael the bad news about the goat.

Michael was standing, hands on hips, in the middle of their field. As Kitty approached, she could see that the soil had dried enough to be able to bring in the harvest – it would not cling too much to their boots and spades. She gazed out to the west – clear skies, no wind. They'd lift a few potatoes by hand today, and then bring sacks and spades in the morning to complete the harvest. She smiled. No matter what Waterman did, he could not take from her the pleasure of harvesting her own crops, laying down the stores that would feed her children throughout the winter. Michael would find other work. Something would happen to change their luck.

'Weather looks good. I think we should lift a few today, and the rest tomorrow,' she said to Michael, when she came within earshot.

His face looked drawn and worried. 'I lifted some. Look.' He showed her his hands. He was holding three small potatoes, which all had ominous veins of black running through them.

Kitty felt her heart sink. 'No! Oh, no, please God, no. Not again.' She sank to her knees and scrabbled at the soil under the nearest plant, raking it with her fingers, reaching into the earth to find the tubers beneath. She found one, pulled it up, and stared at it. It was undersized and discoloured, just like the others. She stared at Michael in horror. He wordlessly pulled a small knife from his pocket and handed it to her. She cut the potato in half. The flesh should have been smooth and white, but was mottled black, brown and grey. 'No! No, no, no!' She scrabbled again in the earth, digging the roots of another plant in a different ridge. This one was worse – the potatoes were completely rotted and inedible.

'Oh my God, Michael, it has happened again! What will we do? We'll starve for sure this winter, just like the little ones before us. What have I done to deserve this? What have any of us done? This—' she stared down at the ruined potato '—this is Ireland's tragedy, so it is. Ireland's ruin. Ireland's end!' She threw the potato across the field, as hard as she could.

'Mammy, Mammy, be calm there, now!' Michael put his arms around her and held her as she sobbed, huge, racking sobs on his shoulder. 'I'll find other work, so I will,' he went on. 'There's talk of a public works scheme starting up. Road building. I'll apply for that. The government won't let us starve this time, not after what happened last winter. There'll be work, there'll be money and food to buy in the shops. We'll be all right. We still have the chicken, and the goat, and the rest of Martin O'Shaughnessy's potatoes.'

Only half a sack left, she thought, and he didn't yet know the goat was gone. They faced yet another winter of starvation. How could they possibly survive?

CHAPTER 9

Maria

I woke up with red-rimmed eyes and a lead weight in my heart. Before I so much as opened my eyes I was reaching for my phone to call Dan. But it went straight to voicemail. Damn it. Right when I really needed to talk to him, and explain things. I couldn't let him go on for a moment thinking it wasn't his child. How painful that must be for him.

There wasn't much I could do about it though, other than try to take my mind off things before I went mad, and try to call him again later. Or maybe he'd call me with any luck.

I spent a few minutes after breakfast writing a list of things I wanted to do while in Ireland, and research angles I should follow up. It was a long list. That sketch I'd seen in the museum, which looked like an example of Michael McCarthy juvenilia, had intrigued me. Why had it hung on display at Ballymor House for years? What was the connection between the then owners of the house and Michael? Who was the man on the horse in the sketch? I added an item to my list to research who'd owned Ballymor House from the famine years onwards. And then go out to take a look at what was left of it.

But first, I wanted to have a look around the various graveyards and cemeteries in the area. Maybe there was a McCarthy grave. I knew Michael himself was buried in Highgate Cemetery in London, and I had been to see his grave, with its ornate carving and Celtic cross, when I wrote my thesis, but maybe other McCarthys were here in Ballymor. I called first at the tourist office to pick up a map of the town and find out where the cemeteries were. There was a small graveyard behind the church, a larger one up the hill beyond the tourist office, and a famine graveyard three miles out of town where, the tourist office lady told me, a mass grave contained an estimated 1,500 people who'd died during the winter of 1848–9. I shuddered to think of so many people in one pit, all unmarked. Whole families buried together with no one left to mourn them. I didn't know whether Michael had any siblings, but most Irish families of that time would have had several children, so I assumed he had. As I perused the map and set off towards the first graveyard – the one nearest the tourist office – I wondered whether any of his family had died during the famine.

This graveyard was well tended, with neatly mown lawns surrounding scrubbed and polished headstones. I wandered among them reading the inscriptions, but realised they were mostly quite recent graves, with dates from the 1950s onwards. Many stones had more than one name on them. It seemed to be traditional for families to buy big plots to accommodate several of their members over two or three decades. The cemetery was moving but not what I was looking for, so I quickly left it and walked back towards O'Sullivan's and the church opposite, guessing that the graveyard nearer the church would be the town's first one, containing earlier graves.

It certainly looked older. A rusty iron gate separated it from the well-maintained gardens and car park immediately around the church, which I realised I had not yet set foot inside. The graveyard itself was unkempt, with waist-high thistles jostling for space with nettles and grass. A couple of paths had been mown through it all, and I followed these, once again reading the inscriptions if possible. Many were too weathered and worn to be able to make much out, but I found a few with dates in the 1840s – O'Dowells, Ryans, McDaniels and O'Shaughnessys. Encouraged by this, I began a more systematic search, going up and down each row, pushing aside the thistles and treading down the nettles, glad I had worn trainers and not sandals, trying not to think about Dan and last night's phone call.

I was so engrossed in this I did not notice Declan until he stood right in front of me. 'Would you be looking for a McCarthy grave?' he said, making me jump out of my skin.

'What? Oh! Hi,' I said, and was annoyed to find myself blushing furiously. 'Didn't see you there. Yes, I thought I'd have a poke around to see if there were any McCarthy graves here. There are certainly some that go back to the time of Michael's parents.'

He smiled. 'Yes, there are many. The McCarthys are over here. Not sure if they are actually buried here, but there's a memorial stone against the wall over there.' He gestured further up the cemetery, near the boundary wall.

'I should have guessed you'd know,' I said, grinning at him, and we both made our way over to the grave he'd pointed out. He held back a couple of brambles for me – the perfect gentleman.

'I should really get this place tidied up,' he muttered. I wondered what his job was, if the graveyard was his responsibility, but did not comment as he'd said it more or less to himself.

The McCarthy gravestone was easily legible and I was almost disappointed that Declan had pointed it out to me. I would have found it myself in time, and that might have been more satisfying. But he'd certainly saved me time and doubtless saved me from some scratches. This headstone was made of white marble rather than the softish grey stone of the others that had weathered so badly. The lettering was still perfectly clear, once I'd pushed aside a couple of nettles with my foot.

In loving memory of
Patrick McCarthy – died 1844
And his beloved children
Patrick 1835–1846
Grace 1837–1849
Nuala 1839–1847
James 1842–1847
Éamonn 1844–1847
Victims of the Famine – Never to be Forgotten
In memory also of Kitty McCarthy, wife of Patrick and mother of the above children
May you rest at peace with our Lord
This stone erected by Michael McCarthy, in eternal gratitude for a mother's sacrifice

I read it in silence. What a lot of children. I counted up – Michael had five siblings, all of whom died during the famine years. And his father died just a couple of years earlier.

'Wow. What a tragedy. They all perished so close to each other,' I said. The words sounded trite and inadequate, and yet this was just one family of so many hundreds and thousands of families that must have suffered similar losses.

'I know. Puts our own troubles into perspective, doesn't it?'

'It certainly does.' I read the names again. 'Interesting that Kitty's name is on here. Yet the legend is that he never found her, and never knew what had happened to her.'

'Hmm,' he said, crouching down to peer at the engraving, 'but if you look closely it seems those last three lines are in a slightly different style to the others. I would say they were added later.'

I looked closely and saw what he meant. 'So the stone originally listed Patrick and the children, and Kitty and the line about the stone being erected by Michael were added later?'

'I think so. Often a family buy a plot when someone dies, and put a stone up with room for more names. Then other inscriptions are added whenever someone else is buried in that same plot.'

'But there are no dates for Kitty. That ties in with the idea that he never found out what happened to her. Perhaps he added that when he finally accepted that she must have died.' I was thinking aloud.

Declan nodded. 'Yes, that seems quite likely. I wonder what he was referring to by the mention of "eternal gratitude for a mother's sacrifice"?'

I shrugged. 'Wish I knew more about it.' I pulled out my phone and took some photos of the gravestone, from various angles. I wondered exactly what sacrifices Kitty had made for her children. All mothers had to give something up – whether it was as simple and short term as giving up alcohol while pregnant (although I'd not entirely given it up, having had champagne on the night Dan proposed, and a Guinness on my first night in O'Sullivan's), or the long-term giving up of eighteen years of your life to dedicate to bringing up a child. Jackie had always complained I'd held her back, that she could have done so much more with her life if she hadn't had me. Parenthood changes you – I'd seen that happen to friends, who'd given up work, stopped going out and spent all their time thinking about their children first, never doing anything for themselves. It could even affect your relationship – the very thing that had brought the child into existence could end up being threatened by it. I was terrified by the idea that might happen to Dan and me – already my pregnancy had driven a wedge between us. Yet again I realised what a life-changing event becoming pregnant was, and I was not sure I was ready for it.

That phrase from the gravestone – *a mother's sacrifice* – played on my mind. It was Michael I was here to research, but I was becoming more and more fascinated by his mother. I wanted to know more about her. Perhaps it would help me come to terms with my own impending motherhood. God knows I felt I needed all the help I could get.

'You should check the church records,' Declan said, shaking me out of my thoughts. 'They will tell you whether all the McCarthys are actually buried here or if it is only a memorial stone. They'll also say whether Kitty was buried in this parish, and if so, when it was.'

'Good idea. I will do that.' I wondered how to go about getting access to the records, and was about to ask Declan if he knew, when he spoke again.

'If you like, I can help you. It's fascinating, all this, so it is. And you with your book – that's the perfect excuse to get properly immersed in some research. I've time tomorrow, if you like. I'll meet you in the church. Any time after one thirty.'

'Perfect,' I said. 'I'll come after lunch then.'

He nodded. 'Well, I'll let you get on. Might see you in O'Sullivan's this evening, perhaps?'

'Sure, I'll be there.' I waved as he left, picking his way through the overgrown cemetery towards the church car park. Again I fleetingly wondered if I needed to be careful. He was a good-looking man, and in another life I'd have fancied him, definitely. But my life was complicated enough and I most certainly did not need to be adding to it. I put a hand on my slightly swollen belly. These jeans were definitely becoming too tight. There was a Dunnes Stores just up the road. Perhaps they'd have some cheap, loose trousers that would do until I needed to buy proper maternity wear. I pictured myself in a tent-like smock dress and shuddered, resolving to put off the moment when I had to wear that kind of thing for as long as possible.

The weather was better again – I was beginning to get the hang of Irish weather. Basically, you couldn't predict it. You had to wait until it was time to go out, look out of the window and then make a decision about what to wear and what to take. And you always had to take your mac. But today looked like it was going to remain sunny, so I decided to have a quick lunch in a café then head off into the moors for another walk. It had been so glorious on the day I'd walked up to Kildoolin, and I fancied a bit more of that. At the tourist office I'd collected some leaflets showing local walks so I decided to pick out one of those over lunch.

In the café, I ate a massive BLT and downed a huge pot of tea – portion size, I had noticed, was enormous in Ireland, as if to make up for the starvation their ancestors had endured during the famine. I bought a bottle of water to tuck in my rucksack and set off, towards Kildoolin initially but then veering off the track, up a lesser-used path, flanked initially by waist-high bracken, giving way to heather higher up the hillside. The leaflet from the tourist office contained a rough map, which showed that a little way up there was a stone circle that I wanted to see, and also some ruins of old copper mines. I remembered Declan had warned me about uncovered mine entrances on the hills. What copper mining had to do with my research into Michael McCarthy's life I did not know, but who cared, I was on holiday and might as well enjoy myself.

As the track wound its way up the hill, becoming quite steep in places, I found myself really missing Dan. We'd done a lot of hillwalking during the years we'd been together – mostly in the Lake District, or Snowdonia. We were both fans of that wonderful feeling of putting one foot in front of the other, each step a little higher than the last, each step taking you that bit closer to the summit and the sense of achievement when you reach the highest point. I missed him now – missed sharing the moment with him, the easy camaraderie that comes with sharing a physical challenge. He'd have been stopping every few minutes to photograph the view. We always ended up with dozens of pictures of every walk we did, no matter what the weather was like. Today it was clear and sunny, and as I'd expected, the view over the moors towards the distant sea became better and better the higher I climbed. In places the path was not much more than a sheep-track through the heather, and indeed a couple of times startled sheep scurried away as I approached. Once again I found myself wishing things were as they used to be. Me not pregnant, Dan having not proposed, but here with me now. Us together, young and free, with no worries.

I pulled out my phone. Now would be a good time to talk to him. But there was no signal on this side of the hill. It would have to wait.

Eventually, the path levelled out, though not yet at the summit of the hill. From here it contoured around, past a couple of rocky outcrops, and then suddenly, there it was – the walk's destination. A ruined building in grey stone, its windows glassless and cold, a tall circular brick chimney reaching to the sky. The old copper mine. I walked around it first, then went inside the roofless building, staring up at the blue patch of sky. There wasn't much left of the place, and no boards or notices to inform visitors about how the building would have been used. The leaflet from the tourist office didn't say much either, other than that it was one of several mines in the area that had been owned and run in the eighteenth and early nineteenth century by the Waterman family of Ballymor. Outside the building, a sturdy wooden trapdoor was set into concrete – an entrance to the mine, I guessed. The building must have housed a steam engine, perhaps for hauling up the copper ore, or for pumping out water.

Again I missed Dan. He'd have enjoyed investigating this with me. I imagined him taking endless photos and then, back at the pub, going straight onto the internet to see what more he could find out about copper mining in Cork.

This thought prompted me at least to take a few photos to show him. They wouldn't be any use for my book but good as a reminder of this holiday.

But would I ever get the chance to show them to him? Or had I ruined things completely between us? No, surely not. Our relationship had to be strong enough. We'd sort this out, as soon as we had the chance to properly talk. I checked my phone. Still no signal.

I put a hand over my belly. Hillwalking was just one of the things that would have to take a back seat when this baby came along. I sighed. At what age can children walk up Lake District fells? Seven? Eight? Older? Would I really have to give up doing something I loved, something Dan and I loved doing together, for eight or more years? Or even longer if we had a second child, I realised with a jolt. Dan would no doubt want more than one child. If we sorted out this mess and I said yes to him, I was saying yes to a potential whole brood of children, and many years in which we could not go walking in the mountains, or spend evenings in the pub without having to pay a babysitter, or go on holidays wherever we wanted. Small things, really, but all were examples of things to be sacrificed. Everything would need to revolve around the child or children – putting their needs first – doing what would suit them rather than what we wanted. It was a huge step and once again I felt terrified that I would not be able to do it. But once you became a parent you couldn't just run away, could you? With a jolt I realised that already I could not simply run away and ignore it. I was pregnant. It was happening, whether I liked it or not.

Suddenly the ruins of the copper mine held no appeal for me. I wanted to be back in my room in

O'Sullivan's, with a cup of tea and one of Aoife's wonderful cakes, and my phone in my hand with Dan on the other end of it, friends again, me apologising, him comforting me and telling me it'd be all right and we'd cope, and we could do this thing, together.

I turned and began walking back down the hill. My mind was focused inwards and I was barely looking where I was going. After a while I realised I was not on the path I'd taken on the way up. I'd veered off on a narrower sheep-track, or possibly just a rabbits' trail, which was petering out amongst the heather. I carried on, heading downhill, struggling through the knee-deep heather and occasional prickly gorse. I knew I'd find the path eventually or, at worst, pop out onto the road a little further out of town.

After a few minutes struggling through the heather it thinned out and gave way to bracken and some gorse bushes, which I had to carefully pick my way around. Away to my left I could see the stone circle, so I headed over in that direction. I was concentrating so hard on avoiding the gorse I almost fell straight into it – a mine entrance set into a rocky outcrop, leading steeply down. A few shreds of rotted wood showed it had once been boarded over but not any longer. I felt my heart pound – it had felt like a close escape. Another step and I might easily have stumbled into it. I crouched and peered into the gloom, carefully pushing back a branch of gorse. It was impossible to see much but it certainly wasn't the type of place you would want to fall into. I wondered if I should report it to someone, so they could come up and replace the rotten boards. But whose responsibility was it? Who owned the land? I realised that as it was not actually on a path it was unlikely anyone else would come this way and fall in.

My mind automatically turned to Declan. I'd mention it to him. He would know what I should do. Funny how after only a few short days in Ballymor I was already beginning to think of him as a good, close friend, someone I could rely on.

I straightened up and began making my way downhill again towards the stone circle, keeping a very careful eye out for more mineshafts. Only a few metres further on I found myself on a track that led downwards, directly to the stone circle. So the open shaft was not that far away from where people would walk. It was worryingly unsafe.

The stone circle itself was not as interesting as I'd thought it might be. It was about four metres in diameter, ten stones each about waist height situated in a rough circle. A *Bord Fáilte* sign declared it to be an ancient monument under the control of the Irish tourist board. Although the gorse and bracken had been cleared from around it, they were gradually reclaiming the area. Tall purple foxgloves added colour, and I took a few snapshots that I hoped were vaguely artistic. Maybe because it was so much older than the Kildoolin cottages and the mine workings, I did not get as much of a sense of the people who'd built it and used it, as I did amongst the other ruins. Or maybe it was because it had no association, that I knew of, with my ancestors.

CHAPTER 10

Kitty

Kitty had scraped together enough money to pay the rent by selling furniture and spare clothes. The little family now only owned the clothes they stood up in and a blanket each to sleep with. The cottage was even more sparsely furnished than before. Michael had insisted they kept one chair. 'Grace and me can sit on the floor to eat, sure we can, but you, Mammy, you must have a chair to sit on properly,' he'd said. She'd acquiesced, but only because she'd managed to raise enough this month, and they weren't yet starving, and the chair could wait to be sold to pay the next month's rent. Not that she liked to look ahead.

Things were becoming desperate. Without the goat, without Michael's wages, without the autumn crop of potatoes, food was extremely scarce. The chicken ceased laying eggs, so Kitty had no choice but to butcher it. At least it provided them with meals for two days, and broth for a third. The store of potatoes was almost gone. Very few had been salvaged from the disease-ravaged potato plot.

Michael came home one day battered and bruised. He'd taken part in a march, protesting at the lack of action from the government.

'They have to do something to help the people,' he told Kitty, as she tended to a cut above his eyebrow. 'They can't just let us all starve again, like last winter. 'Tis inhuman.'

'But how can they give charity to so many people?' she asked. 'And there are many who'd be too proud to take handouts, no matter that they were starving.'

'More fool them, I say.' Michael stared at her. 'If there'd been handouts last year, maybe we could have saved young Pat and the little ones.'

He was right, Kitty realised. She must not be too proud herself to take charity, if it was offered, not if it could keep her remaining children alive. 'Tell me, how did you come by the cut on your head?'

He sighed. 'There was a rally, in Ballymor. We met in the square in front of the church. All working men – or we would be working men, if there were any jobs. The fellow at the front of the march had stuck a loaf of bread on a pitchfork, and he held it aloft. It's all we want – work and a wage to buy our bread. We marched through the town, to the grain store. Word was out that there'd been a delivery, and there were sacks of cornmeal, imported from America, but there'd been no decision on how to distribute it. We went along to help them make that decision, if you get my meaning.'

Kitty nodded. She'd seen crowds building up around the store the last time she'd been in town, but on that occasion there'd been nothing in the store, and the crowd had dispersed, unwilling to waste its energy when there was nothing to gain from it.

'At the store, the constables and warehouse workers were defending the door. They had sticks and clubs, and were beating anyone who came too close. The marching men charged, and forced their way into the store, then an unholy battle took place with everyone lashing out at everyone else, and no one knowing who was on what side, though to be fair the warehousemen look as starved and thin as everyone else. I tried to get out once I saw what was happening, but caught a blow on my head as I ducked through the crowd.'

Kitty shuddered. She could imagine the scene all too well. Thank the good Lord Michael had not been more seriously injured. 'And was there any grain in the store?'

He shook his head. 'A few sacks is all I saw. Not enough to warrant fighting over. They'd either hidden the delivery somewhere else or it was all an untrue rumour. Mammy, if there'd been any food, I'd have got my hands on it and brought it back, sure I would. I'm sorry to come back empty-handed.'

'I'm just glad you've come back in one piece,' she replied, dabbing at the cut which was finally beginning to stop bleeding.

'What will we eat tonight?' Grace had been sitting silently, watching and listening. Her voice sounded weak and plaintive.

'Ah, my sweet colleen, there are potatoes still. I will put some in the pot.' Kitty didn't add that they were down to the diseased potatoes, the shrunken, foul-tasting ones they'd salvaged from the autumn harvest. She'd add herbs to the pot to try to disguise the taste. It was eat those or starve.

If only Patrick was still here. Unbidden, memories of that terrible day, before the famine, before the deaths of the little ones, came rushing into her mind.

*

It had been Martin O'Shaughnessy's eldest, Daithí, now gone across the ocean to America, who'd brought the news. He'd come running down the hillside behind the village, tripping over himself in his haste.

'Mrs McCarthy, Mrs McCarthy, come quickly! 'Tis your husband Patrick, so it is. He's been in an accident, in the mines. Come quickly!'

Kitty had dropped the potatoes she'd been preparing – fat and white they'd been, and plenty of them in those days before the Hunger – and quickly passed baby Éamonn to Grace to mind. She'd gathered up her skirts and run up the hill after Daithí, her thighs burning and her lungs heaving as she forced herself to keep going, faster and faster. What could have happened? Was Patrick badly hurt? She had to assume he was, or else why would Daithí have been sent to fetch her?

Finally, they reached one of the entrances to the copper mines. The hillside was riddled with tunnels and mineshafts, Patrick had told her. Generation upon generation of miners had followed the seams of copper ore, digging or blasting it out, hauling it to the surface in buckets, and handing it over to Thomas Waterman or his forefathers.

There was a clutch of men standing by the entrance, all with worried expressions but no one actually doing anything. Patrick was not amongst them. Kitty knew they'd seen her approach, yet not one of them lifted his head to catch her eye.

'What's happening? Where's my Patrick? Young Daithí here says you're after having an accident in the mine – is that right?'

'Ah, Mrs McCarthy,' said one man, shaking his head sadly. Kitty recognised him as James O'Dowell, Patrick's foreman.

She clutched at his sleeve. 'Tell me, what's happened?'

''Tis a bad one. I'm very sorry, Mrs McCarthy. There's been a collapse, down below. One of the tunnels. We were worried it was unsafe. We'd been telling Mr Waterman we needed to close that one for ages, so we had. But he wouldn't hear of it, said it was still yielding enough ore to be worth working. Patrick was down there. He was the last one inside. We dug and dug, but couldn't reach him, could only reach his foot, and that all crushed beneath the rock. There's no hope.'

At the last two words the breath left her, and she fell to the ground. Someone was wailing, keening, crying as though their heart had been torn from their body, and it was a minute before she realised the sound was coming from her. Patrick, gone, crushed, and no hope of being saved. Memories of their time together crowded through her mind – their first meeting in Ballymor at the midsummer fair; their first kiss high on the moors on a warm summer's day; the delight in little Michael's eyes when Patrick threw him high in the air; their wedding day when the future held so much promise; the births of the five children they'd had together – Little Pat, Gracie, Nuala, Jimmy and baby Éamonn. And now he was gone. He'd never again walk in through the door of their cottage, filling its space with his merry voice and dancing eyes. He'd never gather his children about him to tell them a story of the giant Finn McCool and how he'd tasted the Salmon of Knowledge, or of the Children of Lir turning into swans again. And she would never again feel the warmth and safety of his arms about her.

Someone pulled her up, and she was ushered into a hut and given a cup of tea. As if tea could make up for losing Patrick! She drank it dutifully, and forced herself to appear composed, outwardly at least. She had the children to think about. They needed her. How she would provide for them without Patrick she did not know, but she would not go into the workhouse, that was for sure. Michael was old enough to work. She would take in washing. They could still tend their potato patch. Little Pat could help in the fields and Grace could take care of the little ones. They would manage. They would *have* to manage.

She had walked back down the hillside with Daithí in silence, carrying Patrick's shoe, the only thing of his the miners had been able to retrieve from the collapsed mine. Daithí had stopped outside her cottage, and oddly, awkwardly, had shaken her hand before leaving her to go inside and break the news to the children.

They had never managed to retrieve Patrick's body. She'd been left with not even a grave to visit. At the time, his death had seemed like the worst thing that could possibly happen to her. But losing four of her children from starvation and fever in one single winter had surpassed even that – the loss of the great love of her life, taken in his prime.

*

The following day, Kitty went to Ballymor along with Michael, leaving Grace alone in the cottage, sleeping to conserve her strength. There had to be *something* they could do – some work to be found, some charity. Kitty's great fear was that they would all become too weak to leave the cottage, and no one would come to look for them. They would die in their beds one by one, lying undiscovered and forgotten for months, perhaps years. While she had the strength she had to do something. Anything – to keep her last two darling children alive.

There was a crowd of men and women outside O'Sullivan's pub. Kitty at first thought it was a gathering for another rally, and urged Michael to stay clear. But he asked some men on the fringe of the group what was happening, and received welcome news.

'Public works are starting up. From today. There's to be work widening the road from here to Cork. Employment for all who are fit, and payment at the end of each day. I'm going to stay and get work.'

A woman wrapped in a grubby shawl nodded. 'They'll take women too. I'm going to stay to work, so I am. And there's cornmeal in the stores to spend the wages on.'

Kitty caught Michael's arm. 'I'll stay too and work. This is our chance. Finally, the government are doing something to save us.'

He nodded, but his mouth was set in a grim line. 'It won't be easy work.'

*

It wasn't. The working party – some hundred or so men and women, with a few children tagging along – were marched out to the Cork road, on the other side of town from Kildoolin. The men were given pickaxes and shovels, and set to work levelling the ground to widen the road from its single cart-width to twice that. The women were given lump-hammers, to break stones at the side of the road for the road's foundations. Water was provided for the workers, and in the mid-afternoon a foreman distributed a handful of cooked cornmeal to every worker. It tasted foul, but was better than nothing. Kitty wanted to save some to take home to Grace, but had no means of storing or carrying it. 'Bring a bowl, next time,' advised the woman working alongside her. 'Bring your children too.' She nodded to where the foreman was handing out a ration to some children who'd been lying on the ground near to where their mothers laboured.

To think it had come to this. Stone-breaking, eating tasteless gruel, just to survive.

But at the end of the day she and Michael were paid, as they'd been promised, and they were able to buy a loaf of bread and a bag of cornmeal on their way home. Kitty gave thanks to God that they would live another day.

On the following day, Kitty took Grace with her. Michael carried his sister to the worksite, wrapped in a blanket. She sat beside the road, at one time trying to help grade the stones by size until Kitty forbade her, while they worked. When the rain came, Kitty wrapped the blanket around her daughter's head to try to keep her warm and dry. Perhaps she'd have been better off staying at the cottage after all. But the mid-afternoon ration of gruel would not go to waste, and indeed Gracie wolfed it down and seemed better for it.

Kitty looked around at her fellow workers. They were a sorry lot, indeed. All of them dressed in rags, all far too thin. Everyone moving slowly, deliberately, trying to conserve energy. Her fellow countrymen, the proud Irish race, and look at them! They were not so proud now. Each of them was caught up in their own private fight for survival.

And yet, despite their desperation, she noted little acts of kindness and compassion. A man stumbled, his neighbour caught him before he fell and held him till he was steady on his feet and could swing his pickaxe again. A woman, noticing a child that was not her own eyeing her portion of gruel hungrily, passed the unfinished bowl over. Even the foreman, spotting a man too weak to raise his pickaxe again, bade him sit down and rest until the end of the day, with no loss of earnings. While people cared for each other there was hope for them all, yet.

*

They worked daily on the roads over the next couple of months, as the winter set in. It was a hand-to-mouth existence. Their supply of potatoes at home had finished, even the rotten ones, and they relied entirely on the gruel at the works, and the occasional loaf or cornmeal they were able to buy with their wages. Some wages had to be kept back to pay the rent, for Kitty refused to let them go into the workhouse. No one who went in ever came out – the place was rife with disease, which spread like wildfire amongst the people crammed so close together. They were surviving, and as the year turned and the days began to lengthen again, Kitty allowed herself to hope that things would get better, that the three of them would survive this famine, that they would be able to grow their own potatoes again, find work that was easier and better paid, raise the money for fares to America . . .

And then the day came when the afternoon gruel rations ended. They'd still be paid, but there'd be no food provided during the day. Their only food would be what they cooked themselves when they returned home. A few days later, Kitty watched as a skeletal man laid down his pickaxe, crawled away from the road and lay down to sleep. When he failed to move at the end of the working day, she went over to rouse him, and found to her horror he was dead. Michael came to her side, and together they covered the man in stones as a makeshift grave, until his body could be collected and taken to the mass famine graveyard. The other labourers looked sadly on, but walked on by, too tired and weak to be able to help.

From that day onwards, Kitty left Gracie at home. The child was too weak in any case to walk the three miles to the worksite and back again in the evening, and Kitty and Michael were too weak to carry her. But they had to continue labouring. It was the only way they could eat.

CHAPTER 11

Maria

I was hot and sweaty by the time I got back from the walk up to the copper mines and stone circle, not to mention covered in scratches from the gorse. I went straight up to my room in O'Sullivan's, tried once more to call Dan, but his phone was still going straight to voicemail, then put the kettle on for a cup of tea and stripped off for a shower. Fifteen minutes later, I was clean, refreshed and deciding what to wear that evening. I was only planning a meal downstairs, so it didn't really matter what I wore, but I found myself remembering that Declan had said he might see me later in the bar. I pulled out a pair of loose cotton trousers and a lacy top, and did my make-up carefully. If I was going out with Dan I'd make an effort, so why not tonight? But was I doing this for Declan then? What was I playing at? In another life, one with no Dan in it and no baby in my belly, I might have flirted with Declan, made it obvious I was interested and seen where it took me. But I shook the thought out of my head. That was not the life I was living in. I had Dan. I was pregnant. I'd be a fool if I did anything at all to encourage Declan's attentions. It wasn't fair on him. Or me. Or Dan.

Nevertheless, I found myself putting on some lipstick and dabbing scent behind my ears. Maybe it was my last hurrah as a single, childless woman.

Maybe Declan wouldn't even come to the pub tonight. Maybe I was just being ridiculous.

*

But he did come. I'd finished my dinner, exchanged a few words with Sharon and Dave from the campsite, who'd taken the kids to Blarney Castle that day, kissed the Blarney Stone and got themselves a little sunburnt, and was on my second glass of elderflower cordial when Declan entered the pub. The musicians had not yet arrived, and Sharon was just ushering her family out, so the pub was pretty quiet. Declan spoke for a few minutes with Paulie, who was propping up the bar in his usual spot, ordered a pint of Guinness from Aoife, who was in a Pink Floyd t-shirt today, black with a prism and rainbow design, and then came to sit with me in my nook beside the window, as though we did this every night of the week. I smiled as he approached, feeling myself light up inside. Stop it, Maria, I told myself. You are practically engaged. I noticed Aoife frown slightly as Declan came over and wondered whether she fancied him herself. If she did, she'd had plenty of time to make a move on him. Perhaps she had and he had turned her down. I remembered her comment on the day I'd arrived – you won't get far with that one, she'd said.

'Hi, Maria. Did you go for your walk up to the stone circle?' he said, pulling out a stool and sitting down.

'Hi, Declan. Yes, I did. It's beautiful up there, with all the heather in bloom.' I remembered about the mineshaft I'd stumbled upon, but decided not to mention it after all. I wanted to have a happy chat with him, not moan about the dangers I'd encountered.

He might be offended if he thought I was criticising the local area.

'It is, sure. There's something about tramping through the heather over the moors that puts everything into perspective. Makes all your troubles disappear. Well, it does for me. Do you find that, too?'

I pondered a moment. I seemed to have a lot of troubles at the moment. I was pregnant and still unsure about it all. Terrified of impending motherhood. My boyfriend had proposed and I'd run away. Now he thought the baby wasn't his, and was not answering my calls. 'Kind of,' I answered, with a bit of a grimace. 'Can't really say my troubles disappeared but I was able to forget them for a while at least.'

He smiled, a warm smile that softened his eyes. There should be warning notices. A girl could drown in those liquid eyes. 'Want to talk about your troubles? I'm a good listener.'

Suddenly, totally without warning, I felt tears well up in my eyes. Oh God, this was embarrassing. I hardly knew the man and I was about to blub in front of him. I did want to talk, I realised. About pregnancy, about Dan's proposal, his accusation that I'd cheated, about my fears that I'd be as crap a mother as Jackie was, about the way events were moving too fast, life was railroading me along a very grown-up path that I did not feel ready for.

'Maria? Is something wrong?' He reached out a hand and laid it on my forearm. His touch was cool and comforting.

I shook my head. 'Ignore me. I'm just being stupid.' But, as I said it, a tear escaped and rolled down my cheek, forcing me to brush it away with the back of my hand before it fell into my drink.

'Tears are never stupid, Maria.' His voice was gentle and reassuring.

I was silent for a moment, considering. I realised I did not want to tell him about Dan's accusation – that was between me and Dan. As soon as I had the chance to talk to Dan I'd be able to sort that one out myself, and make it clear to him the baby was most definitely, one hundred per cent, his. I may have been guilty of not telling him about it for far too long but I was most definitely not guilty of cheating on him. I would never do that.

'I'm pregnant and I don't know how to be a mother.' The words came out in a rush, and as I said them I looked at Declan defiantly, as though expecting him to contradict me and tell me I'd be a great mother.

'Ah.' He looked thoughtful, as though he was weighing up his words before he answered. I was grateful for this. Most people would instantly spout platitudes about how mothering would come naturally once the baby was born, that no one knew how to do it but everyone managed all right when the time came. But I knew differently. Jackie hadn't managed naturally.

'I imagine,' he said, 'that motherhood must be the hardest and most terrifying job in the world. Having someone who is so completely dependent on you for everything.' He spoke quietly, his tone kind.

I nodded. 'Yes. Terrifying is the word.'

'Is there someone you can talk to about the way you feel? I don't know if . . . the baby's father, perhaps? Your own mother?'

I snorted. 'My mother is half the problem. She has told me many times she never wanted to have a child, and that I held her back, ruined her chances in life.' My voice had become bitter as it often did when I mentioned Jackie.

His eyes widened. 'Doesn't sound like you had an easy childhood.'

'Well, I wasn't abused or anything like that, and we weren't poor, and my dad was around until I was seventeen. He was a great parent, and tried his best to make up for Jackie.'

'Jackie? Your mother?'

'Yep. I wasn't allowed to call her "Mum".' Those blinking tears began to spill again. Twenty-nine years old and crying because I'd never had a proper mum. I'd loved her, as a kid, and had always tried to please her, but nothing I did ever seemed good enough for her. As a teenager I'd given up trying, and moved out as soon as I could.

Declan seemed to know instinctively not to touch my hand or look at me. The slightest sympathetic glance would have tipped me over the edge. He took a sip of his drink, giving me a moment to wipe away those traitorous tears and get a grip of myself.

'Some people just don't have the right temperament to be a parent,' he said, carefully.

'Jackie didn't. And what if I'm the same?' I looked up at him, hoping he'd have words of wisdom for me, praying he could take away my doubts with a word or a look.

'You're not though, are you? You are Maria, she is Jackie. You don't have to be like her – you can do things your own way. And because you are worrying about this, that tells me you *won't* be the same. You've recognised your mother's failings and that'll stop you from making the same mistakes.'

It wasn't enough. He was missing the point. 'But what if the baby's born and I don't love it? What if

I find myself resenting it, like Jackie said she resented me? You have to give up so much to be a parent. What if I don't want to?' And wasn't I *already* making the same mistakes, hiding my pregnancy from Dan and then running away here to Ireland? Denying the child that was growing in my womb.

He smiled gently. 'What if you find yourself head over heels in love with the baby from the moment you first hold him or her? What if you find the joy the baby brings into your life more than makes up for the sacrifices you have to make? What if being a mother ends up being the best thing that's ever happened to you? No one knows how they will react to enormous life-changing events like this. I'm afraid you will just have to wait and see what happens, so. But try not to worry in the meantime, although it's perfectly understandable.'

He was right. I was being pessimistic, glass half empty, and not seeing that it could all go the other way. Who knew how I'd feel when the baby actually arrived? I gave him a feeble smile as I tried to feel more positive about things.

'Maria, are you religious at all? If so, perhaps asking God for guidance would help?'

'I'm not, really,' I replied. It seemed like an odd question to ask. But then, Ireland's a much more religious country than England.

'That's OK. But He's there, if ever you felt like talking to Him.'

I smiled. 'I think I do better talking to a person, face to face. You're right, Declan, you are a good listener.'

'Thank you. It's part of my job, after all. Cheers. *Sláinte*.' He raised his glass and clinked mine. I was about to ask him what his job was, when the musicians began playing. They'd arrived and set up while we'd been talking. Declan swivelled part-way round on his stool so he could watch them, and I settled back in my chair.

The band began with some traditional Irish folk songs as on the last time I'd heard them. They began with 'Black Velvet Band', then played 'The Fields of Athenry' again. Declan turned to me to speak into my ear. 'That reminds me – the local hurling team are playing tomorrow afternoon. Do you want to go along?'

'Hurling?'

'A Gaelic game. Bit like hockey only they whack the ball at head height. Fast, furious and thrilling.'

'I thought "The Fields of Athenry" was a rugby song?'

'It's actually about the famine – about a man who was imprisoned for stealing corn to feed his children. But it's been appropriated by rugby, so it made me think of rugby, which we also play here in Ballymor, and that made me think of the match. Want to go?'

I grinned. 'Why not?'

The next song was 'The Leaving of Liverpool'. I loved the lyrics – *It's not the leaving of Liverpool that grieves me, but my darling when I think of thee.* I thought of Michael McCarthy, who'd left Ireland as a young man and lived in America for a while, and wondered whether he'd had to leave a loved one. He'd had to leave Kitty at least.

'You're looking pensive?' Declan leaned over and said into my ear.

'It's this song. It's lovely.'

'Ah, yes. It could easily be about all those people who left Ireland during the famine. Most never returned, although their cottages were left empty and waiting for them. Still empty and waiting, as you've seen up at Kildoolin.'

It was a poignant thought – the cottages standing empty for a century and a half, for people who never returned. Michael McCarthy had returned though, after a dozen or so years in America, and that's when his search for Kitty had begun.

I listened in silence to the rest of the band's set and, when they stopped for a break, Declan turned to me. 'Well, I'm afraid I must be away now. Will you be calling at the church to look at the baptism and burial records tomorrow – see what you can find out about your ancestors? If so I can meet you there early afternoon – after one thirty. We could look at the records and then go on to the hurling match.'

'Sounds great – I'll see you then,' I said, and Declan got up to leave. For a moment I thought he was going to bend over to kiss me goodbye, but he was just reaching across the table for his glass to take back to the bar.

*

Back in my room, and before I did anything else, I tried once more to call Dan and as soon as the call went to voicemail I hung up. If he wasn't answering my calls, I needed to contact him some other way. This was too important to let it drag on any longer. I started up my laptop and sent Dan an email.

Dan

Yes, we were always careful. But do you remember that night on holiday in Rhodes, back in April? We were strolling along the beach on a balmy evening, the stars were beautiful

and the silken sea was lapping gently on the beach. The beach was deserted, and it was all so impossibly romantic. We took a risk, didn't we? My pregnancy, Dan, is the result of that night.

I am sorry I did not tell you earlier. Really sorry. I am so scared I'll be a rubbish mother like Jackie has been, and I suppose I was in denial about it all, not wanting to change the perfect life I felt we had. I realise now I should have spoken to you sooner.

Dan, please call me. I can't bear not being able to talk to you.

Love you, always

Maria

CHAPTER 12

Kitty

Kitty was worried – even more so than usual. Grace had developed a dry, hacking cough and was complaining of pains in her stomach. She'd had enough to eat lately – just – Kitty didn't think she was starving to death the way little Jimmy, Éamonn and Nuala had gone, but she was very poorly, and had never been truly strong since the previous terrible winter of hunger had sapped her strength. The dear sweet-natured child. Kitty was fearful that it would not be long before Grace joined her brothers and sister, although she would do everything in her power to save her.

She was sitting at Grace's side, mopping her fevered brow, when Michael returned to the cottage. Darkness had fallen a few hours earlier, Kitty had been back a long time from the worksite, and she'd begun to fret about him. He was carrying something beneath his jacket.

'Surprise, Mammy. Don't give out to me, but I came across a duck, so. I wondered if it might tempt Gracie, and might help make her well again. How is she?' He put the dead duck down beside the fireplace and knelt beside his sister.

'You've been poaching again, have you? You'll get caught, and then where will we be?' Kitty began to scold, but her heart wasn't in it. Her little family was in a bad place even if Michael was never caught. And maybe the food in prison would be better, or at least more regular. 'Gracie's very sick,' she continued, to answer his question.

Michael sighed, and took Kitty's place at Grace's side, also taking the damp cloth from her hand to mop his sister's forehead. 'Come on, Gracie, perk up, would you? There'll be fried duck breast for you soon. I remember how you liked it the last time. Sweet, succulent duck meat. I'll stay with you while Mammy cooks it, will I?'

Grace nodded weakly and murmured something.

'Couldn't catch that, Gracie. But if it's hard to talk you just keep quiet there. Look, Mammy's already preparing the duck. It'll not be long till dinner.'

Kitty smiled sadly as she listened. Michael was such a gentle, caring boy. Before the little ones had passed over, he'd been a great help with them, taking the place of their dear daddy after Patrick's accident. She would never have coped without him. And yet, when she thought of his beginnings, she still, even now after all these years, felt a shudder of revulsion pass through her.

Well, there was a duck in her hands that required attention. Maybe Michael was right and it'd help Gracie fight her fever. She set to work plucking the bird, jointing it, and placed the pieces in the cooking pot with some herbs. They'd eat well tonight.

When the food was ready, try as she might she could not persuade Gracie to take any of it. The child would only sip at some broth Kitty had made from the saved cooking water. It was better than nothing but Kitty was fearful. She resolved to fetch the doctor from

Ballymor the next day. How she would pay him she did not know but there had to be some way she could save her daughter. She had to try.

*

The next day Grace seemed worse, weaker than she'd ever been, moaning in pain, and with a red rash spreading across her stomach and chest. Kitty asked Michael to stay with his sister while she went to town to find Dr O'Reilly. They were both having to give up a day's work on the roads, a day's wages, but Gracie was more important, and the duck Michael had poached had bought them some time.

It was a calm day, but a mist had rolled in from the sea, blanketing everything in white, muffling sounds and making everything seem strange, ethereal and confusing. The kind of day where you needed to watch out or the faeries would take you, as Mother Heaney used to say. Kitty had never believed in any of that nonsense about the old faerie folk who lived in the hills, dancing in the stone circle higher up the hill, stealing children away to be their slaves, leaving changelings in their place. In days gone by, people had been afraid of the faerie folk, and had left appeasement offerings up at the stone circle – loaves, eggs, sacks of potatoes. They were always gone by morning. Kitty thought they were probably taken by the poorest folk in the village, but Mother Heaney had insisted the faeries came at night and took the gifts. If no gifts were left for a month or more, they'd come to the village and take a child instead, she'd warned. Kitty had smiled and paid no heed. It was just the superstitions of the older generation.

But on a day like this one, with everything shrouded in mist, and the endless bad luck they'd had in the years since the last peace offerings had been made to the faeries, it was enough to get you thinking, perhaps there was something in it, perhaps the faerie folk did exist and had ways in which they could influence your luck. There was some duck left over from last night's meal. Perhaps, Kitty thought, she should take it up to the stone circle and leave it there, and maybe the faeries would take pity on her and do something to save Gracie and end their suffering . . .

She shook her head. What nonsense she was thinking. It was only the eerie quality of the mist that made you feel as though someone was following, just out of sight and earshot, behind. Kitty quickened her pace, thankful that she knew the way from Kildoolin to Ballymor so well she could walk it blindfold. She'd done it in the dark many times so the mist held no fear that she would become lost. Nevertheless, the sooner she reached the town and found the doctor, the better.

*

In town, she found herself drawn first of all to the church. She slipped into its quiet, dark interior and sat on a pew, bowed her head and prayed for God to spare Gracie and for some way out of this cycle of poverty and hunger. The faeries couldn't help, but God could, if He chose to. She clung to her faith as a drowning man would cling to a raft. What else could she do?

The doctor's house was one of those in the smarter part of the town. Kitty made her way there, only to discover he was not at home. He was employed on his fortnightly inspection of the poorhouse, she was told by his wife. Perhaps if Kitty waited outside she might catch him when he left there. She walked through the streets, past the National School, now closed, where in happier days before the famine Grace had studied, along with Michael, Little Pat and Nuala. At last she reached the huge brick-built workhouse which stood on the edge of town, its imposing presence looming over all those who went near. 'We'll not end up in the workhouse,' she muttered to herself. 'Not if I can help it. There'll be another way.'

She was there for some time, during which the mist lifted and the sun came out. She wanted to think of it as a sign, a promise that things would get better, but that would be giving in to superstition. It was just a welcome improvement in the weather, that was all.

Finally, the workhouse gates opened and a trim man in a black suit, carrying a bag, came through.

'Oh, excuse me, sir, but would you be Doctor O'Reilly? Only I wondered if you could come and look at my little colleen, she's poorly so she is, but 'tis not the hunger.'

'I am O'Reilly, yes,' said the man. His voice was gentle and kind, but he sounded tired. Kitty felt a pang of guilt for bothering him. Surely he'd had far too much work for one man these last couple of years since the first potato crop failed. 'Where is your daughter?'

'She's up at my cottage, above in Kildoolin.' The doctor's face clouded, and he shook his head.

'I'm sorry. I haven't the time to be going all the way up there. I was after thinking there was no one left living up there anyway?'

''Tis only myself, my son and my poor little Gracie left now. She's too sick to come here. What can I do for her? Only I lost three little ones, and my other son last year, and my husband a couple of years before that, from an accident in the copper mines. I can't lose another child. I can't!' Kitty could not help herself. The tears came, flowing freely down her face. She had not wanted to appear weak before the doctor, but it was too much to deal with.

'Hush now. Sit yourself down here, on this wall, Mrs . . .?'

'McCarthy. Kitty McCarthy,' she replied.

'Well now, Mrs McCarthy, you tell me what your Gracie's symptoms are and I'll see if I can advise you how best to treat her. And if I've time tomorrow I'll come up to see her.'

Kitty described Gracie's pains, fever, rash, the headache that had started it all, the diarrhoea that had begun that morning.

Dr O'Reilly looked grave. 'It sounds like the typhus. There's a lot of it about.' He shook his head. 'There isn't much you, or indeed I, can do for her. Keep her cool and comfortable, give her sips of water if she can take them.'

'Doctor, am I going to lose her?' Kitty looked up at him, imploring him with her eyes to tell her no, typhus was not deadly, Gracie would pull through.

In response he put a comforting hand on her shoulder. 'I'm sorry. I'm so sorry. Here, let me give you this for her at least.' He reached into his bag and pulled out a small bottle. 'It'll help her sleep, so she won't feel so much pain.'

Kitty hesitated. This was the moment when she had to admit she could not pay for the medicine. She could not afford to reduce her child's pain, and ease her passage to the next world.

'It's all right. There's no charge,' said the doctor, as if he could see her thoughts. He smiled at her, his eyes kind and sad, and pressed the vial into her hand.

She was too overcome to be able to answer in any way other than a nod of her head. He patted her shoulder, picked up his bag and went on his way.

Kitty pocketed the little bottle and set off back to Kildoolin. She walked even faster on her way back than she had on the way down, even though she was no longer fancying that faerie folk followed her. She wanted nothing more than to be by Gracie's side, spending every last moment with her until the end came, as she now knew it soon would.

*

Michael met her at the door of the cottage. 'She's no better, Mammy. Did you find the doctor?'

'Yes, and he's after giving me something for her. Is she awake?' The cloying, almost sweet smell of sickness assaulted her as she entered.

'Just about,' he said, standing aside to let her see.

Grace was lying covered in blankets, her face white and sweaty, her cheeks sunken. Kitty pulled back the covers to see the rash, which had extended over most of her body. Grace moaned slightly.

'There now, Gracie. I have some medicine from the doctor. It'll help you feel better. Can you lift your head a little to take it?'

She held Gracie's head and dribbled the medicine into the corner of her mouth. Gracie coughed slightly but swallowed it and sank back onto the bed. Kitty wiped the girl's forehead and held her hand, receiving a feeble squeeze in acknowledgement.

'Sleep now, Gracie darling, and we'll see how you are when you wake.'

Gracie smiled weakly, and closed her eyes. A moment later she was asleep. Kitty hauled herself back to her feet and sat in the one chair they had left. Michael stood beside her, his hand on her shoulder.

'Will she live, Mammy?' he whispered.

She shook her head. 'The medicine will take away the pain, that's all. The best we can hope is that she dies in her sleep. My poor angel.'

'Oh no, Mammy.' He pulled her head against his chest and stroked her hair. She allowed herself a few tears, but not many – she had to stay strong for him, and for Grace while she still lived. But she drew strength from him – strength to face whatever the night would hold.

*

Grace breathed her last in the early hours, in the darkest part of the night. Kitty had kept the fire burning and had sat beside her daughter, keeping vigil, mopping her brow, giving her sips of water and medicine whenever she woke, murmuring prayers and words of comfort to her. Michael sat up alongside Kitty, even though she'd urged him to sleep so that he could work the next day, and that she'd wake him before the end so he could say goodbye to his little sister. But he'd shaken his head and stayed with her, joining in with the prayers, fetching her water, adding turf to the fire whenever it burned low. She'd been glad of his company. So many deathbed vigils in far too short a time. Her darling children, all of them, weakening, hollowing, crying and then just lying quietly, accepting their fate with dignity while she, their mother, thrashed and wailed and fought against it, all the time clinging on to her faith and trying to keep the other children alive, and herself strong enough to care for them. Why, Lord, why did she have to lose another? Grace had been the sweetest, the sunniest of all her children. Everyone had loved her. She'd brought joy into many hearts in her short time on earth. Sure it was God's will to take her, but why, and for what purpose? Had Kitty not given enough children already?

She carefully pulled the blanket up over Grace's head, and looked across at Michael, who made no attempt to check the tears that flowed down his face. 'Well now. She's gone. There's no more pain for the poor child, only warmth and food and love.'

He nodded. 'I'll carry her down to the church in the morning for burial. She'll be with her sister and brothers again.'

'She will. And in heaven she'll be with her daddy too.' She caught hold of Michael and pulled him to her, her voice hoarse with grief. 'My last baby. I'll not see you die. I'll never let another child die.'

*

They buried Grace the next day, in the same plot as her siblings, and with a simple wooden cross to mark the spot. Father John conducted a hurried ceremony, before rushing off to do his rounds at the workhouse, where several people required the last rites. To Kitty's immense shame she could not afford an inscribed gravestone. At least she had not been put into one of the mass graves, where so many hundreds lay unnamed and unmourned.

'I'll never forget you, Gracie,' Kitty whispered, as her daughter, wrapped in a blanket for they could not afford a coffin, was lowered into the ground. 'Sleep well.'

She bowed her head in prayer. Grace would be the last of her children to die. There was only Michael left, but she would make sure he did not die of the hunger or the disease epidemics that ravaged Ireland. He must leave – go to America, where he could live without fear of starvation, and prosper. One way or another she must raise the money for his passage to America. Whatever it cost.

As they walked away from Gracie's grave, Kitty slipped her arm through Michael's.

'Are you all right, Mammy?' he asked.

She gave him a small, sad smile. 'You're all I have left, now, Michael.'

'I'll never leave you, Mammy. I'm stronger than the others. I'll always be here for you.'

She shook her head. 'No, you won't. I don't want you to be. I want you to go, to get away from here, away from the hunger and the disease. Away from this land sucked dry of hope. You deserve more, you deserve better, and I want you to have it.'

'No, Mammy. My place is here with you. I won't be going anywhere, sure I won't.'

She stopped walking and pulled him around to face her. 'You'll die if you stay here. Like all the others. As I will too, no doubt. I *want* you to go – to America, where there's hope, and food, and opportunities. I want you to go and make your fortune, as Patrick and I would have, if we could. Patrick was lost before we had the chance to go, but you're still young and free. You must go, in his place.'

He threw up his hands. 'Mammy, you're not making any sense. How on earth can I afford to go? We've no money to put food in our mouths, no money for a headstone for Gracie and the others, no money to pay the rent. I know you're wanting to save me – I love you for it – but it's not to be. I'll stay here, work alongside you on the roads, earn the money to feed us both. And when the time comes I'll plant the next crop of potatoes and the next harvest will be a good one, you'll see if it isn't.'

'We've no seed potatoes,' she said. 'We ate them long ago. And we've no money to buy any. So there'll be no more crops. Michael, there's no future here. One way or another we have to find a way to buy you a passage to America. Once you're there you'll make your fortune, then you can come back and find me.'

'How will I make my fortune? The streets won't be paved with gold, sure they won't, whatever the rumours say.'

'Your art – you can paint and draw the rich people. They'll buy your work.'

'Maybe I can sell my pictures here, then? Maybe I should try that first.'

'Yes, you should.' But Kitty knew that idea would fail. No one in Ballymor had any spare money to spend on pictures. Most of them were like herself and Michael – they couldn't afford to eat let alone anything else. No one other than Thomas Waterman and his agent had money to spare.

She stumbled then, tripping on a loose cobble in the road. Michael caught her and steadied her. 'It's been a long day, and you're after not sleeping last night. Think no more on my going to America, Mammy. You need to rest now. Come on, and I'll take you home.'

She needed to eat more than she needed to rest, she thought. She still had the bones of the duck Michael had poached. They'd do to make some broth.

The track up to Kildoolin seemed longer, steeper and rougher than it ever had before. And going home to the cottage, knowing there was no Gracie in it and never would be again, was unbearable. She tried to stay strong, to stop weeping, but she could not. The only thing that was keeping her going was Michael and her belief that somehow she must save him.

*

Bereaved they might be but even so, the next day Kitty and Michael made their way to the worksite, and spent another weary day breaking rocks. At least, Kitty thought, she no longer needed to worry that Gracie was too cold or too hungry. Gracie was suffering no longer. Kitty wielded her hammer slowly, methodically, trying to conserve strength. She kept her head down, checking the stones for cracks, trying to use the least number of blows to break them apart. So she did not notice immediately when a man came to stand near her, watching her.

'Kitty McCarthy? Stand up.' The voice was English, authoritative.

She stood, slowly, hoping to avoid any dizziness. It was William Smith, Thomas Waterman's land agent. She hoped he had not come to ask for more rent. Surely it was not yet due?

'Mr Waterman would like a word with you,' Smith said, and indicated where Waterman sat on his horse, on the edge of the worksite. He looked just as he did in Michael's sketch of him – aloof and arrogant.

'Yes, sir,' Kitty said. She dropped her lump-hammer and walked over, wiping her dusty hands on her skirt as she went. She was aware of Michael pausing his work, watching her, ready to step in and protect her if she needed him. As she neared Waterman, that old feeling of revulsion at the sight of him welled up in her. What could he possibly want with her? She approached him slowly, keeping her eyes down.

'Look up at me,' he said, as she drew near.

She raised her head, squinting against the bright sky.

'I suppose you're hungry, like the rest of them? You must be, to want to work here.'

'Yes, sir.' Of course she was hungry, and she was working there because there was no other choice, not since Smith had laid off Michael. She still didn't understand what he wanted.

He looked at her, then back towards Michael, who had not resumed his work but was standing some distance away, pickaxe in hand, watching. 'Your son?'

'Yes, sir.'

His eyes narrowed. He was calculating, she could see, estimating Michael's age, working out how many years it was since he'd come across her working on Mother Heaney's potato patch, trying to remember whether Patrick McCarthy had had dark hair like Michael's or not. She prayed silently: Dear Lord above, don't let him guess the truth, don't let him know it.

He regarded her in silence for a moment, with an expression in his eyes that she could not read, then nodded as though he'd made a decision. 'Come to Ballymor House when you finish here today. It'll be worth your while.'

He didn't wait for an answer, but spurred his horse to turn round and trot away off down the newly built road.

Kitty was left staring after him. What did he want from her? What had she seen in his eyes – desire? Pity? Regret? Perhaps a mixture of all three. Or did he want to know about Michael? She would never tell him the truth. Never.

*

Memories of the last time he'd sat on his horse and bade her go to see him came flooding back to her. Back then, she had been fifteen, naive, innocent and trusting. She'd done as he'd bid her to do.

Sundown, he'd said. She'd arrived and waited behind the stables as he'd asked, just as the sun began to sink below the horizon. She'd told Ma Heaney some of the potato ridges had been damaged – well, that wasn't a lie, they had been, by Thomas Waterman's great horse – and she was going to work on the plot until it was dark. There was no danger of her great-aunt coming up to the field to check on her, not with her lame leg that had left her almost unable to walk.

She sat on a log, her back to the stables wall, her face turned to catch the last rays of the evening sun. Her thoughts turned once more where they shouldn't – what gift would he have for her, would this be the start of a romantic relationship? Of all the girls, he'd noticed *her*, picked her out. What did it all mean? She recalled his long legs, straight back, jet-black hair and handsome features and shivered with anticipation. She couldn't really believe he was interested in her but he had certainly praised her looks, asked her to meet him and promised her a gift, and why else would he have done that unless he wanted to woo her? She decided, with a secret smile to herself, that she would allow him to woo her, if that was what he wanted.

'You came. Good girl.' The voice broke into her reverie, and she leapt to her feet, brushing bark and woodchips from her dress.

'Yes, sir, I came as you asked.' She tried to dip a little curtsey but was clumsy with it, and slightly lost her balance, staggering back against the log she'd been sitting on. She found herself blushing as he laughed at her.

'The maids in the house curtsey to me, Kitty Tooley. That's not what I want from you. Stand upright, and look me in the eye.'

She did as she was told, her stomach churning with excitement.

'That's better,' he said, cupping his hand under her chin to tilt her head back so she was gazing up directly at him. Was he going to kiss her now? She'd never been kissed. What was it like? What should she do? She allowed her mouth to open a little bit, and he smiled wolfishly at her.

'You want me, do you? Good. But not here. Come on.' He caught her by the hand and led her around to the front of the stables. A groom was brushing down Thomas's bay horse, but the man looked away quickly, pretending not to notice them. Thomas crossed the stable yard and pushed open a narrow door. There was a wooden staircase beyond, and he climbed it, taking the steps two at a time, still pulling her after him. She clutched at her skirts to hold them out of the way.

Upstairs was a small room, poor but better furnished than the cottage she lived in with Mother Heaney. There was a washstand in the corner, holding a basin and ewer. A small wardrobe, a bentwood chair and a worn rug on the floor. And a narrow iron bedstead, with a pile of blankets messily thrown across it.

Kitty suddenly had a bad feeling about what was happening. She knew what went on between a man and his wife in bed – her great-aunt had educated her well. But she and Thomas were not married. Why had he brought her into this bedroom? Whose was it, anyway? She supposed it must be where one of the grooms slept. Perhaps that man below, who was brushing Thomas's horse.

She turned back to the stairs, but Thomas grabbed her around the waist. 'Oh no you don't,' he said. 'Come here. Remember I said I had something for you?'

The gift he'd promised. She'd forgotten. She turned back, and he pulled her close and kissed her roughly. His stubbly chin scratched her, his hands on her waist were too tight, hurting her, and she tried to pull away.

'What's the matter? Am I too rough? I won't hurt you,' he said, but he did not let her go. He held her tighter still with one arm, and brought his other hand round to her front, squeezing her breasts. Too hard; it hurt. She tried to scream but his mouth was on hers again, and he was forcing her across the room, the backs of her knees now against the bed. He hooked a leg around hers, and she was toppled backwards, and then he was upon her, pinning her down, a hand over her mouth so she couldn't scream, his other hand pulling up her skirt and fumbling at his trouser fastenings.

She thrashed her head from side to side trying to loosen his grip, and pummelled at his back with her fists, but he was too big, too strong for her. She knew what he was doing and she didn't want it. Why oh why had she come to meet him? Because he was good-looking and had showed some interest in her? Oh, she was so stupid! No English landowner's son would ever truly care for an Irish peasant girl. Why had she allowed herself to think that he might? He'd praised her looks and she'd let herself be flattered by his attention, and now look where that had brought her. She realised the best thing now was to lie quiet and still, let him do what he wanted and hope that he did not hurt her too much.

Afterwards, he rolled off her and fastened his trousers in silence, while she lay with her face turned to the wall. He threw some coins at her. 'Get yourself a prettier dress and come back to me again.'

She sat up and stared at him defiantly. 'I'll never come back. Never.'

He snorted. 'Shame. I'd make it worth your while. A feisty little thing like you is just what I want. I could do a lot for you.'

'I would never take anything from you. You are a monster.'

He shrugged and left the room grinning like a cat who'd had the cream.

She finally left the room two minutes later, leaving the money in a pile on the washstand. The groom was still in the yard, sitting on a stool and polishing tackle, whistling while he worked. He did not raise his head to acknowledge her as she passed. She wondered how frequently Waterman brought a girl back here. She was certain she was not the first, and would not be the last.

*

A hideous memory. Kitty shook her head as if to dislodge it from her mind. She was proud, however, that she had not taken Waterman's money on that terrible day, had never gone back to Ballymor House and had mostly managed to keep out of his way whenever he'd been in Ireland over the years. But now she was desperate.

She spent the rest of the day debating with herself whether to go to Ballymor House that evening. What would Thomas Waterman have to offer her? Surely he could not want her, not now she was old – thirty-three – and so thin and gaunt. She would not be able to fight him off if that was his intention. Did he want to claim his son? Surely not. He had no legitimate children of his own, she knew, but doubtless had numerous bastards across the county. He would not be interested in Michael, and even if he was, she would not let him have the boy. But if he was offering food or employment in return, or free rent – anything to give her and Michael a chance of survival – should she not take that chance? She'd vowed to find the money to send Michael to America, to save him, whatever the cost. So maybe the cost was this – she had to go to Waterman and see what he was offering. Give herself to him, if that was what he wanted. But could she? After eighteen years of hating the man for what he had done to her, could she willingly go to him now?

At the end of the day she had not reached a decision. She had not told Michael of Waterman's command, only that he had asked her name and how long she had been working on the road. She planned only to go home with Michael as usual, make broth with the carcass of the duck, try to find a few potatoes that were still edible, cook and eat and sleep. And wake up sobbing when she realised that little Gracie was not sleeping in her arms and never would again.

*

They reached home, cooked and ate their meagre meal. Michael lay down beside the fire and almost instantly fell asleep, and Kitty lay down upon the straw mattress that she had shared with Gracie. Without her daughter to cuddle it was cold and she wrapped her blanket tightly around herself. There was one fewer blanket now, as Gracie had been buried in one as a funeral shroud. Kitty curled herself up and tried to sleep, her hand tucked into a tear in the fabric of the mattress. There was something there. She pushed her hand deeper in and felt around in the straw. Something hard, with a sharp point that pricked her . . . She grasped it with her fingers and tugged it out.

It was Mother Heaney's brooch – the one the old lady had always used to fasten her shawl, that Kitty had admired when she was young, and which she'd thought was lost or perhaps buried with Mother Heaney. Gracie must have found it somewhere and kept it.

Kitty sat up and inspected the brooch by the light of the dying embers of the fire. It was tarnished, so she rubbed it on her skirts until it began to shine. Mother Heaney had always said it was very valuable. A Celtic knot, in a reddish metal – Mother Heaney said that gold was not always yellow; it could be white, or rose, and this was rose gold.

Kitty's mind worked quickly. If it was valuable then she could sell it. If it was *very* valuable, as Mother Heaney had always insisted, then it might fetch enough to buy Michael's ticket to America. She clutched it tightly, ignoring the stab of pain as the end of the pin dug into her palm. This brooch could be the saving of her last child. If only Gracie had told her she had it, Kitty could have sold it long ago and then could have bought enough food to keep them all alive – even young Pat and the little ones. None of her children need have died. She stared at the brooch, half loving it for being Michael's salvation and half hating it for keeping itself hidden until now, when it was too late for all of Patrick's children. But it could still save Michael.

Thank goodness she had not gone to Thomas Waterman! She did not need to now. She would go into Ballymor the next day, and find a buyer for the brooch. And then she would buy food – good food. Meat, flour, tea, butter, corn – anything and everything she could find to buy. They would not go hungry again! She pinned the brooch to the bodice of her dress and fell asleep with her hand over it and dreams of plentiful, glorious food running through her head.

CHAPTER 13

Maria

After spending the evening in the bar with Declan and making arrangements to meet him to go through church records and then on to the hurling I felt guilty. Had he intended the day as a date? Despite tossing and turning for half the night trying to work out his intentions and my feelings I still didn't know. I eventually fell asleep, only to dream of Dan pulling me one way, towards a pit filled with squalling babies, while Declan pulled me the other way towards a glorious orange sunset. You didn't need to be Sigmund Freud to work that one out.

But I awoke with the sun streaming in through the window and Dan on my mind. I checked my watch – it was 8 a.m. and although it was Saturday he was usually up early. I wondered whether he had seen my email. I grabbed my laptop and quickly logged on.

Maria
Yes, I remember that night in Rhodes. Ring me when you get this. I love you too.
Dan

Oh, thank goodness! I grabbed my phone and rang him. At last it did not go straight to voicemail.

'Hey, babe,' he said, sounding sleepy. 'Wassup?'

'I got your email. Are we OK then? You believe me?'

'Aw, sweetheart, of course I do. God, I am *so* sorry for what I said that night. I'd had a few drinks. Was not thinking straight.'

'I've been trying to ring you ever since. Sent that email in desperation.'

'Ahem.' He sounded sheepish. 'I knocked over a glass of water that night, all over my phone. Didn't notice – as I said, I was pissed – and the phone sat in a puddle all night. Had to take it apart and put it on top of the boiler to dry out. Darned thing has only just started working again.'

Relief flooded through me and I found my eyes brimming with tears. 'I thought you were so upset you were ignoring me. I thought – maybe – we were over.'

'God, no. Shit, I should have called you from work or something. It's all been a bit manic lately. Maria, I am so sorry.'

'And I'm sorry too for not telling you sooner about the baby. I know I should have.'

'We are both rubbish.'

'Yep, we are.' I found myself grinning through my tears. It was so good to know we were OK.

'You should tell Jackie soon, I think.'

'Jackie? She won't care.'

'She's going to be a grandmother. I know you don't owe her anything, but she ought to know. Maybe . . .'

'What?'

'Well, I wondered if it would change the way she acts towards you. I mean, it'll be a rite of passage for her, too, the start of a new stage of her life.'

'Hmm.' I wasn't convinced. I had as little contact with Jackie as possible these days, as whenever I phoned or called round she tended to brush me off, saying she was busy and had no time for me. We met once every couple of months for a coffee, at which we updated each other with news of friends and acquaintances, but never actually talked about ourselves or our relationship with each other, steering clear of any dangerous ground or mentions of the past. We exchanged Christmas cards, and that was about it. But I supposed I'd have to tell her about the baby sooner or later.

'Well, think about it. If you want to wait till you're home and we could call on her together that'd be fine with me. I'm counting the days, no, the hours, till you come home. Four days, five hours and forty-six minutes. I can't wait – to see you and meet The Bump.'

I laughed. 'Not much of a bump yet, although it's growing daily. Yes, I'll be back on Wednesday. Can't wait to see you again, too.'

We were both silent for a minute, holding our phones, just being with each other. We'd both been idiots. And I still hadn't answered his proposal.

'So, how's it going? Done lots of research? What are you up to today?'

'Looking at church records and then going to a hurling match.'

'Hurling? Did your ancestors play or something?'

'No idea. But the local team are playing so I am lending my support.' I avoided mentioning that I was going with a tall, handsome young man who had eyes you could drown in. Even as I thought this, Dan's warm, familiar voice was wrapping itself around me, making me feel secure. He was all I ever wanted.

'Well, hope you enjoy it. I've never seen a hurling match. Give me a ring after and let me know how it went. Love you.'

'Love you too.' I hung up, feeling so much better than I had done for days.

Well, that was decided then. I'd meet Declan today, go to the match with him, enjoy the rest of my holiday and get my research done. Then I'd go back to Dan and put that damned ring on my finger. I owed him, it was the right thing to do, and God damn it, I loved him!

Unlike last night I took little care over my appearance today. Cotton drawstring-waist trousers from the local Dunnes Stores, which were so much more comfortable than my too-tight jeans, a loose t-shirt and hair in a ponytail. That would do.

*

Over breakfast I pondered what Dan had said about telling Jackie. He was right, I knew. And I decided I might as well get it over with, so once I was back upstairs in my room I pulled out my phone again and called her. She worked on Saturdays but didn't start till later in the day, in her admin job for an office cleaning company, so I knew I'd catch her at home if I called early.

'Maria! I wasn't expecting you to call. Really, it's not the most convenient time.' She sounded cross and exasperated.

I felt instantly wound up. How dare I phone my mother! 'It never is convenient for you, is it? You're my mother, Jackie. Most people don't need to warn their mothers that they're going to phone them.'

'I'm busy, Maria, is all I meant. So what have you phoned for?'

'I won't take much of your time. There's something I need to tell you, and I didn't want to wait till I come home from my holiday.'

'I didn't even know you were on holiday. Just let me get my tea – I was just making a cup – then I can sit down and you can talk.'

I listened to the sounds of her moving around her immaculate flat. It was all stripped wood floors, white sofas and huge floor-standing vases of dried flowers. Not at all child friendly. Not a granny-house in any way. But then, I couldn't imagine her being a normal granny.

'Well? What did you want to talk about?'

Best just to get it out there, I thought. I took a deep breath. 'I'm going to have a baby. You'll be a grandmother.'

She was silent for a moment. 'Oh. Well, that's a surprise. I always thought you'd do things properly – you know, marry first, children later. I'm assuming it *is* Dan's?'

'Jackie, for goodness sake, of course it's Dan's!' I snapped. 'I'd assumed we'd marry first as well, but things happen, and here we are.'

She snorted. 'It'll change your life, you know. Completely. You need to be sure that's what you want. I assume it's early days – it's probably not too late—'

'No.' I broke her off before she said too much, before she said something that might damage our relationship still further. She should have been delighted at the thought of having a grandchild. Any other woman would be. Why couldn't my mother be like any other woman? 'I'm nervous, Jackie. I'd be lying if I said I wasn't. But that's for me to deal with. Aren't you pleased at the idea of becoming a grandmother?'

'Won't make any difference to me.' There was a moment's silence, as if she was considering the implications of my news, and then she drew a deep breath. 'Don't expect me to babysit for you – I'm done with all that. And don't think of getting your kid to call me Granny or suchlike. It can call me Jackie like everyone else. Well, look, if that's all you wanted to say to me you can let me get on now. Like I said, I'm really busy today.' I couldn't believe it. She couldn't wait to get me off the phone, despite the life-changing news I'd just given her!

I gritted my teeth a moment, to stop myself exploding. 'Right, well, just thought you should know. Obviously you're not interested. All I hope is that I'll be a better mother than you were.' So much for it being a turning point in our relationship.

'Well, sorry I was so useless, I'm sure. But you're right. I probably shouldn't ever have had you. Your father persuaded me. I sometimes wished I'd never listened to him.'

'Even now? Now I'm adult and off your hands?' I'd heard all this before, years ago. More recently we'd avoided the topic. I'd forgotten how much it hurt to hear her say these things.

'I'd have done great things if I hadn't had a kid to look after. You held me back.'

'Jeez, thanks, Jackie. That's great. How do you think that makes me feel – my own mother rejecting me like that?' As on so many occasions, I tried to let it wash over me, I tried not to care. But now I was going to be a mother myself, I was going to experience the other side of the equation. The hurt of her rejection felt like a physical pain in my chest.

'You pushed me away, too,' she said quietly. 'As soon as your father died you moved out, remember? Left me all alone right when I needed support.'

I shook my head. 'We'd have killed each other if I'd stayed, without Dad to liaise between us. You know that, Jackie.' If I'd stayed, it would have been a disaster. Moving out and seeing Jackie only occasionally had felt like the only answer at the time. I had a sudden, unwelcome thought – maybe if things had been different and I'd stayed then perhaps that could have been a turning point for us. But I'd been still a child at seventeen, only just holding myself together after Dad died, unable to cope with the added pressure of building bridges with Jackie. She'd been the adult. She should have been the one to try to mend our relationship.

She gave a loud sigh. 'All I'm saying, Maria, is if you decide to go ahead and have this child, make sure you've thought long and hard about what it'll mean for your lifestyle, for both you and Dan. It's not easy being a parent, and not everyone can do it well.' She was silent for a moment before continuing in a softer tone. 'You're more like me than you realise, Maria. Some of us aren't cut out for motherhood.'

I felt tears prick at my eyes for the second time that morning. She'd voiced my deep-seated concerns, right there. What if I was too much like her, and would be unfit as a mother? What then? The line from the McCarthy grave came to mind – *eternal gratitude for a mother's sacrifice*. Not something I could say about Jackie. Would my own child be able to say it about me? Would I be a Jackie or a Kitty?

'Well, on that note, I'll go. Thanks for nothing, Jackie. Enjoy your day.' I hung up before I began screaming at her. I should have known she'd react like that. But it could have been worse if it had been a face-to-face meeting. And at least now it was done, and I'd told her.

I sent Dan a quick text to let him know, and had a reply back almost immediately: **Well done, proud of you. xx** He was the only person who knew how difficult Jackie could be. I may not have the support of my mother, but I had Dan's support. And always had, I realised.

*

After mooching around the local shops for the rest of the morning I arrived at the church a little early, and found a number of cars in its car park and several people on their way out after a private christening service. The baby was in a fabulous long white christening gown, being held by a proud mother, surrounded by other family members. As I passed them on my way into the church, I congratulated the mother. The baby, I have to admit, did look pretty cute, sleeping comfortably in his mother's arms. I found myself wondering whether Dan and I would get our baby christened or not – was it hypocritical to do so if we weren't religious? One thing was for certain – there'd be no heirloom christening gown. No heirlooms at all from Jackie. She'd thrown out all my baby and childhood stuff as soon as she possibly could. I remembered a time when she'd sent a sack of cuddly toys to the school fete, before I was ready to give them up. I'd had to rummage through the stall and buy back my favourite teddy with my pocket money.

The priest was still in the doorway of the church, his face in shadow, chatting to the last few christening guests. As I approached, I recognised his voice, and then he stepped forward into the sunlight.

'Declan! Um, sorry I'm a bit early. You did say there was a christening on.' I tried to cover my confusion and pretend I'd known all along he was the priest. Aoife's words from my first evening in O'Sullivan's came back to me – *You'll not get far with that one* – and her smirk. So that's what she'd meant!

'Hi, Maria. Go on through – the record books are in a little room off the vestry. I'll be with you in a few minutes.'

As I walked through the church, which was light, airy and brightly painted in blue and gold, I trawled my memories of the last few days to see if I'd made a fool of myself with him. Had I flirted at all? Catholic priests took vows of celibacy, didn't they? Had I said anything that might have offended him? I blushed as I recalled I'd thought he was leaning over to kiss me goodnight as he left the pub yesterday. Oh God, what an idiot I was!

And then I found myself grinning. I hadn't done anything *too* embarrassing – well, only in my mind. Declan had never said he was a priest, and he hadn't worn a dog collar.

I entered the vestry and found the little office that led off it. One wall was lined with dark wooden shelves from floor to ceiling, which housed hundreds of dusty record books, some old and worn, others looking pretty new. I was standing gazing at them and wondering where to begin, when Declan came in behind me, already tugging his surplice over his head.

'Right, well, the records are in date order, more or less, from top left to bottom right. Eighteen forties I guess about there.' He pointed to a shelf about halfway up. 'Pick one and work your way forward or back as necessary. I just need to get changed.'

'Thanks. Declan?'

He turned back at the door. 'Yes?'

'I didn't realise you were the priest here. I hope I didn't – you know – say anything stupid?'

He stared at me for a moment and then threw back his head and laughed, an infectious sound which soon had me joining in as well. 'Ah, I shouldn't laugh, so I shouldn't, but it must have given you a surprise to see me here in my priest's get-up? It's my own fault. I should wear my collar out and about, but I much prefer polo shirts.'

He stopped laughing and looked at me more seriously. 'Does it bother you? I know you said you're not religious at all. Just think of my calling as a job, like any other, if it helps.'

I smiled. 'No, doesn't bother me, of course not. But it does explain why you're such a good listener.'

'Yes, I get plenty of practice in the confessional. Anyway, I'll be off to change and back with you in five minutes or so. You get started.' He waved a hand at the record books and disappeared back into the vestry, pulling the door closed behind him.

By the time he was back, now dressed in his usual jeans and a moss-green polo shirt, I was still pulling out the ledgers one by one to try to find the right years. I worked backwards from 1850 to begin with, looking for any McCarthy burials. All those children listed on the memorial stone – I hoped at least some of them had had a proper burial, with a priest in attendance and their details written down in a book. It was heart-breaking to think of all those who'd died during the famine and been simply thrown into one of the mass graves, with no record of their passing kept anywhere. In a ledger that covered the winter of 1848–49

I found one – Grace McCarthy. She had been buried in the churchyard, in what was listed as 'the McCarthy plot', but with no stone marker.

'Look,' I said, pointing out the entry in the book to Declan. 'There was a McCarthy plot.'

'Ah, that's good. So at least this little colleen, Grace, was buried with proper rites. Have you found any others?'

'Not yet.' I pulled out the next volume, going backwards, and began leafing through it. The writing took a while to get my head around and of course there were so many entries for deaths in those years. Eventually, back in the winter of 1846–47, I found several McCarthy entries, all within a few days of each other.

'Here they are, the poor little things.' I felt my eyes well up with tears as I passed the book over to Declan. These children were my three great-uncles and aunts, but they'd had such short lives, and had died in such a tragic way.

'It's so sad.' He ran his fingers slowly over the words in the ledger, and was silent for a moment. Praying silently for their souls, I guessed, and I felt oddly comforted by the idea.

'All the children died during the famine. I haven't found their father though, and he is mentioned on the gravestone.'

'But with an earlier date, I think?'

I pulled out my notebook where I had copied down the details. 'Yes, he died in 1844.' I soon found him in a ledger which covered 1839–1844. There were far fewer deaths before the famine and the books covered a longer period. Next job was to try to find christenings for the children so I could work out their exact ages when they died. Although I was supposed to be researching Michael, and perhaps discovering what had become of his mother Kitty, I felt the need to fill in the blanks of his whole family. It would help to add background to the biography. And if *all* his siblings had died that added real poignancy to his search for Kitty. That thought made me realise I could be looking for christenings for more McCarthy children than just the ones on the headstone. Maybe there were other children who'd survived to adulthood. This was going to take a while.

*

It did. Declan helped, but also spent some time on his church paperwork and other tasks, looking up from his laptop whenever I found something new to show him. After a couple of hours, I'd found christenings for all the children except for Michael, and had found a wedding record for Kitty and Patrick McCarthy in 1834. No other McCarthy children. I'd noted everything down and taken photos on my phone of each relevant document. Why no christening for Michael? I did not know his exact date of birth. Where in the family had he come? I knew he'd travelled to America the first time in 1849 alone, so must have been at least in his mid- to late-teens then, which made him older than his siblings. With a jolt I realised he must have been born before his parents married. Well, that was not uncommon, either then or now. My hand snuck down to my abdomen almost of its own accord – here was another little one who'd quite likely be born before his or her parents were wed. The thought made me shudder. Despite having made up with Dan on the phone this morning, I still felt terrified at the prospect of becoming a mother. The conversation with Jackie had not helped.

'You all right there?' asked Declan. I must have been making a face.

'Yes, I'm fine. So, it looks like Michael was the eldest and very likely born before his parents married,' I said, to deflect him from asking more about my state of mind. If we began talking again about my pregnancy I'd soon be blubbing on his shoulder, like last night.

'It happened a lot,' he said, with a shrug. 'But you're assuming that he was definitely his father's child? I mean, perhaps he was from an earlier relationship Kitty had? Because if he was Patrick's child, surely they'd have married quickly when she found she was pregnant.'

'Good point. I need to go back further to look for a christening.'

'Could be in a different church – she might have only begun coming here after marrying, if she moved to her husband's parish then. He glanced at his watch. 'I think we'll need to leave it for now if you want anything to eat before going to the match? Or a cup of tea at least? O'Sullivan's, the café, or I could see what I can rustle up in the presbytery?'

'I wouldn't put you to so much trouble. The café will be perfect.' I put the volumes I'd been looking at back on their shelves and we left the church, arm in arm, companionably.

CHAPTER 14

Kitty

The brooch! Kitty remembered it with a start as she awoke the following morning. She put a hand to her breast where she had pinned it to her dress the night before, and there it was, still securely attached. Michael was already awake and preparing himself for the day's work. There would be no breakfast – nothing to eat until the evening. Unless, of course, she sold the brooch quickly in which case she would buy food and fetch Michael from the worksite.

'Good morning to you, Mammy,' Michael said, as she arose from the bed and straightened her clothing. 'Did you sleep well?'

'I did, thank you, love. I feel a little better today.' She gave him a small smile, and picked up her shawl.

'What's that?' he asked, pointing to the brooch.

'Ah, 'tis an old brooch that was Mother Heaney's. Gracie must have found it and hidden it away in the mattress.' She hadn't wanted him to see it. He would only insist that she bought food with the proceeds of its sale. But her plan was to buy a ticket for his passage to America and present it to him, so he had no choice but to go. The timing couldn't be better – she'd heard the *Columbus* was sailing from Cork in five days' time. James O'Dowell, Patrick's old foreman, was due to sail on it along with his family. So Michael would not be alone on his journey.

'It's pretty, so it is.'

She nodded and knotted her shawl around her shoulders, covering the brooch. She did not trust herself to say anything more. 'There's nothing for breakfast, Michael. I'm so sorry.'

'We'll be paid today. We'll buy food on our way home. Come on, 'tis time we left.'

She dared not look him in the eye. 'You go. I might be along later. There is something I must see to first.'

He gave her a quizzical look, then shrugged as if he was too weary to question her further, kissed her cheek and left.

She felt guilty for deceiving him but if her plan worked, and there was money left over, she'd be bringing home food, and he'd understand. She'd buy beef, if she could get it. Bacon, eggs, bread, potatoes, milk. A new chicken or two.

Her stomach rumbled, as it always did in the mornings, and her mouth watered at the thought of what they might be able to eat. Food such as they'd not had since before the first failure of the potato crop. Food such as they'd never had, not since the early days of her marriage to Patrick, when they'd always kept chickens and pigs and a goat.

*

Despite her hunger Kitty felt full of energy as she walked down the track into town, a half-hour after Michael had left for the worksite. It was amazing what hope could do to a person. Before she'd left she'd put Michael's sketch of Thomas Waterman on his horse in her pocket.

It would serve as a reminder of what could be gained – a future for Michael as an artist amongst the rich. The day was cold, overcast with a chill wind and a light drizzle, but to Kitty it felt as though the sun was shining inside her. By the end of the day their troubles would be over. Michael would have his ticket and she would have food, and maybe some money to spare. If the brooch fetched enough money for two tickets . . . she stopped short in her thoughts. Would she go to America too? Could she leave this place, leave the home she'd shared with Patrick, leave the graves of all their children? No, she decided. She could not. She would have to stay and look after the graves, make sure they were not forgotten, commission a decent stone memorial for them. It was enough that Michael would be able to leave and have his chance in life. That she should live while the children had all died was hard enough to bear, without adding to the guilt by leaving their graves untended.

In the centre of town, she looked about her. She prayed that she would not come across Thomas Waterman today, after ignoring his request that she go to Ballymor House to see him. Now, where would a person go to try to sell jewellery? It was not a situation she'd ever found herself in before. Ballymor was a small town, and there were few rich people living in the area, other than Waterman and a few other landowners and their agents. She decided to ask at O'Sullivan's pub. As a precaution, she unpinned the brooch and re-pinned it on the inside of her dress, knotting her shawl tightly around her shoulders over it. People were desperate these days. Who knew what they'd do to get money for food?

She was in luck. James O'Dowell himself was in O'Sullivan's, settling up his bar bill. He had been luckier than most during these terrible famine years – he owned his own house, and had kept a good job as a foreman at Waterman's copper mines. He'd been able to save enough to buy a passage to America for himself, his wife and three of his children. He'd lost two children to disease rather than hunger, and that had made him decide to go.

'Kitty McCarthy!' he exclaimed, as she entered the pub. 'It's been a long time since I rested my eyes on your fair face. I heard about your little girl. I'm so sorry.'

She shook his hand. His grip was warm and firm. 'Thank you. These are terrible times, to be sure.'

'And how's that son of yours? A good lad, he is.'

She remembered that O'Dowell had given Michael the sketchbook and pencils. 'He's surviving. Working on the new road. Not so much time for drawing these days. But look, here's something he drew.' She pulled out the sketch of Waterman.

O'Dowell studied it. ''Tis a good likeness, indeed. Talented lad, so he is.' He handed it back and regarded her with concern in his eyes. 'And you, are you getting enough to eat?'

'Barely, but we are managing. Mr O'Dowell, I hear you are away to America on the *Columbus* soon?'

'I am that. I'll be sorry to leave the old country, but after losing our two young 'uns I think it's time to go, see if those streets of New York are truly paved with gold like they say they are. I'm away to Killarney today, to say farewell to my sister before we leave.' He paused, as if remembering that she'd lost a lot more than two young ones. 'Kitty, I'm sorry. If I could help you I would, but I only barely managed to buy the tickets for the five of us. I'll let you have any food we have left when we go. 'Tis all I can do for you.'

'Maybe not all,' she said. 'I'm after some advice. I've something I might be able to sell.' She dropped her voice. There were a couple of skeletal-looking men in the corner of the pub, not drinking, just sheltering from the cold of the day. The publican turned a blind eye to those who wished to use his premises as a temporary home, rather than walk miles back to cold, empty cottages. 'I've a piece of jewellery. Tell me, Mr O'Dowell, where might I get the best price for it?'

'Not here, for sure,' he said. 'Unless you take it to Mr Waterman, up at the big house. Perhaps he'd buy it from you.'

She shook her head. 'No. I'll not go to him.'

O'Dowell frowned. 'He'd be your best chance in Ballymor. They say he's beginning to realise the plight of his workers, at long last, after three years of the Hunger. He's finally wanting to do something to help.'

Kitty gave a hollow laugh and shook her head. 'I'd no more believe that, Mr O'Dowell, than I'd believe in the man in the moon. 'Tis not in the man's nature to show any kindness.'

'Nevertheless, Kitty, the word is he's beginning to open his eyes to the people dying all about him. One of his grooms didn't turn up for work one day, and when Waterman went to find the man he was with his parents, nursing them in their final hours. Skeletons, they were. Waterman's own staff have always been well fed, and it seems he didn't realise how bad things were. I heard he went out to the road-building site yesterday, to see for himself.'

'He did, that. I saw him there.' Kitty nodded.

'And now he wants to help. Too late for so many, of course. Still, your best hope to sell the brooch is to go to him.'

Crawling to that monster would have to be her last hope, she thought. 'But Mr Waterman has no wife and no daughters. What would he be wanting with a trinket like this? Is there nowhere else I could sell it?'

He rubbed his chin, thoughtfully. 'You could take it to Cork. There are a few jewellers on St Patrick's Street. I'd try there, if I were you. If you hurry now, I think old Jimmy Maguire will be going that way soon. He'll give you a lift in his cart. Come on, I'll take you to him.'

She smiled. 'Thank you. And, when I've sold it, where do I go to buy a passage on the *Columbus*?'

He stopped and stared at her. 'So you're after wanting to come too?'

'Not me. Michael. I'm hoping you'd perhaps keep an eye on him, just till he finds his feet.'

'Gladly I will. He's a good lad, like his father.'

She did not respond to that. O'Dowell, like most people around here, assumed that Patrick had been Michael's father.

He described to her where in the city the office was for the shipping line, then took her arm and led her out of the pub and through the town, to a storehouse near the Cork road. A man was in the yard, harnessing a sorry-looking horse, its ribs poking through its mangy hide, to a cart which contained a pile of empty sacks. 'Jimmy! Just the man. Will you take this lady here to Cork? She's got some business there. Bring her back again after. She'll be able to pay you, then.' He winked at Kitty.

The man looked at her suspiciously, but then nodded. 'Climb up, then. Sit on them sacks, you'll be all right there. I'm coming back at three, but the cart'll be full then of sacks of cornmeal. You'll have to sit atop of it.'

'Thank you, sir,' she said, as she climbed up, helped by James O'Dowell.

Maguire smirked at being called 'sir', and hauled himself up. He flicked the reins and the old nag reluctantly began to plod out of the yard and along the road.

'Good luck,' O'Dowell called after her, and she waved in reply.

Jimmy Maguire was a taciturn man, who spoke not a word to her for the entire journey to Cork. It took them a couple of hours. Kitty had only been to the big city once before, just after she and Patrick had married. They'd gone to buy furniture, pots and plates for their cottage. They'd hired a cart not unlike this one, leaving Michael with Mother Heaney, and had brought it back crammed with items to set up home with. It had been a joyous occasion. She could remember feeling overwhelmed by the number of buildings, the crowds, the shops and pubs, the magnificent churches. She'd been so happy then – with her man at her side, her future secured and so much to look forward to in life.

There was nothing now for her to look forward to. If today was successful, it would mean she would say goodbye to her only remaining child in just a few days' time. She would be left all alone. But Michael would be saved from the famine.

*

Cork city was as big as she remembered, but not as busy or vibrant. The famine had struck here too. The people they passed in the streets were as thin and gaunt as those in Ballymor, with the same look of desperation on their faces. Shops and pubs in the poorer parts of town were closed and boarded up. A crowd was gathered at the front of the storehouse where Maguire was to pick up his goods, so he drove around to the back entrance. The place was guarded by men with stout sticks. 'The mob overturned my cart one time,' Maguire grumbled. 'Scrabbled at the sacks, filling their pockets, cramming uncooked cornmeal into their mouths, so they were.'

He drew the cart to a halt in the back yard, and turned to her. 'I'll be leaving this place at three. If you're wanting a lift back to Ballymor, be here by then. I'll tell the guards to let you through the gates. Let's hope the mob's gone by then.' He nodded, dismissing her, and she climbed down and made her way out of the yard and towards the city centre.

Kitty wound her way through the narrow cobbled streets, crossed a river and eventually found her way to St Patrick's Street, which she remembered from her previous trip as being one of the principal upmarket shopping streets. She walked along it until finally she found a cluster of goldsmith businesses – Greaves, Teulons and Jennings. She tried Greaves first, entering the premises hesitantly, knowing that she was hardly the sort of customer they would normally expect to serve, dressed as she was in her ragged dress and shawl. Nevertheless, she had something to sell and a right to be there. She took a deep breath and held her head high as she approached the counter in the shop's dark interior.

A thin but smartly dressed young man was standing behind the counter, writing something in a huge ledger. He looked up and wrinkled his nose as she approached.

'No beggars in here. We have nothing for you. The soup kitchen is up the hill in Barrack Street.' He glared at her expectantly, waiting for her to turn and leave.

'Thank you, but I have business here,' she said, trying to keep the quaver out of her voice. 'I have something to sell.'

He raised his eyebrows but said nothing.

She untied her shawl, and extracted the brooch from where it was pinned inside her dress. With a shaking hand she held it out to him.

He did not take it from her. He shook his head, sadly she thought, and then came out from behind the counter to hold the shop door open for her. 'Ten minutes' walk – along the street, cross the river on South Bridge and up Barrack Hill. They'll feed you there.'

'But – my brooch? Will you not even look at it?'

He didn't answer but remained standing there, holding the door open for her. She stared back at him for a moment and then left. There were two other jewellers in this street alone.

She crossed the road to try the building opposite, upon which a painted sign swung in the breeze. *Charles and Samuel Teulon – Gold & Silversmiths*, it read. Feeling less confident after her reception in Greaves, she pushed open the door and stepped inside.

A grey-haired man was holding out a tray of rings for a well-dressed lady, who sat on a velvet-upholstered chair, to peruse. He looked up as Kitty entered, and turned a shade of puce.

'Out, woman! You'll get no charity here!'

'Please, sir, I have something to sell,' she begged. 'Please look at it at least.'

'Indulge the woman,' said the lady in the chair. 'Who knows, perhaps she does have some sweet little trinket that may be worth the cost of a meal to her.' She smiled at Kitty, but the smile was false and did not reach her eyes.

'Thank you, ma'am,' Kitty said, dipping in what she hoped was an approximation of a curtsey. She held out the brooch to the grey-haired jeweller, who took it from her and inspected it through an eyeglass.

'Pah. Worthless. A nice enough design, but made of nothing but copper.' He handed it back.

'But, sir, 'tis my belief the metal is rose gold! Please, look again!' She thrust it back towards him, but he'd turned away.

'It's copper, woman. I know my trade. Rose gold does not tarnish black and green like copper does. Look for yourself!'

She did look at it, and realised he was right. Mother Heaney must have fooled herself that the brooch was valuable. Tears welled up and spilled down her cheeks before she could stop them. All her dreams, her plans, evaporated like mist on a summer's morning.

'Charles, give her a shilling for it, would you? She looks like she needs to eat. She's probably got a cottage full of starving children somewhere. Have a heart, Charles!' The lady in the chair reached out to the jeweller and gave him a beseeching look.

He returned to Kitty and held out his hand for the brooch. Turning it over he said, 'Very well. I'll give you one shilling for it, as an act of charity, to feed your children.'

'Sir, my children are all dead, except for my eldest who is a grown man now.' The words were out before she could stop herself.

'Your children are all dead, but you still live and walk and only *now* try to sell your valuables to save yourself?' gasped the lady.

'I wish that I were dead instead of them,' Kitty replied, her head bowed.

'Well, I think the less of you now that I find you have let them die,' the lady said, turning her face away.

Kitty sighed, her head dipping still further in despair. But then the woman's words sunk in, and she raised her head defiantly.

'Madam, I did not *let* my children die. 'Tis the government that has done that.'

The woman stood up in front of her and sniffed loudly. 'I'll have you know my husband is a member of that government you accuse.'

'Then tell him about me,' Kitty said. 'Tell him there are thousands like me. Tell him about my children, wasting away one by one even though I went without food myself that they might have more. Tell him about the workhouses, crammed with four times as many people as they were built for, where disease spreads like a plague of rats, from where none come out except in a coffin. Tell him—' she was crying openly now, her voice high and shrill '—to open soup kitchens in every town. To pay double on the work schemes. To import more food and ensure it gets to where it is needed. Your husband, madam, can make a difference and stop more children from dying. It's too late for my own dear little ones.'

The woman stared at her, speechless, then sat back down in her chair, facing the jeweller.

'Charles, may we return to our business now? Send this creature out, with or without her shilling as you see fit.'

'Without her shilling, I should think,' said Mr Teulon, his tone stern and disapproving.

Kitty turned on her heel and left without another word. She was exhausted, with no more fight left in her.

There was one more goldsmith. Perhaps Mr Teulon had been wrong, and the brooch was rose gold after all. But in the third goldsmith's shop, the reaction was the same – the brooch was valueless. In this shop – Jennings – she was served by a kind-faced elderly man. He shook his head sadly as he told her the brooch was nothing but copper, probably from local Cork mines.

She tucked the brooch away inside the bodice of her dress and turned to go, but as she reached the door he called her back. 'Take this, at least, for your journey home,' he said, and passed her a bundle. Inside was a small loaf of bread and a wedge of cheese wrapped in paper. 'It was to be my lunch, but your need is the greater, so it is.'

She smiled her thanks, unable to trust her voice. There were still good people in the world, even in these bitter times.

*

The journey back to Ballymor passed in silence – an awkward one after Kitty explained that she had not sold her brooch and therefore had no money with which to pay Jimmy Maguire for the lift.

'Aye, well, I suppose I'll have to take ye anyways,' he said, grumpily, and for this at least Kitty was grateful.

She spent the journey home sitting atop empty sacks, for there had been no corn for Jimmy Maguire to bring back to Ballymor, clutching the package of bread and cheese which she resolved to give to Michael who would have had a hard day's work. As the cart clattered along the rutted road, she mulled over her options. There weren't many left. Whatever happened, she was still determined that Michael should have a place on the *Columbus* when it sailed. As the rain began to fall and she huddled shivering into her shawl, she realised there was only one course of action she could take now. Only one chance left. For herself she would not have taken it, but for Michael she would do anything. Even this. She would go to Waterman that same evening, before she lost her nerve.

CHAPTER 15

Maria

We left the church and had a cup of tea and a sandwich at the café across the square. The waitress, a woman in her forties with a frilly white pinny tied around her ample midriff, flirted a little with Declan, patting his shoulder and fluttering her eyelashes at him. I guessed that women felt safe doing this around Declan, as he was a priest and would therefore never take it too seriously.

After we'd finished the sandwiches, Declan checked his watch. 'So, if we leave now we can walk to the sports ground, or if you'd like a cake or another cup of tea I could drive us there. It's about a mile away, so.'

'Let's walk,' I replied, and he smiled and stood to leave.

The route took us through town and past a row of single-storey cottages which Declan said dated from the early 1800s. They looked tiny but well maintained, their roofs tiled although I guessed they might originally have been thatched. They were all whitewashed, with brightly painted front doors that opened directly onto the street. I felt an almost irresistible urge to peep in at the windows, but didn't dare in case someone was inside. But I did take a photo – I imagined the cottages up at Kildoolin would have looked something like this if they'd been kept up and inhabited over the years.

From there we went through a modern housing estate, across a children's play area where kids from six to sixteen were hanging out, doing their own thing – the younger ones on the climbing frames and roundabouts; the older ones on the swings with their mobiles in their hands. There were no adults in sight. I wondered who was looking after the little ones – perhaps the teenagers were their siblings. If so, they weren't keeping a very close eye on them – they all seemed to be focused entirely on their phones. I resolved to make sure my child was always watched carefully at parks. I'd give him or her freedom to run around, of course, but supervised and with a parent on hand to ensure safety.

There I went again – planning how it would be when I was a mother. Different to Jackie – she'd never taken me to the park, not once. That had always been Dad's job. He'd push me higher than anyone else on the swings, spin the roundabout so fast I'd be squealing for him to stop, and was always there to catch me at the bottom of the slide.

After what Jackie had said on the phone, it was a fair bet that she wouldn't be the kind of grandparent who took her grandchild to the park either. Dan would love to, I was certain. And I – well who knew, but I'd definitely try to be the kind of parent Dad had been, rather than Jackie. Kids deserved to have fun.

'Good to see the kids playing, isn't it?' Declan commented, as if he could read my thoughts.

I nodded and smiled.

At the far end of the playground was the town's sports centre and a pitch, with what looked like a cross between rugby posts and football goals at the end – a tall H with a net at the bottom. A large noticeboard welcomed visitors to Ballymor GAA Ground.

'GAA is Gaelic Athletic Association. In other words, hurling and Gaelic football, which are both played on the same pitch,' Declan explained.

There was a small crowd already gathered, and excitement was building. We bought our tickets and took up places in the small stand that lined one side of the pitch. I noticed whole families who'd turned out to watch the match, from aged grannies sitting on deckchairs to toddlers in their fathers' arms. The local team's colours were apparently maroon and yellow, judging by the garish scarves and shirts many were wearing. The visitors – a team from Kerry – were in blue.

The match began and I watched in awe as men in helmets with faceguards ran at full pelt along the pitch with the ball balanced on the end of what looked like a fat hockey stick, then flicked the ball up in the air, took hold of their stick ('hurley' – Declan corrected me) and whacked the ball half the length of the pitch over the top of the goal, between the uprights. The crowd roared – obviously that meant a point had been scored.

'You get one point for hitting it between the posts, and three for scoring a goal in the net,' Declan yelled in my ear, over the cheers.

I'd been in the hockey team at school, but Jackie had never watched me play. It had always been Dad dropping me off for Saturday morning practices, or cheering my team from the sidelines. I couldn't get the phone call with Jackie out of my mind. Why couldn't she at least have said congratulations to me? Why had she brought up that whole thing about her having not wanted me, and how I was more like her than I realised? I didn't want to be like her. I wanted to be the kind of parent who took their kid to the park, and who cheered them on at their chosen sport. There was a middle-aged woman wearing a maroon sweatshirt and with a yellow scarf tied in her badly dyed hair sitting a couple of rows in front of me. She was holding a home-made banner which read *Up Ballymor! No tea for Dermot unless he scores!* I picked out the player I guessed was Dermot, the one for whom she cheered loudest whenever he had a touch of the ball. Her son, I supposed. I loved her for her loud, unembarrassed support of him. If I was going to be a parent, I wanted to be *that* kind of mum. If I had it in me.

Soon I was cheering as loudly as everyone else whenever the Ballymor players scored. I had no idea of the rules, but the game was fast and furious and very watchable. At one point there seemed to be some kind of penalty awarded, and all the visiting team players lined up to block their goal along with their goalkeeper while a Ballymor player – it was Dermot! – took a shot. The crowd fell completely silent as he lined up his shot.

'It'll hurt if he hits one of the players,' I whispered.

'He won't aim directly at them – he wouldn't score if he did,' Declan replied, and sure enough the player aimed high and managed to put the ball into the top corner of the net, to his mother's and the crowd's absolute delight.

Ballymor won, two goals and fifteen points to the visitors' zero goals and ten points. Everyone was in good spirits leaving the ground – even the visiting fans.

'So, what did you think?' Declan asked, as we walked back across the park.

'Great fun! How long has it been played in Ireland? I have never heard of it before.'

'Ah, sure it's an ancient game, been played for thousands of years. The GAA standardised the rules in the late nineteenth century.'

'Michael McCarthy might have played it, perhaps?'

'He might have, indeed.'

I loved the idea of Michael, perhaps pre-famine, before the death of his father Patrick (if indeed Patrick was his father) playing hurling at the local school or with his younger siblings. I fervently hoped there had been happy times for the family before the disasters struck.

Declan had to leave me back in town – he had an evening service to prepare for and other parish business. 'Thanks for your company today,' he said, giving me a brief farewell hug.

'Thank *you*. I've had a great day and learned so much.' Not least that you're a priest, I thought, and that I would rather be like the player Dermot's mum than my own.

*

I had an early dinner at O'Sullivan's then, as it was a beautiful evening, I decided to go for an evening stroll. It'd be better for me than sitting in the bar sipping sweet drinks for hours and brooding on the phone call with Jackie. My first thought was to head up to Kildoolin and watch the sunset from the top of the hill, and indeed I headed out of town that way, but after the long walk earlier to the hurling match I couldn't face the hill. Instead of taking the track left to the abandoned village, I turned right, along a lane which was signposted 'Clear View Camping'. I remembered that Sharon, Dave and their kids were camping here and wondered if they might be around – they hadn't been in the pub today. Dave had said something about there being ruins of an old stately home at the campsite, which I assumed would be Ballymor House. It'd be interesting to take a look at it.

The lane wound its way between hedges sloping gently downhill, then through a pair of ancient stone gateposts into the campsite, which occupied the old landscaped parkland. Huge beech trees were dotted around, spreading their branches wide, with tents and caravans pitched in the spaces between them. I walked through the site, keeping an eye out for Sharon and Dave, following the signs to Reception. At the top of a little rise there was a line of poplars and beyond that I could see some buildings. The ruins of the main house were on the right, and the old stable block was on the left, now converted into various campsite utilities including the reception, shower blocks and a communal kitchen.

I stood in the middle of the courtyard and looked around, trying to imagine it as it would have appeared in the mid-nineteenth century. Maybe there'd be some pictures of it – paintings or early photographs – which I might find online. I walked over to the old house for a closer look. Its roof had fallen in, and saplings grew in abundance inside. All the doorways and glassless windows were secured with sturdy iron bars and hung with signs saying 'Dangerous structure: keep out'. It certainly didn't look like the kind of place you'd want your children climbing all over, although I was sure kids would love to explore it. Peeking through the grilles, I could see an internal wall leaning at a very nasty angle. It had clearly been left to rot a very long time ago. I wondered about its history. Perhaps it was like so many country houses in the UK – the First World War had left families unable to afford the upkeep of large estates, often with no male heir to take over, so the houses had fallen into disrepair and been abandoned. But at some point, while it was still habitable, someone must have made the decision to move out and leave it to be gradually reclaimed by nature – at least until some enterprising person had the idea of building a campsite.

I was supposed to be researching the McCarthys, and as far as I knew they had no connection with Ballymor House. Then it struck me – the owners of the house would also have been the landowners around here, and therefore Patrick McCarthy and perhaps Michael too, before he became an artist, might have worked for them. I remembered too that unnerving Michael McCarthy sketch of a man on a horse at the museum in Cork, which had apparently hung in this house for many years. Perhaps there was more of a link than simply that of landowner to farm-worker.

'Maria, hello!'

I turned, to see Dave and his younger son Sammy walking up the path from the camping field. The boy was filthy dirty as though he'd been rolling around in mud, and Dave was half dragging him towards the shower block, a towel slung over his shoulder.

'Hey! Wondered if I might bump into you. Looks like you've got your work cut out with that one.'

Dave grimaced. 'Yeah, think I'll just chuck him in the shower with his clothes still on. There's an overgrown duck pond at the far end of the campsite. Little tyke thought he'd try to make a boat out of a plastic food container, using a tea towel tied to a wooden spoon as a sail. He waded in through the mud at the edge of the pond to launch it and fell in.'

'Oh dear! And what happened to the boat?'

'It's out in the middle of the pond, unreachable. Except for the tea towel, which was last seen sinking without trace. Sharon'll go spare.'

I couldn't help but laugh. Dave was grinning too. Well, wasn't this the sort of thing kids were supposed to do while on holiday? I had a sudden memory of a family holiday we'd taken when I was about eight or nine years old. Dad and I had spent hours mucking around in a rock pool – trying to entice a small crab out from under its stone, catching minnows, trying to identify species of seaweed. I'd kept everything I found in a bucket to show Jackie, desperate to impress her and include her in our fun. At some point I had leaned over too far, fallen in and grazed my knee on the sharp rock. Jackie had given us both hell when he'd brought me, dripping wet and oozing blood, back into the rented holiday cottage, but Dad had dried me and patched up my knee. 'What is childhood for, Jackie,' he'd said, 'if not to make discoveries and push boundaries? There are bound to be some accidents along the way, but no real harm done.' He'd then mopped the floor and put my clothes in the wash, while Jackie had sat on the sofa with a cup of tea and a sour expression until he'd finished his chores and could sit beside her. She'd snuggled up to him then, happy to be once more the focus of his attention, and I'd retreated to my bedroom. All I'd needed was a get-well kiss from her.

'Sounds like a fun thing to do,' I said to Sammy, and he grinned at me, his teeth shining white against his muddy face.

'So what brings you here?' Dave asked me.

'Just fancied an evening stroll, and I also wanted to see the remains of Ballymor House.' I fell into step alongside them, walking in the direction of the old stables.

'There's a brief history of the house written up in the campsite leaflet,' Dave said. 'You can get one from Reception. If they're closed, we've got one in our van you can have.'

'Thanks, that'd be great,' I said. There was some connection between the great house and the McCarthys, back in the mid-nineteenth century, I was sure of it.

*

I read the leaflet, given to me by Dave, later that evening when I was back in my room at O'Sullivan's. There were only a couple of paragraphs about the history, and a single photo of the house from around 1900. It had been owned for many years by an English family named Waterman – the same family, I recalled, who'd owned the copper mines in the hills. Around the time of the Irish famine one Thomas Waterman lived here, splitting his time between Ireland and England. He'd left no heirs and on his death the Irish estate had passed to a cousin who had sold most of the land and rarely visited Ireland. The house had been emptied of its furnishings and abandoned in 1922 after the Irish War of Independence, and the remaining land bought and turned into a campsite just ten years ago.

I searched online for Thomas Waterman to see if I could discover anything more about him. There was a portrait of him on the National Gallery's website which I was very excited to find, but sadly it was not by Michael McCarthy. It had been painted around 1865 and showed a grey-haired man, sitting in a high-backed armchair, his hands folded on top of a walking cane. His eyes looked rheumy, his face lined, and his overall expression was one of deep disappointment with life.

Nothing online linked Waterman with Michael McCarthy. I was no nearer working out why a rough McCarthy sketch would have been framed and hung in pride of place in Waterman's house.

CHAPTER 16

Kitty

Kitty jumped down from the cart as soon as Jimmy Maguire had brought it to a stop, back in his yard in Ballymor. She thanked him, and hurried off as fast as she could, through the town centre, and out along the road that led towards Ballymor House. Her legs felt weak, and she realised she had not eaten all day. The hunk of bread and cheese was still wrapped up and tucked in her skirt pockets, but that was for Michael, whose need was greater than hers. She would have to manage without. She debated making a detour via the road-building site so she could pass the package to him, but it was the wrong direction and besides he would insist on sharing it with her and she wanted him to have it all.

She needed to go ahead with her plan, now, before she stopped to think too hard about what she was doing, before she lost her nerve. She'd seen desire in Waterman's eyes. If things worked out, much as it made her shudder to think of it, she might have money enough to buy food for the next few days as well as money for his ticket. And if she did, what did it matter where it had come from? What she was prepared to do for the money was a sin, but it would save a life and give a deserving young man a chance in life. God would forgive her.

She pinched her lips together resolutely, and marched as fast as her jelly-like legs would take her, along the well-surfaced lane that led to the big house. It was lined with majestic poplar trees, and lush green lawns studded with wide-spreading beeches sloped away on both sides. So different to the rough track through the heather that led to Kildoolin. She felt as though she was stepping into another world. Which, in a way, she was – his world. Thomas Waterman's privileged, easy, selfish world.

As she neared the imposing house, her resolve began to fail her. Memories of her previous visit here surfaced – Waterman's cruel abuse of her when she was not much more than a child. The abuse that had resulted in Michael. It seemed fitting in a twisted way that she was returning here only as a last resort, in a bid to save him. She reminded herself of what James O'Dowell had said about Waterman being changed, more sympathetic, perhaps more willing to help. She still could not believe that of him. It did not fit with the man she had known.

Should she go to the front door? It would be opened by a maid, or a butler, she supposed. Or should she look for him in the stables? What if he was not at home? Or was entertaining guests?

'Be strong now, Kitty,' she told herself. 'He asked you to come, so he did, so pull on the bell cord at the front door as a lady would.' She smoothed her skirts, tucked a stray lock of hair behind her ear and held her head high as she climbed the polished stone steps to the grand main entrance. She tugged on the bell rope and heard a distant jangling somewhere inside. A moment later, the door was opened by an elderly man in a black suit.

'Yes?' he said, looking her up and down and wrinkling his nose.

'Mr Waterman asked me to come to the house,' she said, her voice wavering. 'Is he at home?'

'What on earth would Mr Waterman want with you?' said the man. 'If you're wanting charity, try round at the kitchen door but I'm not sure you'll have any luck. If we start doling out food to one then we'd soon have the whole county on our doorstep.'

He began to close the heavy door, but Kitty put out her hand to him. 'Please, sir, Mr Waterman really did ask me to come, yesterday. Is he in the house? Or I could go to the stables if he's there? Please, sir, tell him it's Kitty McCarthy come to see him as he asked.'

The man frowned, then seemed to believe her. 'Very well. Go to the stable yard and wait. I shall tell the master your name. But I very much doubt he wants to see such a one as you.'

She opened her mouth to say something further but the butler had already closed the door in her face. She sighed, and walked around the house to the stables. She shivered as she glanced up towards the small window of the groom's lodgings, remembering what had happened the last time she was there. On this occasion there was no one about. The stables were almost empty – just two horses stood munching hay and stamping their feet. One was the huge black one Waterman had been riding yesterday, the one in Michael's sketch. The door to the tack room hung open, but there was no one inside. She remembered what O'Dowell had said about the groom nursing his dying parents, and wondered if he was still with them. She stood in the centre of the yard, twisting her hands in her skirts, wondering what to do, where to go, how long to wait.

It was only a few minutes before she realised a door on the side of the house had opened, and Thomas Waterman was striding across the yard towards her. She forced herself to hold her head high, although her stomach was turning somersaults. It was lucky it was empty, she thought, or she might have been sick.

'Kitty McCarthy,' Waterman said, as he drew near. 'I thought I told you to come to me yesterday?'

'You did, sir, and I'm sorry I'm late.' She tried to curtsey, but her legs felt too weak to hold her and she stumbled slightly.

He put out a hand to steady her. 'Come inside. You look as though you need to sit down and eat something before you do anything else.'

She nodded. He was right about needing to eat. What the 'anything else' he might require of her would be she didn't dare to think about. She would face it when it came.

He began walking back to the big house, obviously expecting her to follow him, but she hesitated. There would be servants inside – the butler she'd already seen, but there'd also be maids, kitchen staff, footmen. She didn't know anyone directly who worked at the hall, but she was sure if she was seen there with Waterman the word would get out and the townsfolk would assume the worst. Her reputation would be ruined. The butler was unlikely to gossip or sully his master's name but the lower servants would have no such scruples. But did it matter? What was a reputation, when the alternative was probable death by starvation for both her and Michael?

Waterman had noticed she was not following. 'What's the matter? Scared of entering the house, are you? Very well. I seem to remember the last time you were here I entertained you in one of the grooms' lodgings. Perhaps that will serve us again, although I shall have to fetch food from the kitchens. Here, go inside and up the stairs and wait for me.' He held open the door to the groom's cottage where he had taken her all those years ago.

It took a huge effort of will to go through, passing as she did so close to him, but he made no move to touch her or even to catch her eye, and as soon as she was through the door he let it close and was gone. She let out the breath she hadn't realised she was holding, and climbed the stairs with effort, on all fours. The room at the top was almost exactly as she remembered it, but dustier as if it had not been used for some time. The narrow bed still stood against the back wall. She sat down upon it. She did not want to, but she felt too weak to stand any longer and there was nowhere else to sit. He had gone to get her some food. She would have to find a way to keep some to take back to Michael, along with the bread and cheese package she still had tucked in her skirts. What food would Waterman bring? Suddenly it was all she could think of. Her mind emptied of why she had come and what he might desire of her, and filled itself with thoughts of the food he might bring, the food she might save to take to Michael . . .

It was only a few minutes before he returned, bearing a tray upon which was a plate of bread spread with butter, a selection of cakes, slices of cold beef, ham and cheese, a jar of chutney, a pot of tea and two cups, a dish of cream. She could not remember when she had last seen so much food, all together, and all for her. Her eyes widened greedily as Waterman placed the tray down upon the small table which stood near the window of the room.

'Here,' he said. 'I shall take a cup of tea, but the rest is for you. Eat whatever you want; we will talk when you have finished.' He dragged the table carefully over towards the bed so that she could reach it from where she was sitting. He poured two cups of tea, left one on the tray for her, and picked the other up for himself, to sip as he stood beside the window, watching her eat.

She felt self-conscious at first, wanting to cram her mouth full of a bit of everything, relishing the taste of meat and butter in her mouth, and cheese, and those sweet cakes – when had she last had *cake*? She was careful to leave at least half of everything to take home to Michael – he would feast tonight, and if they were careful there'd be more for tomorrow, and the package of bread and cheese from the goldsmith might yet last them another day.

At last, and with the food only a quarter gone, her shrunken stomach told her it could take no more. She finished her cup of tea, wiped her mouth with the starched white napkin he had laid at the side of the tray, and looked up at him. 'Thank you, sir.'

He nodded. 'You needed that, I could see.' He put down his cup on the tray, and sat beside her on the bed. She tried not to flinch away from him. Her mind was working fast – if he thought he could have her body as payment for the food, she was in trouble. She wanted much more than a couple of days' worth of food from him, if she was to submit to him again.

'You're still a beautiful woman, Kitty McCarthy. You are too thin, but you have kept your looks. That hair's a bonus,' he said, as his eyes roved over her. 'I went to England for many years after our first, ahem, encounter, with only occasional trips to Ireland.

If I had not, I think I should have seen a lot more of you at that time. I should have searched you out.'

She was not sure how to answer him. There was nothing honest she could say that would not anger him, and she did not want him angry. This quiet, gentle, reflective mood he was in was much more tolerable than the arrogant brusqueness he'd shown when he came to her cottage with Smith, and when he came across her on the road-building works. This was not the Waterman she remembered. Perhaps it was the Waterman James O'Dowell had told her about. But still she was on her guard. He might change at any moment.

'I never forgot you, Kitty,' he said quietly.

She raised her eyes to his, and was surprised to see a hint of compassion in them.

'I did you harm. I was young and foolish. I lusted for you. My father had taught me to grasp whatever I wanted with both hands and never take no for an answer. It's no excuse, but as a foolish young man I extended that advice to mean I should take you as well. Afterwards, when I'd gone away from here and could not forget the defiant look in your eye, I realised how very wrong I'd been and how much I must have hurt you.' He paused, as if waiting for her to say something, but she knew not what to say.

'You did me a very great wrong,' she whispered, hardly daring to look at him in case her words angered him and made him want to abuse her again

'I married, in England,' he went on, as if he had not heard her response. 'A girl with hair almost as vibrant as yours, skin almost as ivory. A rich young heiress, who loved me, I think, as I loved her.'

She looked at him, startled, for she had only heard unconfirmed rumours that he had taken a wife.

'It might have worked. She – Lydia – and I would have made a good team in life.'

'What became of her, sir?'

'She died, in childbirth. Twins. The babies died too.' He was quiet and thoughtful as he said this, and she realised that he had suffered also. Not as much as she had, but they both knew what it was to lose a spouse and children.

But she could not bring herself to sympathise with him. She gave a small nod in response, and lowered her head, as a tiny, personal tribute to the unknown woman and her babies who had not had a chance to live.

'You have lost children too, I understand?' he asked. 'Smith informed me.'

She nodded.

'I am sorry for your loss.'

She looked up at him, and saw genuine remorse in his eyes. Not just sympathy for the loss of her children, whom he had not known and who meant nothing to him, but something else – regret for his past actions, sorrow for what he had done to her. And something else – a longing. For her? For her body?

'I should not have let Smith raise the rent and take your goat. I have spent too much time in England and let that man do what he liked. I have been meaning to speak to you since that day. How fares your little girl?'

'She is dead now, too.'

'I am sorry,' he said again, with a sigh. 'You have lost such a lot.' His eyes fell on her brooch, which was pinned to her shawl. He fingered it, as she held her breath – his hands so close to her breast. 'A pretty piece. Where did you get this?'

'Sir, it was my great-aunt's. She brought me up.' She realised suddenly that this was her chance.

She must seize it, think of Michael and his future, and get what she could from Waterman. He owed it to them both. 'I-I have been trying to sell it, sir. To raise some money for my only remaining son, so that he can have a future, away from here and away from the hunger.'

He frowned. 'It is pretty, but it is only copper, and surely worthless.'

'That is what I am told. But it is all I have to sell.' That, and her body, she thought, ruefully. She kept her eyes raised to his. She would not beg, but neither would she leave here empty-handed.

On impulse, she remembered she still had in her pocket the sketch Michael had made of Thomas Waterman astride his horse. She pulled it out and unfolded it.

Waterman took it from her, and stood, crossing over to the window to hold the picture in a better light. 'Why, that is me, on Charger,' he said. 'A fine drawing. When did you make this?'

'Sir, I didn't. It was my son, Michael. Mr O'Dowell gave him the sketchbook and pencils long ago. He saw you once, in the fields, and drew this, so he did.'

'Michael. The boy I saw you working with, on the road building?'

'Yes, sir.'

'How old is the lad?'

'He's . . . s-seventeen, sir.' She held her breath.

'Seventeen, hmm. And you were married to a fellow called McCarthy, who died in my copper mines, were you not? I remember hearing about the accident. I was in England at the time.'

'I was, sir. He was a good man.'

He nodded, and stared at her. There was an excitement in his eyes. When he spoke again his voice was quavering with emotion. 'Michael is not McCarthy's son, is he? He's mine, isn't he?'

She remained silent, realising that what he wanted from her now was not her body, had never been her body. He wanted her son.

He strode across the room and seized her by the shoulders, shaking her. 'I must know it – is he my son? I suspected it when I saw him at the worksite – that is why I told you to come here, to find the truth. You *will* tell me!'

She turned her head away.

'Tell me!' He growled the words.

She flinched and pulled herself away from him. He took a step back and shook his head, as if considering a new tactic. When he spoke again his voice was once more sad and thoughtful.

'I lost my two sons when Lydia died. It was a terrible time. You know yourself how it feels to lose a child. I told myself I could not go through such agony again. All that hope for the future, all that potential in those tiny beings, all dashed away within minutes of their birth. It was a cruel blow, indeed. And now I learn I have another son living, one already grown, past the dangers of infanthood. The only child I will ever have, for I will never marry and risk facing such loss again. So you see, you *must* confirm that I am his father!'

She looked him in the eye, and saw a middle-aged man disappointed with life. No wife, no heirs. No joy, for all his wealth and status. And now he saw the possibility of a son, a fine young man. A relationship with such a son could make him happy after his losses and disappointments.

But Waterman deserved no such happiness. She pitied him for the loss of his wife and babies, but it did not change the fact that he had grievously misused her, and she could never forgive him that.

'Patrick McCarthy was his father,' she said, quietly. It was not a lie. Patrick had acted as father to Michael – taken him in as his own, provided for him, played with him, nurtured him and taught him. Loved him, as much as he had loved his own children.

He sighed deeply. 'It is what I deserve, I suppose. To be denied my son, for what I did to you. I thought I had suffered enough, losing Lydia and the twins. It seems the good Lord thinks otherwise.' He had turned away, and was speaking almost to himself, as though he had forgotten she was in the room. He picked up the drawing again and studied it. 'It is a fine likeness.' He was silent for a moment, as though considering, and he looked from the picture to her face, a half-dozen times.

'I'll not see him suffer, whether he acknowledges me or not,' he muttered. Then he turned back to Kitty. 'How much?'

'Sir?'

'How much do you need, to give your son his future? I assume you want to send him to America. That seems to be where all Irish men and women aspire to be.'

She named the price of passage on the *Columbus*. A part of her screamed out to add to it – to get more from him, the price of a second passage, or enough to keep her own body and soul together during these dark times. But the stronger part of her – her pride – would never take charity for herself from him. Only for Michael, his son, though she would never admit it to him, even if he had guessed the truth.

He nodded. 'I shall buy this sketch from you, for that amount. Send our son away, and wish him luck.

Tell him, also, that if ever he comes back to Ireland, he should call on me if he requires any assistance.' He took a deep breath. 'I would never turn him away.'

She felt tears rush to her eyes, and blinked and swallowed to try to stop them falling. She would not let him see her weakness. 'Thank you, sir,' she said, in a voice as steady as she could manage.

'Wait here. I will go back to the house to fetch a basket for the remaining food, and the money.' He turned and left the room before she could respond.

Kitty's mind was in turmoil as she sat alone in the cold, damp room, awaiting his return. Less than an hour ago she had sat here, expecting to be given a little bread and cheese and then to have to give herself up to him, and beg for money in return. Instead, she'd eaten a feast, heard what almost amounted to an apology for what he'd done to her. Not only that, he'd agreed to pay for Michael's ticket, and had offered assistance in the future. Thomas Waterman – Michael's saviour – who would ever have thought that would happen?

A moment later, he was back, with a basket in which to pack the rest of the food (and she noted, there were other wrapped parcels, presumably of more food, already lying in the bottom of it), and an envelope containing banknotes for her. She hesitated momentarily before accepting the money. She had not taken his money at fifteen. It was hard to do so now, even though it was what she had come here for.

'Take it, woman!' he said. 'There's enough there to cover the cost of the passage, and a little more. Buy your son the ticket. Send him away with a few coins in his pocket. He deserves a chance in life.' He sighed. 'And you, Kitty McCarthy, don't suffer yourself. Come back to me for food, money, shelter or anything you need, but only when you are prepared to admit to me the truth and allow me to acknowledge my son. Otherwise, stay away.'

He held out the envelope and basket. She took them, and prepared to leave. But at the door she turned back to him.

'Sir, there is more you could do. Not for me, for I will take nothing from you, but for your workers. So many are starving and dying, and yet you have so much. Does it not pain you, when you could do so much to help them? You could save many lives, sir, if only you were willing.'

He looked taken aback that she had spoken to him like this. He opened his mouth to reply but before he could she left the room and descended the narrow stairs as quickly as she could. He'd shown kindness and compassion to her for Michael's sake, that was for sure, but she would never come back for more. And she would sooner die than give him Michael, his son.

CHAPTER 17

Maria

I'd been so lucky not having morning sickness at all, but on the day after the hurling match and my walk to Ballymor House I felt decidedly iffy when I got up. I'll be all right after a cup of tea and some breakfast, I told myself, so I dressed quickly and went downstairs to find Aoife. She was busy vacuuming the bar, but switched off as soon as she saw me.

'All right there, Maria? Will I make you the full Irish today?'

I blanched – I could not face a fry-up. 'Just tea and toast, if you would, please.'

She looked at me with concern. 'Grand, coming right up. You're after looking a bit peaky. Sure you're all right?'

That was the moment when my insides heaved and I had to dash out to the ladies' toilets. Aoife followed a moment or two later. 'Maria? Is there anything I can do? I'll fetch a flannel for your face, will I? You're not a drinker – is it something you've eaten?'

I shook my head, and wiped my mouth with some toilet tissue. 'Not something I've eaten, no. I'm pregnant.'

'Pregnant! Well, that's fantastic news! Congratulations!' Aoife looked genuinely delighted for me. I smiled at her enthusiasm, despite the way my stomach still churned. 'I'll get that tea and toast, to settle your stomach, so.'

'Thanks.' I followed her back to the bar, and sat within easy reach of the loos, just in case.

Aoife pulled up a stool and sat beside me when she brought my breakfast a few minutes later. 'Life's about to be all change for you then?'

'Yep,' I replied through a mouthful of toast. It was going down and helping.

'I'd say your boyfriend is over the moon, is he?'

I nodded.

'And your parents? Your mum – all mammys are ecstatic when their little girls are going to have a baby. Mine is always wanting to know when I'll settle down with a nice man and a clutch of kids and give up this ridiculous notion of running a pub.'

'My dad's dead, and my mother isn't much interested, to be honest.' The understatement of the century.

'Aw, sorry about your dad. But your mammy'll feel differently when the baby's born, sure she will. I'll leave you in peace now – shout if you want anything more.' Aoife patted my hand and went back to her chores.

I wondered if she was right – would Jackie soften once the baby was born? I couldn't imagine it, and her response to my news on the phone did not make it seem likely. I tried to imagine taking our baby to meet her – if we continued our monthly meet-ups I would have to take the baby with me, so whether she liked it or not, Jackie would meet her grandchild sooner or later. Would the actual, physical reality of a warm little body wrapped in a shawl make her feel differently?

Would she want to hold the child? Would she even look at him or her, or just turn away, uninterested?

*

After breakfast I decided to go back upstairs and sit quietly in my room for a while, catching up on emails and the like, in case I began to feel sick again. There was time enough for a walk later – I had planned to go up past the abandoned village and mines, to the top of the hill. The leaflet of local walks from the tourist office described fabulous three hundred and sixty degree views from the summit.

I sat on my bed, leaning against the headboard, with my laptop on my knees and fired it up. There were a few emails, one – I gasped when I realised – was from Jackie. She rarely contacted me via any means. I hesitated to open it. If it was a continuation of our phone call, containing more accusations that I had ruined her life, it would upset me again. I tried not to let her attitude affect me but it always did, every time. I'd always longed for a normal, loving, supportive mum, and every time we interacted I was reminded that was not what I had.

But I'd have to read it, sooner or later. Whatever she said in it, I had to hear. It was too much to hope that she might be emailing to apologise for what she'd said on the phone, and to congratulate me and Dan, and to say she couldn't wait to meet her grandchild. Far more likely to perhaps be setting down in writing that she wanted nothing to do with it, as she'd said on the phone.

With shaking fingers, I clicked on her email and, as I read it, my jaw dropped open. It was not at all what

I was expecting to find. Typical of Jackie to tell me something like this via an email rather than in person or over the phone, but, I conceded, at least she had told me.

Maria,

I hope your pregnancy is progressing well. I have been thinking about you a lot since you phoned me with your news, and have decided it is time to tell you some things about my past that I have always kept hidden. It is very difficult for me to do this after so many years so please forgive me if I don't word this too well, but I will do my best.

You never knew my parents – I told you they had died long before you were born. The truth is, I never knew them either. I spent the first seven years of my life in a children's home. I was a shy, withdrawn child, and must have seemed unappealing to couples wishing to adopt. Finally, I was placed with foster parents. They were called John and Margaret, and I loved them and was very happy with them, for almost a year. They were beginning to make plans to adopt me, I think, but then John became seriously ill and Margaret was struggling to nurse him and look after me as well, so I was sent back to the children's home. 'Just until Daddy John is better,' Margaret told me, and I accepted my fate stoically, believing they would come back for me as soon as they could.

But John died, and Margaret never returned for me, and so I stayed in the children's home, becoming even more withdrawn than before.

In my early teens, I went 'off the rails' a bit, and ran wild, experimenting with life, not caring about the consequences. I ended up pregnant at the age of fifteen, and despite pleading with social services to be allowed to keep the child, I was forced to give her up for adoption. Yes, somewhere out there, Maria, you have a big sister. I don't know her name or where she lives. I didn't even get to hold her – she was taken from me within moments of her birth.

When I was eighteen, I had a boyfriend I thought I loved, but when I found I was pregnant by him he left and I didn't see him for dust. Nevertheless, I determined I would keep this child no matter what, love it and raise it as best I could, to make up for that earlier little girl I'd had to give up. Maria, I loved that baby-bump with all my heart. I read books on pregnancy, I saved every penny I could from my job as a supermarket cashier, I bought little Babygros and a second-hand pram and planned, planned, planned for our future. I was determined to be the very best mother I could be.

When he was born, he was blue. He didn't so much as take a single breath. They let me hold this child, even though he just lay limp in my arms, his tiny, perfect features in an expression of eternal serenity. I named him Jonathan, I dressed him all in white and I scattered his ashes into the sea.

And then I swore I would never again give my heart to another. Losing foster parents, a boyfriend and two babies had proved to me love was too painful an emotion for me.

Your father changed all that – I could not help myself from loving him. The early years of our marriage were the happiest I'd ever known. Andy taught me how to be happy. He wanted children, but I did not – as you know. I wanted us to remain as we were, just the two of us in our own little bubble. It took him years to persuade me. I'd had one child taken by the authorities and another taken by God, and I did not want to put myself through all that again. Having children opens you up to all kinds of potential heartbreak – I knew that all too well. But for the love of him I agreed to have one child – you. While pregnant, I refused to feel attached to the growing foetus inside me in case it was stillborn like Jonathan. And when you were born I kept worrying you'd be taken away, and didn't dare relax and love you. I suppose it became a habit – the not-loving you. Andy tried to make up for it – he was the parent you deserved. I remember the expression of besotted wonder on his face when he held the newborn you, while I felt nothing, except perhaps jealousy that he might spend more attention on you than on me, regret at the loss of our cosy life together, and fear that you might drive a wedge between us.

And now that you are to become a mother yourself, I can only hope firstly that you never have to go through the heartbreak that I did. Don't become too attached to your child before it is born, just in case. I hope also that if all goes well, you are able to be a better and more loving parent than I was.

I am not yet sure how I will feel about my first grandchild. I am not daring to think that far ahead, in case things don't go well and you lose the baby. You took me totally by surprise, you know, when you phoned me and made your announcement. I would have preferred to have had the news in writing, so I could have pondered it alone and worked through my feelings before responding. That is why I have written to you now, to tell you my story in a way that gives you time and space to come to terms with it. I suppose you thought you were doing the right thing in telling me on the phone, so I won't blame you for it. It would have been worse still if you'd told me to my face. Some things are better done at a distance.

Well, I have written enough here now for the moment. You and I both have some adjusting to do, I think, as we move into a new phase of our lives. If all goes well and your baby is born healthy, I shall set up a savings account in his or her name.

Yours,
Jackie

I read the email twice, struggling to take it all in. How like Jackie to email this sort of thing, but then she had explained why, and I could understand that. Two babies born before me! An older, adopted sister! I did a quick calculation – she'd be in her early forties now. And the stillborn brother Jonathan. I felt a pang of grief for the siblings I'd never known, for the heartache my mother had suffered, for the life she might have had if Jonathan hadn't died, if her foster father hadn't become ill . . .

I stared at the ceiling. That line about wanting to stay just the two of them – I could identify with that feeling. It articulated how I felt about my own pregnancy, how I'd been too scared to tell Dan in case it changed things between us. Oh God, was I more like Jackie than I realised, as she'd said on the phone? But then, she'd felt a connection to her babies during her first two pregnancies. I hadn't, yet. It was still just a small bump to me, not a living being. What if I never could feel that connection?

I wasn't sure how I felt about Jackie's revelations yet. It would take a while to make sense of it. She was right that I would need time and space to think about it all. Was this another way in which we were alike – needing to work through our feelings slowly, gradually and on our own? It's why I'd come to Ireland, after all, to try to come to terms with the approaching changes in mine and Dan's life.

And how should I reply to Jackie's email? Not something to be rushed, I knew that much. Something to be talked through first, with a sympathetic friend. I picked up my phone to call Dan, but then realised he'd be out cycling and unable to spend long talking to me. Aoife was downstairs, but she'd be busy.

Declan, then. He'd listen, and advise.

I read through the email one more time, then grabbed my phone and bag and went downstairs.

'Feeling better, hun?' Aoife asked.

'Loads, thanks.' At least, my insides were churning for wholly different reasons now. 'I'm off out. See you later.'

Where would I find Declan? As it was a Sunday I tried the church first but there was no service on. The early Mass was over, and the next one wasn't for a couple of hours. Would Declan be out on parish business, or at home? Was it all right to just call on a priest at his presbytery? I had no idea of the etiquette here, but I was in need, and helping people was part of his job, as he'd told me himself. I plucked up courage and crossed the square behind the church, to approach the imposing grey-stone house behind. A sign to the left of the door listed Fr Declan Murphy and Fr John Maguire, as living in the house. I hadn't realised there'd be more than one priest for the parish.

I knocked, and the door was answered by a middle-aged woman, wearing jeans and a paint-splattered sweatshirt. She had a pleasant, welcoming smile.

'Hello, is . . . erm . . .Father Declan in?' I asked. It felt so strange to use his title.

'Sure, he is. I'll holler for him.' She turned away from me and yelled, 'Declan! Young lady here to see you!'

She ushered me inside and, a moment later, Declan came clattering down the stairs.

'Maria! The very person. I've something to show you. Come on, this way.' He beckoned me into a room that led off the hallway. It was a library – floor-to-ceiling bookcases covered two walls, armchairs flanked a marble fireplace on another wall and a bay window overlooking a tidy garden filled the fourth wall.

'What a gorgeous room!' I could imagine curling up on one of those chairs with a book, with a fire roaring in the grate on a winter's day. You'd never get me out of there. I began perusing the titles on the spines of the books. Mostly religion or history: volumes of Victorian sermons jostled for space alongside biographies of prominent Irishmen such as Michael Collins or Éamon de Valera. Incongruously, the entire Harry Potter series was tucked in amongst them all.

'Ah, those would be mine,' Declan said, obviously noticing me eyeing them. 'Light relief from more worthy reading. What I wanted to show you is this.' He crossed the room to the bookcase furthest from the door, ran his finger along a row of books and extracted one. It was a slim paperback, old, but looked cheaply produced. He handed it to me.

I turned it over and read the title on the cover: *Michael McCarthy: Ballymor's Famous Painter. A brief biography* by Martin O'Dowell.

'Wow! That's fantastic!' I quickly opened it and checked the flyleaf. It had been published in 1912, in Cork.

'You can borrow it, of course. For as long as you like. I found it when I was looking for inspiration for next Sunday's sermon. It belongs to the parish. It's quite brief but there may be some information in it you don't already have. The author claims his great-uncle sailed to New York during the famine on the same ship as Michael McCarthy.'

'This is really helpful. Thank you so much!' I wanted to sit in one of those armchairs and get reading straight away, but I'd need my laptop to take notes on. 'I'll read it over the next few days and bring it back before I go home.'

'You can take it back to England if you need to. Post it back when you've finished with it.'

'Cheers!' I tucked the book into my handbag.

'Now, you called on me before I had the chance to come and find you to tell you about the book. Was there something you wanted?' Declan looked at me with that searching way he had, as though he could see right into my soul.

I took a deep breath, but before I could begin, Declan waved towards a chair. 'Sit yourself down. Will I ask Jane to make us a pot of tea? She's painting the utility room but she'll take a moment to make us tea, I'm sure.'

'No, thanks, don't bother her. I'm all right.' I perched on the edge of the chair, while Declan settled himself opposite. And then I told him the full contents of Jackie's email. I'd barely begun when the tears arrived, but without saying a word, Declan reached to a side table and passed me a handful of tissues.

When I'd finished speaking, Declan waited a moment while I composed myself.

'That is quite some email to receive from your mother,' he said. 'How does it make you feel?'

I shook my head. 'I don't know yet. I don't know what to feel. I mean, she had a rough time – all that rejection, losing two babies. She was a rubbish mum, still is a rubbish mum, but this – well, I suppose it explains it, and that means . . . am I supposed to feel sorry for her?'

'You're not *supposed* to feel anything, Maria. Whatever you feel is all right. Confusion to start with is only natural, but give it time and your thoughts will settle down.' He looked at me carefully, before continuing. 'It's a brave thing your mother has done, to set all this down in writing. I'd say, don't respond to her just yet. Wait a while until you can get your head around it all, and work out your feelings.'

I nodded. 'Yes, I'd already thought that. I'll go for a long walk. Always helps clear my head.'

'I'd offer to accompany you but I'm afraid I have a busy day. I hope to be in O'Sullivan's for a quick one this evening. Will you be all right? The forecast says rain, but this is Ireland, so who knows.'

I smiled. 'I'll take my mac, then. Yes, I'll be fine. You've helped, just by listening. And thanks so much for the book.'

I got up to leave. As Declan held the door for me, he said, 'It could be an olive branch, you know. She might be hoping for a reconciliation, before your baby is born.'

That was something to consider. But how could we be properly reconciled? She'd ignored me throughout my childhood. And, I realised uncomfortably, I'd pretty much ignored her since I was seventeen, when Dad died. On the phone she'd said I'd pushed her away, left her alone when she'd needed me most. *Needed* me? I'd never heard her say that before. I felt heat rise through me as I wondered if perhaps I was as bad as she was.

I hadn't even invited her to my graduation from university. By then, at twenty-one, I'd been surely old enough to act the grown-up, but it had been easier to go on as we were, polite but distant. Was it time to change? Was Declan right, that Jackie's email was a kind of olive branch? There was a part of me that wanted to ignore it, to continue as we had been since

Dad's death. And then the other part of me – I put a hand on my bump – was growing up at last, soon to be a mother myself, and realising that as an adult it was at least partly up to me to change things here. To make things better for both of us, and for my baby as well.

The last line in Jackie's email said something about opening a savings account in the baby's name. So she wasn't going to ignore her grandchild completely then. She'd taken the first step. I realised I should stop blaming her and start thinking of what I could do to build a better relationship between us.

CHAPTER 18

Kitty

Kitty left Ballymor House with something of a spring in her step. She had a full belly, a basket of food over her arm, and a pocket full of banknotes – enough to buy Michael his future. And she had not had to compromise her integrity to do it. Thomas Waterman may have guessed the truth about Michael that she'd never wanted to reveal, but at least it meant that he had done some good and paid for his ticket. While she would never fully trust him and would always despise him for what he had done in the past, she was grateful that he had tried to make amends now, when she and Michael needed it most. Time would tell whether her parting words would have any effect – whether he'd do anything to help those who were suffering or not.

But, whatever happened, she would never go to him again. Not once Michael was safely aboard the *Columbus* and on his way to the land of freedom and opportunity. For her part, she would rather starve than throw herself on Waterman's mercy.

It was growing dark as she walked up the long track towards Kildoolin. For the first time in many months she did not feel weak and tired – the meal she'd eaten had put strength in her legs and hope in her heart.

It was a pleasant, mild evening; the dusk sky shimmered purple and orange and the vanilla scent of the gorse hung heavy on the evening air. At a time like this, she felt glad they lived away from the town, up here in the hills, tucked away amongst the rocky crags, the gorse and the heather. She smiled as she adjusted the heavy basket on her arm. Michael would feast tonight, and she would feast her eyes watching him eat his fill. Tomorrow she would buy him a passage on the *Columbus* and present him with the ticket. She decided not to tell him she had enough money for the ticket today, in case he insisted they spend it on food. No, she must buy the ticket first so he had no choice but to take it, and go. Her heart would break to lose him, but she would comfort herself with the knowledge that she had secured a future for him, away from this land of sorrow and hunger. She was determined that this was how things would be.

Michael was already home when she reached the cottage. She found him lying on her mattress, his boots still on, his face grey and shrunken, lined beyond his years. She dropped the basket beside the fireplace and rushed to his side.

'Michael, my love, my son, what is the matter? I have food for you. One minute and I'll have it on a plate in front of you.' She felt his forehead, praying he was not sickening as Grace had done. Not now, not when she was so close to saving him.

'I'm all right, Mammy. I'm just after having done a long day's work. I'm tired, is all it is. Did you say you have something to eat? You have your share first, while I rest a while.'

'I've eaten already. Here, look, there's bread, cheese, ham, a tomato chutney . . .'

He opened his eyes wide and stared first at her, and then the food that she was pulling out of the basket and setting out for him on the battered old table. 'Where did you get that?'

'I was given it,' she said. It wasn't a lie.

'Who by?'

And now it *was* time to lie. She couldn't say she'd sold the brooch. Not until she had the ticket. That lie was for tomorrow. 'James O'Dowell gave it to me. He's away on the *Columbus* in a few days' time, and has food to spare.'

'When did he give it you?'

Why wouldn't he just accept it and eat it? she wondered. It was food, wasn't it, such as they'd not seen in this cottage for far too long. 'I saw him in town on my way home.'

'I'd heard he left for Killarney this morning to say goodbye to his sister. He wouldn't be having cakes like these anyway. Mammy, where did you really get the food?'

'Ah, Michael, does it really matter? Eat up now, fill your belly, and the world'll seem a better place.'

'Mammy, what are you after doing to get this food? There are no shops in Ballymor selling this kind of thing. I want to eat it, I do, but I must know where it came from.'

She turned away, tears of frustration pricking at her eyes. 'It doesn't matter. It's food, and you'll eat it if you don't want to die. I've lost enough children to the hunger. I'll not lose you as well. Eat it!' These last words came out as a scream, her voice sounding harsh even to her own ears. She hadn't had to do anything immoral to get the food, but so what if she had – it was her choice. She'd do anything to save him. The least he could do would be to accept what was given with good grace and not ask too many questions.

'I'll eat it, Mammy, for you need me to be strong,' he whispered, but she noticed out of the corner of his eye that he'd shaken his head sadly.

He ate in silence, while Kitty busied herself about the cottage, and made her plans for the next day. She'd need to go back to Cork to buy Michael's ticket. She hoped Jimmy Maguire would be travelling that way again. At least this time she would be able to pay him a few pennies for his trouble.

*

By the following evening, Kitty had been to Cork city, purchased a ticket for the *Columbus*, and returned to Ballymor. She'd even been able to pay Jimmy Maguire for the ride this time. A mix of emotions churned inside her – delight that she had the means of saving Michael, sorrow that she might never see him again once he was on the ship, and fear that he might come to some harm on the crossing or in the New World. But she was sure she was doing the right thing. Her faith, rocked by the loss of Grace, was back and she had prayed endlessly for Michael to be kept safe on his journey and in his new life.

When Jimmy Maguire dropped her off, she realised it was about the time that Michael would be walking through town on his way home from the road works. She decided to try to catch him, to tell him he'd not have to break stones any more, to show him the *Columbus* ticket – the boat sailed in just a couple of days! – and to take him to O'Sullivans for a pint of stout, as she had a small amount of money left over, and if you couldn't have a drink with your son who was going away to start a new life, when could you have a drink? There was still food at home so there was no need to save every penny. Kitty realised she was not thinking beyond Saturday, beyond the day that she would wave Michael off on the ship. It was as though there was no life for her beyond that. There was, of course, and she would have to begin again the daily battle – working to earn enough to buy food to keep body and soul together – but on her own.

She caught sight of Michael as he passed the church, and hurried to catch up with him.

'Michael! There you are! Come with me – let's just sit a while in O'Sullivan's.' She took hold of his arm and began to pull him across the town square towards the pub. He looked worn and weary. Thank goodness they had food and he would not have to work on the roads any more. A few more days of the hard labour and little food and he might have collapsed, like so many before him.

'O'Sullivan's? But the landlord won't like people to sit inside if they are not his customers, Mammy.'

'He doesn't mind, sure he doesn't. But anyway, we can be paying customers today! I have some spare money – enough to buy us each a glass of stout. And there is something I must talk to you about.'

Michael's face clouded with suspicion again, as it had last night. 'Where did you get the money?'

She ignored his question and instead steered him into the pub, where she ordered two glasses of stout from the barman. There was a small table free, in a snug near the door. She sat on a stool and patted another for Michael. But he remained standing.

'Mammy, the money. Where did it come from?'

She smiled, in what she hoped was a reassuring way. It was time to lie, and may God forgive her for it. 'You remember that brooch I found? The one Gracie had hidden away under her mattress?'

'Yes?' Still he would not sit, although she knew his legs and back must be aching after his day's work. The barman brought the drinks through and placed them on the table. Kitty put her hand in her pocket to find some coins to pay him, and realised she still had her brooch in there. Thankfully it did not fall out. She paid the barman and watched as Michael took a first sip. The pint of stout would do him good.

'Mother Heaney always said it was valuable. I took it to Cork, to the goldsmiths there.' She had not lied yet. Perhaps he would make a guess at what had happened and she could just let him assume the brooch had sold for a good amount of money.

He rose to the bait. 'You sold it?'

She simply smiled in response.

She watched as his face split into the widest possible grin. 'So that's how you could afford the food we had last night. Why did you tell me you were given the food?'

'I wanted to tell you over a pint, as a celebration, but you were too tired last night to come back into town.' It was a poor lie, but it would have to do.

'Well, I will enjoy my pint, 'tis long enough for sure since I last had one. But the rest of the money you must keep to buy food for tomorrow, next week, next month – however long it lasts.'

'I have already spent most of it,' she said, and pulled the envelope containing the ticket for a place on the *Columbus* out of her bodice. 'This is for you. And I'll hear no arguments about it.'

'What is it?' He stared at the envelope, but did not reach for it.

'Well now, open it and see!'

He did, and she noticed his fingers were shaking and his jaw set firm. 'The *Columbus*? Is that not the ship James O'Dowell and his family are sailing on?'

'Yes, it is.' She nodded.

'There is just one ticket.' He raised his eyes to hers, and she saw heartbreak in them.

'Just one, yes, for that is all the money I had. It is for you.' Be strong, she told herself. Don't let him see how hard it will be to lose him.

'I cannot leave you alone.'

'You'll go, my son. You are young, with your life ahead of you. This is your chance!'

He smiled sadly and reached his hand across the table, to take hers. 'But, Mammy, you need me here. On your own you cannot earn enough. I won't see you in the workhouse.'

'I'll manage. And when I'm after saving enough money, I'll buy a ticket on another boat and come to join you.' Even as she said the words, she knew they would never come true. How would she ever be able to save any money? An image of Thomas Waterman flashed through her mind, but she banished it quickly. She would not go to him again, under any circumstances. Besides, she could never go so far from the graves of her little ones. She hadn't been able to save them, so the least she could do was to stay near their final resting place.

'If I went, and earned enough, I could send you the money for a ticket,' Michael said, thoughtfully. 'But how I'd earn money I don't know. I suppose they will need road builders over there as much as over here.'

She squeezed his hand. 'Michael, you have a talent for art. There are rich people in New York, who will pay you to draw their picture. That is how you will make your money. And perhaps, yes, perhaps you will earn enough to send for me.' She smiled. 'But only after you have bought yourself a house, settled down with a wife, and have enough money for all that you need. I won't come, otherwise.'

He looked down again at the ticket in his hand. 'This ship sails on Saturday. That's just two days away.'

'I know.' She gazed at him, blinking to stop tears from falling. He must not see her weakness in case it stopped him from going.

'Two days,' he repeated.

'We'll go and find James O'Dowell tomorrow, when he comes back from Killarney. We'll tell him the good news that you have a passage on the *Columbus* too. He and his family will be company for you on the crossing, and perhaps you can help each other out when you reach New York.'

'It's so soon,' Michael said.

'It's your chance, your time,' she whispered in reply.

CHAPTER 19

Maria

After leaving the presbytery I went back to O'Sullivan's, my mind still reeling with shock at the revelations in Jackie's email. I needed to spend time really thinking about it all. I'd planned a walk, but decided to have an early lunch at the pub first. I could begin reading that biography of Michael McCarthy while I ate. Sometimes when you've got something really huge to get to grips with, it helps to think about something entirely different for a while. Let your subconscious continue to process the problem while your conscious mind is otherwise occupied. The biography would be perfect for this.

So I ordered a plate of cod goujons and chips from Aoife, sat in a window seat and opened the little book.

The first chapter was a brief account of Michael's early life, growing up in Kildoolin. The author, Martin O'Dowell, had clearly been able to talk to folk who remembered the village before the famine, and it was a wonderful little insight into what it might have been like. There was a mention that Michael was a few years older than his next sibling Patrick, but the author made no indication of any different parentage.

In the second chapter, the author claimed that his great-uncle had been a kind of surrogate father to

Michael after Patrick McCarthy senior had died, and had even given him his first ever sketchbook and pencils, thus starting a great career. I suspected a bit of embellishing here but nevertheless felt pleased that perhaps someone had kept a fatherly eye on the teenage Michael.

After the deaths of all his siblings, Michael had sailed for New York during the famine, on a ship named the *Columbus*. Not a 'coffin' ship – the name given to the roughest ships in which starving and destitute people tried to escape their poverty, only to die at sea – the author stressed, but a relatively comfortable one. The McCarthys had been amongst the poorest people in Ireland, and it was not known how Michael had paid for his passage. O'Dowell made much of the way his great-uncle had looked after the teenager while on-board ship, and had kept in touch when they reached New York.

My food arrived before I could begin the third chapter. Aoife hesitated a moment after she put it down.

'Glad to see you're eating a big lunch after your sickness earlier,' she said. 'Any time you need someone to talk to, you know where I am. I mean, I've not gone through pregnancy myself – not sure I'm cut out for all that – but I could listen for Ireland. Goes with the job.' She patted my shoulder.

'Thanks, Aoife,' I said, putting my hand on top of hers on my shoulder. 'You're being a good friend to me. I feel I've known you for ages. And Declan, and old Paulie.'

'Ha, your Irish family, so we are,' she laughed, and returned to her work.

*

It was mid-afternoon before I got myself organised for my walk. The weather wasn't great – the wind was picking up and it was overcast – but it suited my mood. I wouldn't mind getting wet and blown about a bit. Sometimes battling the elements helps put everything into perspective. So I donned my walking trousers, which no longer buttoned up, a fleece, and my mac and boots, and set off towards the abandoned village. Declan had said it was a good place to think.

There were a few spots of rain as I made my way up the track, but the fresh air and exercise felt wonderful. I pushed my hood back and let the wind send my hair whipping around my face. My older half-sister – what colour hair would she have? Black, like mine, which I'd inherited from Jackie? Would my sister look anything like me? After a childhood as an only child it was hard to get my head around the idea that there was someone else out there who'd been born from the same mother.

I reached the village, and perched on a broken down wall about halfway along, just to the side of the stream which ran through the village and across the track. The thick cloud was still high enough not to spoil the view across the moors to the sea, and I gazed into the distance while trying to put my thoughts in order.

I might have had a brother. I tried to imagine Jackie's anguish at the stillbirth, and with a jolt realised that could also happen to me. Even though I hadn't been – still wasn't – entirely sure I was ready for a baby, the idea of carrying it to term only to lose it was unbearable. I put my hand on my bump, protectively. My feelings were so conflicted still – I hadn't wanted this baby but I couldn't bear the thought of losing it either. What I wanted, I suddenly realised, was to begin to love it. I wanted to feel a connection to it – the connection Jackie had felt with her first child and then with her stillborn son, but which she'd refused to let herself feel for me. How did that work? You might assume it would come naturally, but as yet that had not happened for me.

I gazed around the ruined village. Kitty had lived in one of these cottages. She'd lost so many children, and yet her surviving son had gone to some trouble to express his gratitude for her sacrifices. She must have felt that connection to her eldest, to have done whatever it was that had inspired him to write those words on the memorial stone.

The rain was a little heavier now, so I pulled up my hood, tucking strands of wet hair inside. My trousers were soaking but they were made of a quick-drying fabric, and despite the rain and wind it wasn't cold.

When I'd been born alive and well, why hadn't Jackie let herself love me then? She was happily married, not a schoolgirl as she'd been when her first daughter was born, so there was no danger I'd have been taken from her. Why hadn't she relaxed and enjoyed finally being able to be a proper mother? I tried to remember what she'd said in the email about this. Something about fearing I'd drive a wedge between her and Dad. But he'd loved us both, unconditionally. Jackie didn't seem to realise that love was not a finite resource – you could love more than one person at a time without it diminishing your supply. Could I do this? I loved Dan unreservedly. Would I be able to love our child as much? Or would he or she come between us and spoil what we had?

The backs of my legs were beginning to hurt from sitting on the crumbling cottage wall. I stood up, stretched, and debated what to do next. At that moment the rain stopped, and a break in the cloud over the hill revealed a rainbow. Didn't the legends say that leprechauns hid their pots of gold at the end of a rainbow? On a whim I decided to continue along the track, past the mine ruins and on to the top of the mountain. It looked like the weather might clear up. Might as well take the opportunity to go to the summit and check out the views from there.

Beyond the village, the track quickly petered out into little more than a sheep's track. I passed the stone circle and the ruins of the mine buildings, looking stark and unwelcoming against the grey skies. The rainbow was short-lived, and soon the cloud and rain had returned, making me wonder whether I'd made the right decision in going on. But I felt committed to my quest, and the summit wasn't too far away, so I persevered.

The rain grew heavier, the path ever less distinct, and soon I found myself wading through knee-deep heather and in thickening mist. There'd be no view from the top. Still, I wasn't a quitter – if I set my mind to do something I did it – so I pushed on upwards and, in a little while, the ground became rocky and then flattened out and I realised I must be at the top. The wind here was pretty fierce, raging over the mountain from the west, and the near-horizontal rain stung my face like a million tiny javelins.

'Well, this isn't quite what I had in mind,' I muttered to myself, twisting away from the wind to protect my face. The backs of my trouser legs clung soaking to my legs. There was, of course, no view in any direction. The cloud had sunk lower and I was in a thick, swirling mist. No point lingering on the summit, so I turned to make my way down. As soon as I was in the lee of the hill the wind dropped and the walk down – once I'd found the path again – was relatively pleasant. The fog had intensified, so by the time I was back at the mines, visibility was just a few metres in each direction. For a moment I felt disoriented – which way was the path to the abandoned village? I felt more confident descending by that route than via the other path I'd used when visiting the mines before, which meandered near to those open, dangerous mineshafts. I had a compass app on my phone, but that wouldn't help much as I did not have a map or know which direction I needed to go. At least the paths from the ruined mine buildings were distinct, so I picked one and headed off down it, striding purposefully as if by pretending to be confident I'd actually feel confident.

It wasn't long before I realised I was not on the path that led through the village. Was it the other one that I had taken before? Nothing looked familiar, but as the mist closed about me there was nothing to anchor me, nothing to guide me. However, the path was still heading downhill, and it must come out somewhere eventually. I decided to push onwards, through the swirling mist and relentless rain.

A little further on, I heard voices and then figures loomed out of the mist ahead. I recognised Sharon from the campsite, with her older kids, Kaz and Nathan. Kaz was stabbing at her phone and swearing.

'There's no fucking signal, Mum, like I told you.'

'Keep trying! Oh God, where is he? Sammy! SAMMY!' Her shout was whipped away by the wind.

'Sharon?' I said. 'Is everything OK?'

'Maria? Help! We've lost Sam; Dave's up there looking for him.' She clutched my arm. 'I and the other two are supposed to be heading down to raise the alarm but we're not sure—'

'We're fucking *lost*, Mum,' Kaz butted in. 'Maria, do you know the way down? Do you have a signal on your phone?'

'We keep on this path and it'll lead us back down to the road,' I said, sounding more confident than I felt. Nathan was looking thoroughly miserable and scared. 'Where did you lose Sammy?'

'I don't know, up there – we were exploring the old mines and then the mist came down and then – oh God – what if he's fallen down an old mineshaft? Oh God, Maria, what if that's what happened? He was there with us and then he wasn't, and we walked round and round shouting for him and then the wind and rain and all, and no signal, and Dave said I should take the other kids and raise a search party, and how on earth – I mean who can help us?' Sharon's eyes were wide with terror. Sammy was her baby and he was lost and alone, out here somewhere on the moors.

'We'll find him. Don't worry. He will be OK.' But I remembered those rotting wooden covers on the mineshafts I'd seen on my other walk, and felt a wave of fear for his safety wash through me. 'Listen, I think I've got the number for O'Sullivan's on my phone. I'll call Aoife. She can alert the police.'

I pulled out my phone, but, as for Kaz, there was no signal. 'Come on, we'll get going downhill. Once we're nearer the town we'll get a signal.'

We stumbled onwards, ever downhill, along the narrow path through the heather. I found myself praying silently that the path would lead us back to the road as I'd promised Sharon it did. The relief when we finally spotted the ribbon of tarmac through the mist was palpable. I pulled out my phone again and saw it finally had a signal. Kaz tried to call Dave while I scrolled through my contacts to find the pub's number.

Aoife answered after a couple of rings. 'Maria? Is everything OK?'

'No, it's not. Listen, there's a child lost on the moors. We need a search party. The family were exploring the old mines and they're worried he might have . . .' I glanced at Sharon's terrified face and broke off. No need to spell it out.

'No problem, I'll call the Gardaí now. How old's the child?'

'Five, I think.' Sharon nodded confirmation, her hand over her mouth. 'We're on our way back into town now, but the father, Dave, is still up there searching.'

'Leave it with me. Bring the rest of the family here.'

'Will do, thanks.'

I hung up, tucked my phone back into my pocket and put my arms around a shaking Sharon. 'Listen – it's going to be all right. Aoife's calling the police. We're going to get to the pub as quickly as possible, tell them what we know and get ourselves warm and dry. Come on.'

The fact we had a plan of action, and that someone else (me!) was taking control, seemed to calm her down a little. She grabbed Nathan's hand and began marching along the road towards Ballymor, with Kaz and I scurrying along behind.

We'd come out a good bit further along than either the turn to the campsite or the one to the village. As we passed the campsite turning, Sharon stopped and patted her pockets. 'Damn. If I'd had any sense, I'd have taken the car keys from Dave and could have driven us the rest of the way.'

'It's almost as quick to walk, Sharon,' I said. 'Come on, keep going.' The rain was torrential now and I couldn't wait to get inside the pub. I felt a pang of guilt – thinking of my own comfort when that poor frightened little boy was still up there on the moors somewhere.

We almost ran the last hundred metres to the pub, where Aoife was standing in the entrance, holding the door open for us.

'Go on, through to the bar. The Gardaí are waiting to talk to you.' She pushed Sharon through, and I followed. There were two policemen waiting beside the bar, and Sharon went to tell them what had happened. Aoife steered Kaz and Nathan away, and gave them each a towel to dry themselves off. I looked around the pub. There were a half-dozen men, not drinking, all in their coats. Paulie was on his usual bar stool. Behind us, another three people entered – two women and a man, all togged up for the weather.

'What can we do?' one of the women asked Aoife.

'We're just finding out what's happened then I expect one of the Guards will get everyone organised,' she replied.

'Aoife, who are all these people?' I asked.

'They're the search party. After you called, I put the word out and they've all come to help look for the little fella. We pull together, here in Ballymor.' She patted my shoulder. 'Ugh, you're soaking. Why not go and get yourself some dry clothes on? I'll find something of my own for the boy's mum and sister, but the other kid will probably have to stay in wet clothes.'

'Ah, I'll fetch something of my Tommy's for him,' said one of the women who'd just entered, and she hurried out again. As she left, Declan entered. He had his dog collar on under his coat. I wondered if he'd be offering spiritual support or practical help with the search party.

'I came as soon as I could,' he said. 'Where's the child's mother?'

I pointed Sharon out and he went to speak to her, laying a comforting hand on her shoulder.

A few minutes later, the police had organised everyone into teams and allocated search areas. The woman came back with a tracksuit for Nathan. The searchers set off, Declan included. Sharon had managed to phone Dave and tell them they were coming. Dave refused to leave the moors, and it was all Aoife and I could do to stop Sharon from rushing out to join him.

'Sure, and aren't there enough people searching now. Your place is with your other kids,' Aoife told her. 'Come on and let's get you dried and changed. Paulie, can you hold the fort for me a while, please.'

'Aye, I will,' he grunted, and then I noticed he'd been left with a list of names and phone numbers, and the pub phone beside him, coordinating communication amongst the searchers. It brought a lump to my throat to see how the entire town was working together to help a family they did not even know.

I followed Aoife, Sharon and the kids upstairs, and went into my own room to change out of my wet clothes. It felt good to be warm and dry again, and a little later we were all back in the bar, sipping tea Aoife had made.

I watched Sharon, now dressed in one of Aoife's heavy metal t-shirts and a dressing gown, hands trembling as she held her cup. It must be horrendous to think of your child suffering, perhaps hurt, certainly frightened and all alone. I remembered her blind panic on the moors, her wild eyes and frantic screams.

She caught me looking at her, and attempted a smile. 'What do we do now?'

'We wait,' I said. 'Pray if you feel it helps. He'll be found and he'll be all right – I am sure of it.' I smiled back, hoping I sounded at least a little bit reassuring. To tell the truth, I was worried sick about little Sammy. I didn't even know the kid but his mother's anguish was heartbreaking.

What if something like this happened to my own child? How on earth would I cope? I thought again of Kitty, and all those children she'd lost. How would you ever move on from the death of a child? I shivered a little. In the past infant mortality had been much higher, and it was perhaps usual to lose one or more babies. Did you not allow yourself to care as much for your children, in case you lost them? Was that how Jackie had felt? There was a quote, wasn't there, something about it being better to have loved and lost, than never to have loved at all. That could apply to love of a child, I realised, as well as love of a partner. Jackie had held back from loving me as I developed inside her, and after I was born, in case she lost me as she'd lost her earlier children. And look where that had left us. I didn't want to be the same. I wanted to love my child, unconditionally. Even if the worst happened and I lost him or her too soon.

At that thought I found myself silently praying that Sharon was not about to lose Sammy too soon. That poor, sweet child. I remembered his mischievous mud-splattered grin when I'd seen him and Dave at the campsite. Please let him be all right, please let them find him!

CHAPTER 20

Kitty

When you are dreading an approaching event time speeds up, Kitty thought, as she awoke on Saturday morning. The two days since she'd bought the *Columbus* ticket for Michael had flown past in a blur of activity, as Michael said his farewells to friends, paid his respects at the graves of his siblings and gathered together his meagre possessions to take on-board the ship.

Kitty hauled herself out of bed, lit a turf fire and put a pot on to boil. There was a crust of bread and some cheese left from the food Thomas Waterman had given her. That would do for his breakfast. At least on-board the ship he would get a meal each day, and once he was in New York, well, there was no starvation in America, was there? He would go ashore with little money but endless chances, and she knew he was the type of person who would make the most of them.

Michael was stirring too, and in a few minutes he was up, washing his face in the bucket of water, and putting on his breeches and shirt that Kitty had washed for him the night before and hung to dry in front of the fire. It was a small thing, but she liked to think that she had done her best for him, and would send him to his new life in clean clothes and with a full belly. She did not allow herself to think about what she would eat that evening, or the next day. The last of her money would go on paying Jimmy Maguire for the lift into Cork city today.

'Here's tea, and there's some bread and cheese to set you up for the day,' she said to Michael, as she laid the items on the table.

'What'll you be eating?' he said, frowning at her as she pushed the plate of food towards him.

She shook her head. 'I'm not hungry.'

'What about later?'

'I'm after having some money left over. I'll buy something on my way home after the ship has sailed.' And please God forgive her for the lie. It was all she seemed to do now. She made a mental note to go to confession. Soon there would be no need to lie, and, indeed, no one to lie to in any case. She smiled at Michael, and bustled around the cottage making sure he had everything ready for his journey.

Soon it was time to leave. The sun was shining, sparkling on the distant sea across the moors. Michael closed the cottage door and sighed. 'Strange to think 'tis the last time I will walk through that door and see this view.'

Kitty could not trust herself to reply, but instead put her hand through his arm and pulled him close.

'Sorry, Mammy. I should say, the last time for a few years. I'll come back for you as soon as I have saved enough money, I promise.' He bent to kiss the top of her head.

She smiled up at him – her tall, handsome son, with his shock of dark hair so unlike her own, and his strong jawline. He'd look better with some weight on him – he'd break hearts then. God willing he'd have a better life over the ocean, and wouldn't ever go hungry again.

He gazed at the view across the heather towards the coast. 'Maybe you'll see the ship from here, Mammy. Give it a wave for me. And remember, when you see the sun in the day or the moon and stars at night, they're the same sun, moon and stars that'll be shining on me. We're not so far apart.'

'You'll always be with me in here,' she said, tapping her heart, her voice choked. 'Now come on, Jimmy Maguire will be waiting for us.'

*

During the journey to Cork, first by foot and then in the back of Jimmy Maguire's cart, Kitty tried to savour every last moment of being with Michael. She could not believe the time had come to say goodbye to him. For whatever he said about saving the money to send for her, or coming home for her, she knew, deep down, that she would never see him again. Chances were that she would not survive the next winter. But for now she knew she must keep a brave face on it, and not show him her fears. Michael himself wore an expression of trepidation mixed with excitement. He was young, he was going on an adventure. Of course it was an exciting time for him.

All too soon the journey was over, and Jimmy was dropping them off at the quayside where the *Columbus* was docked. It was a scene of near chaos – people hurrying back and forth, men loading crates and hauling trunks onto the ship. There were coils of rope, huge sacks of supplies, sailors running hither and thither, and groups of passengers standing, looking lost and confused, many with children in tow. Kitty looked about for James O'Dowell. She would feel happier if Michael could meet up with him before boarding the ship. But perhaps the O'Dowells were already on the ship. She twisted her skirt in her hands, unsure what to do next.

Michael seemed more certain of himself. He picked up the small bundle that was all his worldly possessions, and drew the ticket out of his pocket. 'That fellow over there looks like he's in charge,' he said, indicating a man in a black jacket and battered hat who was standing beside the gangplank. There was a throng of people around him, asking him questions and waving their tickets.

As Kitty looked over, a whistle blew, and the activity around them grew more frantic. Sailors were beginning to untie the thick ropes that moored the ship to the quay. Steam tugboats were already in position, to heave the ship away from the dock and out into the main channel of the River Lee, which flowed out to the ocean. The man in the black jacket began ushering people up the gangplank.

'Well, Mammy, looks like this is it,' said Michael. 'Ah look, there's Mr O'Dowell, see, he's already on-board.'

Kitty looked up at where he was pointing and saw James O'Dowell with his wife and children leaning over the wooden rail that ran around the deck. She waved up at him and pointed to Michael. He waved back.

'Go up and find him as soon as you can. He'll look after you,' she said. But she clutched hold of Michael's arm tightly, unwilling to let him go just yet.

'Mammy, I'm grown, I can take care of myself,' Michael replied, a smile on his face.

'Sure, but I feel better knowing there's someone who knows you on-board, who'll look out for you if you need it.' She reached up to stroke his face. 'You'll always be my baby.'

He wrapped his arms around her and hugged her. 'I love you, Mammy. Thank you, for everything. You've done so much for me, more than I deserve. Look after yourself, now.'

'Write to me as soon as you get to New York,' she replied, her voice muffled against his chest. Her beautiful boy, the last of her children, leaving Ireland! In those happy days, before the famine, before Patrick's accident, who would ever have thought it would come to this? Images of her lost children flitted through her mind – Little Patrick, Nuala, Jimmy, baby Éamonn and, of course, sweet, gentle Gracie – all gone, lost to hunger or disease. And now Michael, but he would be lost only to her.

She squeezed him one last time. 'Good luck, Michael, my precious son. Make your fortune. Do it for those little brothers and sisters of yours who did not get their full chance in life. Don't forget them, now, will you?'

'Never,' he said, his voice thick with emotion. 'And don't you forget me, either. I'll be back for you before you know it.'

The ship's whistle sounded again, and they broke apart. The man in the black jacket was shouting at them, beckoning Michael to board the ship.

'I must go now,' Michael whispered. He bent to kiss her cheek, and then turned to run across to the gangplank.

'*Dia duit*,' she called after him. *God bless you*. She watched as he bounded up the gangplank and was swallowed into the ship. The last ropes were loosened, the gangplank was pulled ashore, and tugboats began to ease the ship away from the quayside. Kitty kept her eyes trained on the upper deck where she had seen James O'Dowell. Finally, when the ship was almost too far away for her to be able to make out the figures, she saw a tall, dark-haired young man waving energetically. She waved back, running along the quayside after the ship, until she could go no further and the ship was out in the main channel. She watched until it reached a bend in the river, still controlled by the tugs, and then, too soon, it was out of sight.

Still unwilling to turn her back on Michael, she stood for a moment alone, at the end of the quay, gazing after the ship. She was all alone now. There was no one left. The children were at rest in Ballymor churchyard, Michael had sailed, Patrick was buried deep underground where the mine had collapsed, Old Mother Heaney was long gone too. And all her neighbours from Kildoolin – either dead or emigrated. She was truly alone.

But Jimmy Maguire had promised to wait for her and give her a lift home. So she turned away and began the lonely walk back across the city to where Jimmy had said he would wait with his pony and cart.

She caught a glimpse of a man on a black horse standing on the quayside. He was gazing out along the river after the *Columbus*. As she watched him, he seemed to sigh and slump a little in his saddle, then turned his horse around to walk into the city, away from the docks.

It was Thomas Waterman, she realised. Thank the Lord he had not come to speak to her. She wanted to be alone with her thoughts, clinging tightly to the vision of Michael's excited face as he boarded the ship – her last view of him, which she wanted to imprint on her memory for ever.

*

Jimmy Maguire dropped her off in Ballymor town centre as usual. 'Thank you,' she said, as she handed him the last of her coins in payment and climbed down from the cart. 'I won't be wanting to go back to Cork city, now.'

'Ah, well, if you do need to, sure you'll know where to find me,' he said gruffly, flicking the reins to make the tired old horse walk on, back to his yard.

She watched him go, then began the familiar walk home to Kildoolin. The track to the village was too rough and rutted for a cart nowadays. With no one but her living there, there was no point in Waterman paying to keep the track maintained. She set off up the path, her head down, her thoughts still with Michael, wondering what he was doing now on the ship – was it dinner time? What was his berth like? Were the other passengers and crew friendly? Was he missing her? No. She mustn't think about that. He had gone to his new life, and she must make the best of hers. Although it didn't feel as though there was much life left here for her now. What was the point of staying in Kildoolin, all alone? It was her home, but what was home when there was no one left to share it? Anyway where else could she go, with no money and no family?

'Kitty McCarthy.' The voice came from behind her, and she stopped and turned about on the path. Thomas Waterman, astride his huge black horse, was behind her on the track. He'd come looking for her, she realised. There was no other reason for him to come to the empty village.

'Yes, sir?' she said, a touch of defiance in her tone. She'd got what she wanted from him, a kind of payback for what he did to her all those years ago. She had no more need to be deferential to him.

'Your boy, Michael, he's gone on the *Columbus*, then?'

He knew damn well Michael had gone, she thought. Hadn't he been at the quayside watching? 'Yes, sir, he has.'

'And did you pass on my message? About contacting me if ever he needs any assistance, whether he's in America or back here in Ireland?'

'He'll be all right, sir. He's a clever lad, honest and hard-working, and I'm sure once he's in New York he'll make his own way.'

'Hmm.' Waterman nodded, his eyes still on her. She wished he would just go and leave her, so she could go home, scrape together a meal (although from what, she could not say), and go to bed. Each day that passed was a day closer to Michael arriving in America, a day closer to when she might receive a letter to say he was there, safe, and free from hunger.

'Come to the Hall again, Kitty. Tomorrow.' His words were a command, but his tone was gentle enough.

'For what reason, sir?' She stared up at him.

'There'll be a job for you. In the kitchens, or, if you prefer it, as a housemaid. As long as you're not frightened of hard work, there's a room in the attics and regular food for you. And wages. You've nothing left here. I'll be spending no money repairing these cottages, and yours is almost tumbledown.'

She regarded him carefully. Was there an ulterior motive to him offering her a job, food and board? It was a tempting offer, and coming from anyone else she would leap at the chance. It would be the saving of her. But coming from Waterman – why did he want her living under his roof? Would she find herself with a frequent night-time visitor perhaps? She shuddered at the thought. While he had not made any advances on her since that terrible time eighteen years ago, he had a way of looking at her that said he still desired her, given half a chance.

'Well? Surely it's a good offer – somewhere to live and decent food in return for a bit of housework? Your Michael can write to you at the Hall, and if or when he comes home, there'll be a place for him as well.'

She pulled herself up straight and looked him once more in the eye. So that was what he wanted – to keep her close as a way of hearing news about Michael, and to get to Michael if ever he came back to Ireland? Why on earth hadn't he offered Michael a job then, when they were starving? He'd put Michael *out* of work – at least his agent had.

'I won't take your job, sir,' she said, fighting to keep her voice steady. 'I'll stay living in the cottage, and will earn money on the road building to pay my rent. You don't need to be worrying that I'll not be able to keep up my payments. I have some seed potatoes to plant for next season's crop, sure I have.' That last was a lie. But she would not take his charity.

He sighed. 'You don't trust me, do you? I suppose that's to be expected. Well, with the village as good as empty, Smith won't be collecting any more rent from you. Stay as long as you like, and when the road building is too harsh or the next potato crop fails, call at my kitchen door and ask for a job. You'll not be turned away. Think about it.'

His eyes travelled down her body and back up again, then he nodded curtly, turned his horse around and spurred it into a canter.

She let out a sigh of relief. He'd gone, at last, and she could be alone in her misery. Whatever happened she would not go to him for charity. It was one thing to beg for help for Michael, but not for herself. Not after what he'd done to her. She'd sooner die.

CHAPTER 21

Maria

I sat with Sharon, Kaz and Nathan in the pub for hours, murmuring words of comfort, drinking endless cups of tea provided by Aoife, and jumping up in hope every time the pub phone rang. Sharon was also constantly texting Dave, until he replied that his battery was running low and he needed to save what was left in case there was real news.

I'd fetched my laptop and loaned it to Nathan and Kaz, so they could distract themselves with online games while we grown-ups fretted, worried and voiced platitudes to each other.

'Oh God, what if they don't find him?' Sharon said, for what must have been the hundredth time.

'They will.' I rubbed her arm, hoping the gesture might reassure her a little. If the truth were told, I was becoming more and more worried by the minute. I'd thought with so many people up there searching, it would be no time at all before a call came through to say Sammy had been found, safe but wet, and was in his father's arms.

'I'm just so scared for him.' Sharon glanced across to the older children, then leaned in close and spoke confidentially. 'Sammy's my only child, you see. Those two are Dave's but not mine. Their mother died when they were small.'

'Oh, how awful. What happened?'

'There was a house fire. Faulty wiring in a house they were doing up. Kaz was three and Nathan just a tiny baby. Dave was at work. Their mum – Caroline – had been in the garden hanging out washing when she realised there was smoke pouring out from upstairs. She got Nathan out, then went back inside for Kaz who was napping upstairs, though a neighbour tried to stop her. She dropped Kaz out of a window into the neighbour's arms, but then she was overcome by smoke. The fire brigade brought her out, dead.'

'Oh, Christ.' I didn't know what to say.

'I know.'

We both looked over to the kids, but they were engrossed in their games, earbuds firmly plugged in, and had not heard a word of our conversation.

Sharon looked anguished. 'Caroline gave her life to save her daughter. Since Sammy was born, I've often wondered whether I could do the same for him. Run into a burning building to fetch him. And now . . .' she gave a sudden sob '. . . now this feels like some kind of test. Oh, Maria, I should be up there on the moors, risking my life for him! And I'm not – I'm warm and dry in here, and he's up there, maybe lying hurt and wet and cold . . .'

'You brought the other two down, Sharon, and raised the alarm. That was the right thing to do. You had to think of them as well, and you need to be able to comfort Sammy when he's found. Don't beat yourself up. You did the right thing.' I took her hand and squeezed it. What an amazing thing Caroline had done – giving her life to save her child. I guessed you'd never know if you were capable of such self-sacrifice until you found yourself in that kind of situation, and

God forbid you'd ever have to be put to the test. But being prepared in theory to do such a thing – that was all part of being a parent. I wondered if Jackie would have run into a burning building to save me. Who knew – perhaps dormant maternal instincts would have kicked in and she'd have done it. I liked to think I would, too. Surely that was what it was all about?

'I'll never forgive myself if . . . if . . .' Sharon couldn't finish the sentence, and just shook her head, as tears rolled down her cheeks.

Kaz looked up then from her game, and tugged out her earbuds. 'Mum? What's the matter? It'll be all right, you know. They'll find Sammy, I know they will. And he'll be all right.' She took Sharon's other hand, and Sharon shot her a grateful look then pulled her close for a hug. Kaz held her stepmother's head on her shoulder, stroking her hair and murmuring words of comfort in a perfect moment of role reversal. I'd never held Jackie like that. I envied them their closeness.

A memory surfaced – Jackie sobbing uncontrollably when we got home and were alone after Dad's funeral. I'd stared at her, crying quietly myself but without the noisy hiccupping sobs she was making, and then I had turned away and gone to my bedroom to grieve alone. That was the moment. That was when I should have taken her in my arms and held her, the way Kaz was holding Sharon now. That was the moment when we could have laid the foundations for a new relationship, but I had chosen to turn my back. Our lack of a good adult relationship, I was finally realising, was as much my fault as it was hers. But she'd made a move towards reconciliation by way of that email. Perhaps it was not too late for us.

*

By 9 p.m., the rain had eased off although the mist was still thick outside. Daylight was fading, and a call from the Gardaí confirmed that with regret they were suspending the search for the night. Aoife took the call with a grave face, then sat down beside Sharon to give her the news.

I held Sharon tightly as she wailed and howled with despair. My heart broke for her. Nathan was crying, and Kaz watched with her mouth open, her face drawn.

'They'll find him in the morning, so they will,' Aoife said, but her words sounded lame.

'Can't they, like, send out a helicopter or something?' Nathan asked.

'Yeah, with heat-seeking equipment?' Kaz added.

'I guess not while it's so foggy,' I replied quietly. 'In the morning, at first light, I am sure that's exactly what they'll do.'

'Where will he spend the night? My baby, alone out there in the dark and the cold!' Sharon wailed again, and I pulled her head against my shoulder.

'It's not so very cold. If he curls up in the heather . . .' It wasn't a pretty image though. That poor little boy.

Soon after, the search party returned, wet and dejected. Aoife brought out bowls of chips and plates of sandwiches, and offered everyone a drink on the house. The mood was horribly subdued. Dave, his expression grim, took my place at Sharon's side, and she sobbed onto his shoulder.

'You've done a good job, supporting Sharon.' Declan had come to sit beside me.

I grimaced. 'It's been difficult. In many ways, I'd have preferred to have gone up the mountain again.'

'You'd done enough. Better for you to stay in the warm and dry, in your . . .' He broke off as I glared at him. Just like Dan, talking about 'my condition' as though I was suddenly a fragile flower.

'I'll help with the search tomorrow, that's for sure,' I said.

'There'll be more Gardaí here at dawn; they are bringing in extra from Cork, including sniffer dogs. But I imagine they'll still need local help. You're a good woman, Maria. Well, I must go and get some rest. I hope you can sleep too.'

His words made me realise how very tired I was. It had been one hell of a long day. Was it really only that morning that I'd had the momentous email from Jackie?

I went to where Sharon was still sitting with her family. 'Sharon, I'm sorry, I really need to go to bed now. I'll do everything I can to help in the morning.'

She caught my hand. 'Thanks for everything, Maria.'

'We've been offered a lift back to the campsite,' Dave said. 'Need to get these other two into bed.'

I nodded. 'See you tomorrow.'

It was with a heavy heart that I climbed the stairs to my room. And yet I could not go straight to bed. I had to speak to Dan. I'd wanted to talk through Jackie's revelations with him, but that would have to wait. Right now, I needed to talk to someone unconnected with this drama, to tell them the full story from the start, unburden myself a little. It'd be the only way I'd get any sleep.

Dan answered after just one ring, and I had the impression he'd been waiting for me to call. But before I was able to say anything more than 'Hello, how are things?' he butted in with his own news.

'Your mother sent us a cheque today,' he said, his voice shaking a little with incredulity mixed with excitement. 'It was addressed to both of us so I opened it, but the cheque's payable to you. The note inside said we're to use the money for things for the baby.'

'Bloody hell,' was my response. Though after her email to me it was not as surprising as it might have been.

'Don't you want to know how much?' he asked.

'Go on then, tell me.' I imagined fifty quid or so.

'A thousand.'

'What?!' Jackie was not that well off that she could throw that kind of money around.

'Yes, really! I had a quick look at baby stuff online and that will easily cover everything from the pram to the car seat, the cot, everything. Will you call her to thank her or wait till you come home to see her?'

I'd have to see her, thank her in person. And talk through her revelations in the email, and my realisation that as an adult I could have been a better daughter to her. We needed to meet, talk and make that new start, which I think Jackie wanted for us as much as I did. She must do. Why else send that email, and then the cheque? She was making an effort, reaching out to me. And I would reach back.

I took a deep breath and told Dan all about the email. I needed to hear his views on it, and listen to his advice on how to respond. More than that, I needed to feel his arms around me. God I missed him! There were still several days left of my holiday – my flight home was booked for Wednesday. In some ways I felt inclined to cut it short and go earlier, but then with a jolt I remembered little Sammy.

'Something else has happened,' I said, wishing more than ever that Dan was here beside me, his strong arms around me and his shoulder available for sobbing onto.

'What, darling?'

I related the events of the afternoon and evening.

'And he's still out there now. They've called off the search for the night. That poor little boy, cold and alone out there on the moors somewhere. Or fallen into a mineshaft. Oh, Dan, it's too horrible for words. He's only little. I met him, here in the pub, and he's a real sweetie.'

'Poor little chap,' Dan replied. 'Listen, Maria, look after yourself, won't you? I mean, help them out, of course I know you'll do that, but don't put yourself in any danger. Let the police do their job. God, I hope the little boy is found safe and well.'

'Me too.'

'I'm worried about you, Maria.'

'I'm OK. And yes, I'll look after myself.'

'Look after that little bump of ours too, won't you?'

I nodded, stupidly as I was on the phone and he couldn't see, but the lump in my throat made it impossible for me to answer. Eventually, I managed to squeak something I hoped he'd realise was a 'yes'.

We sat in silence for a minute, the width of Ireland, the Irish Sea, Wales and half of southern England between us, phones to ears, just being with each other, separated by distance but held together by love.

*

There was far too much on my mind to sleep well that night. I was too hot; my mind was churning as it flitted around from Jackie's news to little Sammy's plight to my own pregnancy; I was terrified I'd sleep too late and not be up to help with the search. I must have checked the time on my phone a dozen times. I tried drinking a camomile tea, opening the window, meditating – but nothing worked. Eventually, at some time after 3 a.m., I fell into a fitful sleep.

I was in a cottage. There was a fire at one end; a blackened pot hung over it with steam rising up to the roof. The smell of boiling potatoes filled the room. A bundle of rags lay near the fire, but as I approached I realised it was a child, wrapped in blankets. Was it Sammy? I peered through the gloom but it was a girl, older than Sammy and sickly looking, her eyes far too big for her hollowed-out face, who looked back at me.

A woman spoke, and I turned to face her. She was thin too, but her hair shone in the firelight, a glorious deep red. She nodded at the child on the floor. 'She's not long for this world, the poor wee mite. But I'll not let another child die. Never.'

And then I was the child on the floor, unable to get warm, with a deep ache of hunger in my belly, and the red-haired woman was stroking my face and trying to spoon a thin hot broth into me. The cottage was in ruins about us and a howling wind blew all around. Rain fell, heavier and heavier, soaking through the thin blankets that were wrapped around me. The woman knelt, pulled me into her arms and held me tight, her arms imparting warmth and strength, in a way I'd never felt from Jackie, and I knew while I was wrapped within them I was safe.

*

I'd set an alarm on my phone but woke before it, disturbed by both my dream and the dawn chorus outside my window. The dream dissolved around me as I struggled to recall it, like trying to catch wisps of smoke on the breeze. Although the images were gone I was left with the feeling of security I'd had in the arms of the red-haired woman, the way her love had kept me safe and warm. It was still dark, but there was a glimmer of light in the eastern sky, and I was filled with the urge to get out there and find Sammy. I made myself a cup of tea using the kettle in my room, and added cold water so I could drink it quickly. There were some little packs of ginger biscuits, so I ate those too, hoping that Aoife's advice that ginger staved off morning sickness was accurate. It wasn't raining and looked like it was going to be a fine day. There were worse things to do than go for a walk on the moors as the sun rose, and I had a feeling I knew where Sammy might be. My dream had to have meant something. *I'll not let another child die. Never*. That phrase rang again in my head and I knew what I needed to do. I threw on my walking trousers – thankfully they'd dried overnight – and a warm fleece, and left the pub a full hour before the Gardaí had expected to resume the search.

It was still dark as I walked through town, but the eastern horizon was gradually lightening so I could easily see my way. The air was still, fresh and invigorating. I wasn't usually an early riser but on a morning like this I could see the attraction of early morning dog walks or pre-work jogs. I headed out of Ballymor up the now familiar route to the moors, and turned left up the track to the abandoned village, walking quickly. It was some way from where the boy had last been seen, and I wasn't sure that the search party had covered that area last night – they had rightly concentrated on the old mines and the thick heather moors surrounding them.

It was a tough climb in the half-light. I tripped a couple of times and felt the lack of breakfast inside me. I was pushing myself hard – the sooner I reached the village the better – if the child was indeed there he needed to be found as soon as possible. Was it my dream that had made me think of the village? I wasn't sure, but it was worth a punt.

At last, as the eastern sky turned pink and orange, the row of ruined cottages came into sight. I began calling Sammy's name, startling a rabbit, which bounded across the path in front of me. Up above, a skylark was singing somewhere, sounding full of joy at the new day. Didn't it realise a child lay frightened, possibly injured, somewhere on these moors? If only we could see through the bird's eyes, maybe then we'd be able to spot him. I hoped the police would be able to deploy a helicopter today.

I reached the first cottage, and went in and around it, but there was nothing out of the ordinary. Same with the next few. The stream that cut through the village was much faster and deeper than it had been – yesterday's rain had massively increased its flow. It was now severely undercutting the already broken side wall of one cottage. I didn't want to go into that one – the remains of the wall looked extremely precarious. But something inside me insisted I check out every cottage, this one included, so I ducked under the lintel and entered.

'Sammy?' There was a dark bundle lying amongst the rubble of that undercut wall. A rivulet from the stream was coming through the cottage now, and the floor was a muddy quagmire apart from the area where the bundle lay. 'Sammy, is that you?' I picked my way across and crouched down. Oh God don't let him be hurt . . . or worse . . . I was shaking as I reached out a hand to touch his shoulder . . .

CHAPTER 22

Michael 1849–1860

April 1849

Dearest Mammy

I'm writing this letter on-board the Columbus, but of course I will have to wait to post it when I reach New York. Starting it now, while still on the ship, is a way of passing the time. I think of you constantly, and hope you are well, and that you have plenty to eat, and that you aren't missing me too much.

Life on-board the ship is hard as I knew it would be, but because I know it is only for a short while that makes it easier to bear. There are many people here, sleeping side by side in the hull of the ship, but I have a space near a porthole for light and air when it is not stormy, and I have a blanket and am comfortable enough. James O'Dowell and his family have their own cabin and he lets me come and lie in it during the day when they are strolling on deck if I haven't slept well in the night. I suffered a little from the seasickness in the first few days but that has passed and now I am quite well.

The steerage passengers are all given dried biscuits with a cup of tea every day and beef jerky every three days. Of course for most of us it is more food than we've had regularly for some time, so although our bellies are still sunken we are not as hungry as we were. The richer passengers, including Mr O'Dowell and his family, have brought some food of their own.

There is a family here with six children, many of them with auburn hair. Their mother is expecting another and is tired and needing to lie down most of the time; their father stays with her, nursing his wife. I have taken it upon myself to do what I can to amuse the little ones. They remind me so much of my own dear brothers and sisters. Mammy, I know you will shed a tear reading this part, and I admit I have found it painful to look upon these children and wonder why did they survive while Gracie, Little Pat, Éamonn, Nuala and Jimmy did not. It seems unfair that you lost so many and this family lost only one, a baby of under a year, as I understand it. But these children are happy and lively and they deserve a chance, just as you insisted that I deserve a chance. I have swallowed my grief so that I can help out this family, and Mammy, playing with the children has brought me some comfort – I see Gracie living on in the little girl, who smiles coyly at me from her blanket; I see Éamonn in the youngest, who burbles happily if tickled after he's eaten; and Jimmy in the cheeky boy who hides behind a bulkhead and tries to startle me as I pass.

I paint a happy picture of life on-board, but, Mammy, you should wait until I can send you enough money to buy a passage in a private cabin. I would not want for you to lie cheek by jowl with the other steerage passengers. You deserve better than that – a cabin such as James O'Dowell has.

It is three days since I began this letter and Mammy, something horrible happened – the mother I wrote of went into labour and delivered a stillborn child, a girl, right here in the middle of the deck. She had no privacy. Her husband helped, and James O'Dowell sent his wife down to assist and I did what I could to keep the other children calm and out of the way. The poor little mite did not draw a single breath, but was wrapped in a shroud within an hour, and 'buried' at sea.

Only ten hours later a man, who'd been sickly since he boarded the ship (I suspect with typhus, and I have tried to keep the children away from him), died peacefully in his sleep. He was also buried at sea, after a few prayers.

We are less than a week from New York, and I pray that we will have no more tragedy.

Mammy, yesterday we docked at last in New York, and what a relief it was to leave that dark, stinking hull. The red-haired children looked about them with eyes wide with wonder, and I think I had much the same expression on my face as well. It is hard to describe the differences I can see between Cork and New York, and for the moment I am not going to try, for I promised I would write and tell you of my safe passage the moment I landed, and so I must hurry with this letter to the post office. And then I must go in search of lodgings and work.

With all my love,

Michael

May 1849

My dearest Mammy

It is now two weeks since the Columbus *docked in New York and already the time on-board seems like a distant memory. You will not yet have received my first letter and, indeed, you might get this one at the same time. I send them in good faith that sooner or later they will make their way onto a homeward-bound ship, and once in Ireland will be ferried by the usual routes to Ballymor and thence to the post office, for you to collect as we agreed.*

Anyway, my principal news is that I have found a job, and it comes with food and board, and so I am very comfortable here. I am washing pots in a hotel on Manhattan island – a lowly job, I am told, but one which ensures my basic needs are met, and after breaking rocks and road building, indeed, after potato farming, it is easy work, to be sure. I have a small room at the top of the hotel. It contains an iron bedstead with a couple of blankets, a washstand, basin and ewer, a bentwood chair and a small cupboard for my belongings. There is a small fireplace and I can fill a basket with wood from the store in the basement. Along the passageway is a bathroom, with a flushing toilet and taps you twist for running water – something I never thought I would see, let alone use daily! Mammy, it is luxury indeed for those just off the boat from Ireland, and I thank God daily for my good fortune, in having a mother such as you who enabled me to come here and live like this. Think me foolish, but I thank God too for dear old Mother Heaney's brooch, that made all this possible. I pray too that you will be able to join me before too long. I have opened a savings account in a bank and am putting money aside every week towards your passage. I have met up with the O'Dowells once or twice – they have found lodgings and work as well. Truly this is a land of opportunity!

The chef in the hotel, Mr Corbin, caught sight of my sketchbook yesterday and he was impressed. I was after wondering if he was just being kind to the poor Irish waif, fresh off the boat, but it seemed not. He suggested I take my sketchbook, walk into Central Park on my day off if the sun is shining, and offer to sketch the well-to-do couples who stroll there, arm in arm. I will try this tomorrow. Mr Corbin says people might buy my drawings. I don't expect they will, but I enjoy sketching, and it sounds like a pleasant thing to do on my day off.

At the top of this page I have included my address at the hotel – you may write to me there. I think of you daily and cannot wait until I hear from you and know you are safe. Please God the hunger is over and the potatoes grow blight-free again this season.

Your ever loving son,
Michael

August 1849

My dearest Mammy

I am calculating that the first letter from you will arrive next month at the earliest, for you would have to wait to hear from me, my last letter, to know where to write to. And then the letter must survive the six-week crossing of the Atlantic. Still, although I know I must be patient, I cannot wait to hear from you.

My most momentous news to report in this letter is that Mr Corbin, the chef of the hotel where I am employed as pot-washer, was right. I took my sketching things as he suggested into Central Park and installed myself on a bench, sketching the smartly dressed couple who sat opposite. After a while the gentleman came over to see what I was about, and when he saw my work he called his fiancée (as I was to learn she was) to see. They exclaimed with delight, sat down again in the same position to allow me to finish, and then offered me a dollar for the picture. Mammy, a whole dollar – more than a day's wages! – and for just a simple sketch!

So now, on my days off, which are one a week, I come to the park whenever it is not raining, and I hunt to find someone to sketch and I draw them, and on maybe three occasions out of four I sell the sketch. Yesterday I was accosted in the park by a young lady who had heard of me from her friend, and she pleaded with me to sit for me, and I drew her with her little dog in her arms, and she was delighted with the result and paid me two dollars.

This money, Mammy, is all going into the savings account to pay for your ticket. At this rate it will not be long, and I will be able to arrange for your passage here to join me, and live as you should live – in comfort, not in fear of starvation or disease, not labouring in freezing conditions, not wondering where your next meal is coming from. You deserve better and I have the means to ensure you get it.

Your loving son,

Michael

May 1850

Dearest Mammy

I cannot believe I have been here in New York for a year already. The time has passed so quickly. My life in Ireland feels like a distant memory – except for when I think of you, Mammy, you are as clear in my head as you ever were, and as you always will be. I miss you, Mammy, and I wonder daily when a letter will arrive from you. For surely by now, enough time has passed, and at least one of my letters to you (I have written two dozen now, I believe) must have safely crossed to Ireland and found its way to Ballymor.

Anyway, I will continue to write every fortnight, to tell you of my news. My biggest news for this letter is that I have given up my job at the hotel – the first time ever that I have turned down work. The reason for this is that I am making enough money from selling my art, and I no longer need or want to spend the time pot-washing when I could be painting or drawing. I have rented a room in a boarding house, a very smart room which I only wish I could show you – well, I can show you! I shall sketch it, and include the sketch with this letter. The rich folk of New York commission me now, to paint their children, their loved ones, their pets, and themselves. I say 'paint' rather than 'sketch' as I have progressed now to using oil paints, and have set up a corner of my room in the boarding house as a studio.

One young lady who sat for me recently is named Eleanor. Mammy, she is beautiful and kind, and since I finished painting her portrait we have met and strolled together in the park on a couple of occasions. I wish you could meet her.

Do not worry that the expense of the lodgings means that it will take me longer to save the money for your passage, for I already have enough, and am saving now so that you may have a private cabin on your crossing so you are in greater comfort than I was. Only, I beg you, write to me soon so that we can make the arrangements.

Your son, waiting and hoping for a word,

Michael

July 1852

Dearest Mammy

I painted a picture of you this week, using oils. I wonder why I never thought of this before. Your face is so clear in my mind, even though the time since I saw you last in the flesh draws ever longer, like a thread stretching through time, but a thread that will never break. In the painting I imagined you on the quayside in Cork, dressed as a lady, waiting to board a ship, with a huge trunk beside you. Your expression is one of hope and joy, and on the bodice of your gown I painted the brooch – that beautiful Celtic knot brooch that you sold to buy my passage. The brooch that made it all possible.

I cannot enclose that picture for you, for it is oil on canvas. But I will copy it in a sketch and send you that instead, and hope that you like it.

You will see from the address above that I moved on from the boarding-house lodgings. I have taken a small apartment in a block in mid-town Manhattan. I have a whole room to use as a studio now, and I am booked for many weeks in advance, painting pictures of the rich and noteworthy people of this great city. The apartment is more suitable for receiving guests, such as Eleanor, whom I continue to see each week. Mammy, I intend asking her father for her hand in marriage, very soon now. She is truly the most precious of all women, and worthy of becoming your daughter-in-law.

In Ireland, the people imagine that the streets of New York are paved with gold, and if they could only travel here they would be able to simply pick it up. Well, Mammy, it is not quite like that, but it is certainly the case that if you seize opportunities when they present themselves you can find that gold and make your fortune. I am not a rich man compared with many others here but I am beginning to think of myself as well off.

I always knew myself to be fortunate, for having had a mother like you, who did all she could to give me a chance in life.

I live in hope of a letter from you. As soon as I receive one, I shall send for you.

Your loving and grateful son,
Michael

September 1853

Dearest Mammy

It is done! I have married my beloved Eleanor! We had a simple ceremony by New York standards: her four sisters were bridesmaids, and some five dozen people attended, all who needed to be wined and fed afterwards. When I looked at all the food provided – paid for partly by me and partly by Eleanor's father – and remembered how little we had in Ireland during the famine (thank God that is over, as I read in the newspapers), I could hardly believe how much my life has changed. I pray that your life has changed too, and for the better, perhaps away from Ballymor and that is why you have not responded to my letters. I cannot bear to think there is any other reason.

So now Eleanor and I live together in my apartment in Manhattan. We are as happy as newlyweds should be, and the only thing that could make me yet more content would be hearing news of your safety and wellbeing.

Yours in love and hope,
Michael

March 1860

My dear Mammy

I write to you in the vain hope that somehow this letter will reach you, where perhaps none of my others did. I write with news – momentous news that, if God wills that it reaches you, will delight you. I am to return to Ireland, home to the dear country of my birth! I can wait no longer to hear from you. I am coming home, to find you. And when I do, Mammy, I shall bring you back to New York with me. I am a rich man now, Mammy, and I can easily afford to do this, and, indeed, we shall travel first class on our way back to America. There shall be no expense spared.

I sail on Monday on the Victory, *which is due to dock in Queenstown in mid-April. From there I shall travel to Cork city and onwards to Ballymor, to search for you.*

Why, you might ask, have I left it so long and not come to search for you before now? I have been easily able to afford such travel for some years, as you know, if you have received and read my letters. But the truth is, there were other things detaining me in New York. I wrote to you of Eleanor, of course, my love, my wife. I was reluctant to uproot her from her family and sisters. I know only too well what it is to be alone in the world without parents or siblings around and I did not want to inflict that on her. So forgive me, dear Mammy, for staying in New York, in my comfortable easy life, with my wife and her family, and with my ever-increasing income from my art.

Dearest Eleanor succumbed six weeks ago to the consumption that had plagued her for years. My heart was broken, but I was thankful she should suffer no longer, and that we had no children to grieve for their mother. Eleanor's parents and sisters have each other, but without her here I feel life in New York to be empty and worthless. My parents-in-law understand this, and have given me their blessing to return to the country of my birth to seek my own mother.

And now I find myself just days away from sailing. I have given up the lease on my apartment, put my furniture into storage, cancelled my outstanding commissions and completed any that I had already begun. My affairs on this side of the Atlantic are in order, and I can spend as long as it takes to find you, in Ireland. Or, find what has become of you.

God willing, I shall be with you in just a few short weeks.

Your loving son,

Michael

'Land ahoy!'

Michael was on deck when the cry went up, confirming that after several weeks at sea the south-west tip of Ireland, Mizen Head, was finally visible. The mood among the passengers changed instantly, from morose boredom to one of excitement and expectation. There was still some way to go as the ship passed by the treacherous rocky coastline of the south of Ireland. But finally the captain changed course to head towards land and navigated into Queenstown harbour, picking up a pilot en route and eventually docking alongside the quay.

Michael felt a surge of elation as he set foot upon Irish soil for the first time for eleven years. So much had happened in that time. He had left Ireland a pauper and returned wealthy. He had married and been widowed. He had become a man. And now he was back again. The homeward crossing had been vastly more comfortable, in a first class cabin, than his journey westwards eleven years earlier. He sighed, smiled, and breathed in the sweet, fresh Cork air.

The ship had docked late, so he stayed that night in the Queen's Hotel, then took a coach to Cork city the following day. The city looked very different to the one he had left. Gone were the hordes of starving people in rags, congregating on street corners, despair in their eyes, waiting for the soup kitchens to open so that they might obtain a bowl of thin broth and stave off death for another day. Instead, the people looked well nourished, warmly dressed and were occupied with work. It was like Ireland before the famine, except, he knew from reading the newspapers, there were far fewer people living here than before.

In Cork, he hired a pair of horses, a covered carriage and a driver. Once his luggage was on-board – so much more than he had left Ireland with! – he directed the man to drive him to Ballymor, with an extra shilling to be paid if he got there in under two hours. For now that his journey was nearly at an end, he found himself impatient to complete it, to be back in Ballymor and beginning the task of finding Kitty.

As the carriage neared Ballymor, the gorse on either side of the road was in full bloom, its vivid sunshine yellow brightening the day and lifting his spirits. How had he stayed away so long? He should have brought Eleanor here. Maybe the mild climate of Ireland would have suited her better and cured her consumption. But she'd been American born, of English descent, and Ireland had held no appeal for her. It would never have worked. As the spire of Ballymor church came into view over the hill, Michael realised with a jolt the carriage was now on the piece of road he and Kitty had helped to build, back in those dark, hungry days.

His stomach lurched with sudden nerves. What would he discover? What had happened to her? Why had he never received any letters?

Michael's first job on arriving in Ballymor was to find lodgings. O'Sullivan's had rooms, and he supposed that although they were inferior to what he had more recently been used to, they were far above what he'd had when he left Ireland. So O'Sullivan's it was, with the landlord (a new man, not the fellow he remembered from eleven years earlier) astounded that someone as rich and smartly dressed as Michael should want to stay in his humble inn.

His second job was to call at the post office, where his worst fears were confirmed. Almost every letter he'd sent to Kitty was still there – a thick bundle tied up with twine. He flicked through, and found the very first two or three from 1849 were among them. Kitty had not collected a single letter.

He paid the post office for their work in keeping them, shrugged off the sympathetic looks from the clerk, and tucked the bundle of letters into his coat pocket with shaking hands. All those letters, all his news, and Kitty had not heard any of it. She had not even heard that he had arrived safely in America. What had gone wrong? Why had she not collected them?

The obvious reason was one he did not dare to dwell on, and refused to accept. But the church had to be his next port of call, even before he took the lonely walk out to Kildoolin. He remembered how so many who'd died during those black years had been buried unceremoniously, with no coffin and no marker, sometimes in mass graves on the edge of town. Please God don't let Mammy be one of those poor people, he prayed, but in his heart he could not believe it. She would not have died of the hunger. She had survived that terrible winter of 1846–7 when the little ones had died despite her efforts; he could not believe that she would have succumbed in the end to either starvation or disease. She was too tough, too resourceful. And she was his mother. She could not be gone.

The priest, another man Michael did not recognise, had not heard of Kitty McCarthy.

'Kildoolin? 'Tis nothing but ruins up there now. No one lives there, sure they don't. Not for many years and, for certain, not since I've had the living here,' he told Michael.

That did not have to mean anything. He would not have expected her to go on living at Kildoolin, alone. Nevertheless, he would pay a visit there, in case there was something left in the old cottage that would provide him with a clue.

The priest checked the burial records, but found no mention of Kitty McCarthy.

'But that does not mean she did not die,' he said, with compassion in his eyes. 'You have been in America a long time. Perhaps you're not after knowing how bad things were, at the height of the famine. So many died, so many poor souls, and not all of them had a proper funeral, God rest their souls.'

'I know,' Michael said. 'I was here then. My own brothers and sisters were all lost, and were buried here. Not all had coffins.' A sudden thought struck him. 'I would like a headstone for them, even though I cannot be certain exactly where they are in the graveyard.'

The priest nodded. 'There are so many who died in those dark days that have no one remaining to remember them at all. It is good that you are left to remember your family. I can check the records to see where your brothers and sisters were buried, and I am sure we can make space for your memorial. I'll send the stonemason to see you at O'Sullivan's.'

'Thank you.' Michael spent a few moments in church, praying to a god he was no longer sure he believed in, a god who'd allowed so much suffering and death to occur in just a few short years. He should go to Kildoolin next, but, first, he was in need of some refreshment. A pint of Guinness, for the first time in eleven years, the first one since the pint Kitty had bought him on the day she gave him the ticket.

CHAPTER 23

Maria

Tentatively, I placed a trembling hand on the bundle, on what I thought in the gloom might be Sammy's shoulder, and I gently shook it. As I did so, the sun finally rose above the horizon and filled the ruined cottage with a golden light. A ray of sunshine now shone across the boy's face, and I saw with immense relief that he was breathing, he had colour in his cheeks and he was merely sleeping.

'Sammy? Come on now, wake up. I need to take you back to your mummy.' I spoke gently, quietly, to wake him but not frighten him. I was worried too about the state of the broken wall he lay beneath. It was listing badly inwards and I knew that outside the stream was undercutting it severely.

'Mmm?' he said, lifting his head and looking at me with sleepy eyes. How he could have slept, in the cold and wet, lying on a pile of rubble I had no idea. But he obviously had slept, and deeply.

'Come on, sweetie,' I said. 'We need to get you out of here. Are you hurt?'

'Nnh-hn.' He shook his head, and gazed at me with confusion in his eyes. I wondered if he recognised me at all.

'Let's get out of this cottage, hey? The sun's just coming up over the hill. Want to see?'

He nodded, and lifted his arms to me. I found myself gathering him up instinctively, my hands under his arms to lift him. He wrapped his legs around my waist and his arms around my neck. He was heavy, but perfectly manageable like this, and I carried him outside, breathing a sigh of relief when we were out of the danger of that cracked and leaning wall.

The next door cottage was the one with a low, broken wall – the one where I'd seen Declan sit and where I too had sat yesterday, as I'd pondered Jackie's email. I placed Sammy down upon it. Despite his night out he didn't seem cold, or upset in any way. He was warmly dressed in joggers, a fleece and a waterproof coat and I supposed the remains of the cottage had offered him some shelter.

'I need to make a phone call now, Sammy, and let your mummy and daddy know I've found you, OK?'

He nodded, and I pulled out my phone. I didn't have Sharon or Dave's number so I called Aoife at the pub. She had the list of contact numbers that Paulie had compiled yesterday.

'I've found him,' I said, as soon as she picked up. 'Little Sammy. He's all right. I'm up at the abandoned village with him. We'll start walking down, but can you contact his parents and maybe Dave can come up and meet us.'

'Oh praise the Lord, that is fantastic news, so it is! The Gardaí have just arrived to start organising the search party. I'll tell them now.'

I listened as she announced the news, and heard whoops and cheers. Obviously the whole town had gathered at the pub already to start the search.

'They said to stay where you are – they'll pick up Dave and Sharon and come up to you. Oh, Maria, well done for finding him!'

I hung up, and went to sit on the wall beside Sammy. I wished I'd brought some water and something for him to eat.

'Your mummy and daddy will be here soon. They will be so pleased to see you again. What happened?'

He shrugged. 'We were walking in the fog, and Nathan said it was cloud come down to earth, and I said it wasn't, and he ran ahead to ask Daddy if it was cloud or wasn't, and I sat down to wait, but he didn't come back and then I couldn't see anyone.'

'Must have been very frightening?'

He shrugged again. 'Nope. Was all right. I walked and walked through the heather and it was very scratchy and I fell over twice but I didn't cry and then I found the little house and it wasn't so rainy in there.'

'Good idea to take shelter. Were you cold in the night?'

'No. The lady put her arms round me to keep me warm.'

'What lady?' I noticed he was fiddling with something he'd pulled out of his pocket.

'The lady what give me this.' He held up the item in front of my face.

'Can I see?' He nodded and I took it from him. A blackened piece of twisted metal, a couple of inches across. I turned it over and realised it was a brooch, its pin broken off. It was in the shape of a Celtic knot. 'Where did you get this?'

'The lady give it to me,' he said, again. 'The lady what cuddled me in the night. I don't want it, so you can keep it.'

'Thank you.' I felt a shiver as a scene from last night's dream came to me – the red-haired woman telling me she would not let another child die, tending to the sick girl, holding the child-me in her arms. And that brooch – where had I seen something like that before? So many questions, so much to think about, but now was not the time.

'Do you want a cuddle now?' I asked him.

He regarded me silently for a moment, then nodded. I held my arms open and he climbed onto my lap, snuggling his head against my chest. His thumb sneaked into his mouth. I realised I had never held a child like this before. I'd held a couple of my friends' babies, but never an older child. I couldn't remember Jackie ever cuddling me like this. And yet it felt so right, just as in my dream being held by the red-haired woman had felt: a connection. His warm little body gaining comfort from mine as we waited for his parents to arrive. I realised he was not the only one being comforted. I could feel his little heart beating against my chest, and his free hand was absently stroking my fleece jumper. I bent my head until my chin rested on his hair and I could breathe in his scent – earthy from his night outside. So this is what motherhood might feel like. It wasn't at all bad.

I realised then that while I was descended from Jackie I had the choice not to be like her, but to be like my more distant ancestor Kitty – the kind of mother who would do anything for her child. And that was what I would be.

Jackie had experienced such loss. I felt a pang of pity for her. I had the choice too, to try to forge a new relationship between us. An adult one, of forgiveness and understanding, and perhaps in time, friendship and love.

Sammy and I sat there in silence, cuddling, each thinking our own thoughts. I had the brooch in my hand still, and I turned it over and over, pondering. Presumably he had found it in the ruins of the cottage. Where had I seen it before? I was tired, from the early start and lack of sleep, not to mention lack of breakfast, and my brain was not thinking straight. It was just an old brooch, lost long ago. Sammy's talk of the kind lady who'd kept him warm – well, he'd been dreaming, of course. Or hallucinating. Who knew.

The sun was well above the horizon now. The sky was blue and clear, in total contrast to yesterday. We were beginning to feel some warmth from the sun, and Sammy shuffled in my arms as if he was too hot. So was I, but I did not want to let go of him to take off my fleece.

Something changed about the way Sammy was snuggled into me, and when I shifted a little I realised he was asleep. There was something very special about knowing this little person trusted me enough to fall asleep in my arms. I felt honoured. I raised my face to the rising sun, took in the view that I would never tire of, across the purple moors to the sliver of distant ocean, and felt myself to be blessed. I had a sudden, strange feeling that someone was standing behind me, her hand on my shoulder, smiling down at the sleeping child in my arms. Someone who cared for me. Kitty? Or Jackie?

'Sammy! Maria!' The shouts woke Sammy and roused me from my musings. I looked around and saw Sharon and Dave running ahead of the police towards me.

'Mummy and Daddy are here,' I whispered in his ear, and the spell was broken. He clambered off me and ran towards his parents. I watched as he stumbled across the rough track towards them. Sharon scooped him up and buried her face in his neck, and Dave wrapped his arms around the two of them. The two Gardaí who'd accompanied them stood grinning awkwardly at the reunion. I stood up, feeling a bit stiff as Sammy's weight had sent my left leg to sleep, and hobbled over to them.

'Good work, miss. We'll need a full statement when we get back to town. We've a car waiting at the bottom of the track. Where did you find him?'

I pointed at the remains of the cottage in which Sammy had been curled up. One of the policemen frowned and went over for a closer look. 'That wall looks dangerous, so it does. Could fall at any moment, the way the stream has undercut it. We'll need to get it made safe before some tourist gets hurt.' He came back over to join the other Guard and me. 'Praise the Lord that the wall didn't fall on that young man while he sheltered there last night.'

I shivered. Yes, it could all have been an awful lot worse.

'Well, thank you, miss, and we'll catch up with you back in town. You're staying at O'Sullivan's, I think?'

'I am.'

'Fine pint of Guinness they do there. Grand place to take your statement, it'll be.'

I smiled, and began the walk back down the hill. I didn't get far before Sharon caught up with me. Sammy was now in his father's arms.

She flung her arms around me and squeezed me tight. 'Maria, I can't thank you enough. How did you find him?'

'I don't know. I woke early this morning, before it was light, and just had a feeling it'd be worth coming up to check the village.' I didn't think it worth mentioning my strange dream. She'd think I was going mad. In my pocket, I closed my fingers around the ancient brooch Sammy had found. There was definitely something familiar about it.

At the bottom of the track, we climbed into the two police cars that were waiting there, for the short journey back to Ballymor. O'Sullivan's once again seemed to be the centre of operations and I wondered if the Gardaí even had a police station in the town at all. There was quite a crowd awaiting us – all people who'd come to join the search party this morning. They cheered as we walked in. Aoife was doing a roaring trade in teas and coffees. As soon as Sharon, Dave, Sammy and I entered, she waved us to a table near the window and brought out full Irish breakfasts for each of us. Nathan and Kaz were already there; Kaz hugged her little brother tightly and Nathan ruffled his hair, grinning. I was pleased to see Sammy tuck in to his breakfast and wolf down his sausages, fried potato, bacon and egg, liberally covered with tomato ketchup. He needed that after his night out in the wild. He pushed his black pudding off onto his father's plate. Too spicy for a little one, I guessed.

I found it hard to eat as people kept coming and slapping me on the back, congratulating me for finding the child. I hadn't done much, I told them. The search party would undoubtedly have gone to the abandoned village today and found him. But I admit I enjoyed the attention.

When Sammy had finished eating, Dave began asking him questions – how had he found the cottage; had he been scared in the night; had he been cold. The little boy was tired and overwhelmed but answered as best he could.

'The lady kept me warm,' he said. 'And I wasn't scared when she was there.'

Dave smiled at me. 'Once again, thank you so much,' he said.

I was about to say something, to get Sammy to explain about the other lady he'd mentioned, when I heard my name shouted from across the busy bar.

'Maria, the hero of the hour!' Declan arrived, leaned over and gave me a kiss on the cheek. 'Well done, you.'

I blushed, and put down my cutlery. I'd more or less finished the breakfast and Declan was someone I needed to talk to. 'Do you have a minute?'

'Sure,' he said, and led the way to a snug at the back of the pub, which was a little quieter than the main bar.

He sat down on a stool, I sat opposite, and blurted out: 'Do you believe in ghosts, Declan?'

His eyes widened and he leaned away from me a little. 'Well, sure I believe in the *Holy* Ghost, of course, but I'm after guessing that's not what you're referring to?'

I told him then of my dream, and how I had the distinct impression Kitty had come to me to tell me where to look for the child.

'And Sammy says that he was kept warm by a lady who cuddled him all night. He said she gave him this.' I reached into my pocket and pulled out the Celtic knot brooch. Suddenly I remembered where I had seen it before. 'Declan, some of the Kitty portraits show her wearing a brooch just like this to pin her shawl in place.'

'Maria, it's a lovely thing to believe that our ancestors are able to speak to us in our dreams and help us out, but . . .'

'I know. You're going to say it can't be true. That Sammy must have found the brooch, and hallucinated or dreamed the lady cuddling him. And that I dreamed of Kitty only because I've been obsessing about her recently. We've no way of knowing if the cottage he was in was even hers.'

'Someone was certainly watching over Sammy during the night,' Declan said, quietly. 'I prefer to believe that it was our Father in heaven. But there is a lot we don't know about what happens to our souls after death. Whatever it was that made you have your dream and decide to check out the ruined village, we should give thanks for. Sometimes we must accept there is no earthly explanation.' He smiled.

I smiled too, but I wasn't sure I was ready to accept what he so obviously believed – that God had led me to the village and had protected Sammy. I wasn't sure either that I wanted to believe in Kitty's ghost. I'd always prided myself on being rational, scientific, down-to-earth. But my dream had definitely led me to Sammy; more than that, it had helped show me what a mother's love felt like. And cuddling Sammy had taught me I was capable of giving that love, too. I glanced down again at the brooch I still held in my hand, and gave it a rub with a tissue. It looked like it could be made of copper. Could it really be the same one Michael McCarthy had painted on all those portraits of Kitty?

CHAPTER 24

Michael

No one in O'Sullivan's knew what had become of Kitty. Michael was encouraged a little that no one confirmed her death, but many of the men drinking at the bar either had not heard of Kitty McCarthy, being new to the town in the years since the famine, or if they were men Michael recognised they knew nothing of what had become of her. No one remembered seeing her on the road-building scheme after Michael had left. They assumed she must have gone away, perhaps to Cork to the workhouse, or to some other town in search of food or work, or perhaps – they shook their heads sadly – perhaps she had perished alone, away from home, and been buried in a nameless grave. There was sympathy in the men's eyes as they spoke to him. They had all lost someone, or even their entire families, during the Great Hunger.

'What became of Thomas Waterman's agent, William Smith?' Michael asked them. He'd written to Smith, a year after arriving in New York, enquiring after Kitty, but had received no reply.

'Smith? Died, back in '49, or maybe '50, so he did. Famine fever, it was.' The man who answered Michael, a man named Riley who Michael vaguely recognised, grimaced and shook his head. 'No loss to the town, he wasn't. 'Twas him raising the rents when we were starving, lining his own pockets, so he was. I shouldn't speak ill of the dead but there were no tears shed when Smith died. Waterman paid for his funeral – he's in the churchyard yonder, with a stone engraved and all. No mass grave for him, like so many ended up in, like my own poor Eileen and three of my little ones.'

'I'm sorry,' Michael said. So many people had stories like Riley's – losing loved ones and children, and not even being able to bury them decently. And his own family – his siblings were all buried together in the churchyard, but with nothing at all to mark the spot. There'd been a wooden cross eleven years ago, he remembered, but it must have rotted away over the years. That was something he would need to sort out, while he was here. They deserved to be remembered properly.

'Waterman's still up at the big house,' the man continued. 'You might ask him if he knows anything of your mother.'

'Waterman?' For a moment Michael could not contemplate calling at Ballymor House. Surely the servants there would not even open the door to the likes of him. And then he remembered that he was a rich man now, a gentleman, and the equal of Thomas Waterman.

'He'll see you, so he will,' Riley said. 'Done a lot for the town since the Hunger – employing people, rebuilding, making sure that it can't happen again, not here.'

Michael raised his eyebrows. He'd barely ever seen Waterman – just once or twice as a distant figure on a horse surveying his lands. He'd never spoken to him. He dimly remembered sketching him once. But he remembered how Kitty spoke of the landowner, saying he was evil, the devil incarnate, a man who abused his position of power and authority and who did not care about the ordinary people at all. 'Really? That's not the man I remember. When I was here he seemed to be turning a blind eye to our suffering.'

'Aye, he did to begin with, 'tis true. Kept away at the big house or over in England. But, in the last year or two of the Hunger, he seemed to take pity and began to use his money and position to do some good. I don't know if up till then he'd been ignoring what was going on or was just ignorant as sin. Either way, I'd say he'll do what he can to help you now.'

'Thank you. I'll go and see him,' Michael said, passing Riley a few coins to pay for his next drink. It couldn't hurt, and he was intrigued now, to meet this man his mother had despised but whom the townsfolk seemed now to like and respect.

*

The following day Michael awoke to a day that was grey and wet, with low clouds and a faint drizzle that clung to your face but did not penetrate clothing. He considered borrowing a horse from the stables at O'Sullivan's, but it would feel wrong to approach Kildoolin on horseback. And Ballymor House was in the same direction as Kildoolin – it would not be worth riding there and then returning back to town with the horse before going to the village. No, he would walk everywhere, as he had always done in his youth. It was a shame the weather was not better – he had hoped to see the view across the moors with the distant glimmer of the sea from outside the old cottage, the view he remembered so well. But Irish countryside was beautiful in any weather. In New York, the weather was predictable with bitterly cold winters and scorching hot summers. Not so in Ireland, where summer days could be chilly and winter days balmy. Today looked like a grand, soft day. He would walk and the exercise would be good for him, especially after the weeks cooped up on-board the *Victory*.

After breakfasting on black pudding, rashers and eggs – a meal the like of which he had never before eaten in this town – he donned his hat and travelling cloak, and set off towards Ballymor House. He remembered the roads well, although plenty had changed since the old days. The National School was still there, where he had learned to read, write, and draw. The workhouse on the edge of town had closed down. It had been full to bursting when he'd left Ireland, but now the windows were boarded up. It was a grim place, made grimmer still by Michael's memories of passing the pitiful people outside its gates, clamouring to be allowed in to save themselves from starvation, only to die of disease instead. Today, a group of half a dozen children were playing in the street outside the old workhouse, running around laughing, involved in a game of tag. Michael stood watching them for a moment, smiling. It was good to see such energetic, healthy, well-fed children. They were Ireland's future, and may God forbid they ever have to suffer the way his brothers and sisters had.

There were numerous empty and decaying cottages on the way out of town, but also a few new buildings with sparkling whitewash and tiled roofs. Evidence of the horrors of the '40s was everywhere, but Michael could also see that lives were being rebuilt. Was Kitty out there, rebuilding her life, somewhere away from here? As soon as he had this thought he dismissed it. She would not have left the place where her children were buried.

Out of town, he turned right down the lane towards Ballymor House, although he longed to go on, and then left, up the track to Kildoolin. But better that he spoke to Thomas Waterman first and find out if the landowner had any news for him. He had never before been right up to the house; he'd only caught glimpses of it from a distance, when he was poaching ducks from the small lake in its grounds. He smiled wryly at the memory.

It seemed strange to be marching up to the front door of such a house, here in Ireland. But he was a gentleman now, a rich one, and the front door was where he would be expected to enter. He climbed the stone steps and tugged on the bell rope. It was answered by an elderly butler with an English accent.

'My name is Michael McCarthy,' Michael said, his throat feeling inexplicably dry. 'If Mr Waterman is at home, I would very much like an interview with him.' He realised that although he knew how moneyed society operated in New York, he had no idea of the niceties of social interaction here in Ireland, the land of his birth. He hoped he was not making a fool of himself. Should he have left a calling card first?

'Please enter, and I shall see if the master is at home,' the butler replied. Michael was shown into a large wood-panelled hall, hung with numerous oil paintings. As the butler disappeared along a corridor in search of his master, Michael perused the pictures with his artist's eye, interested to see what kind of paintings an English gentleman collected. They were mostly family portraits of past generations of Watermans, but, nestled among them, framed and behind glass, was a small pencil sketch of a man on a horse. Michael approached and peered closely at it, recognising his own work from so many years earlier. How on earth had that come to be in Waterman's possession and hung in this house? It made no sense.

He was still staring at it when a discreet cough made him spin around, expecting the return of the butler. But instead he found himself facing a silver-haired, well-dressed man of upright bearing.

'Michael McCarthy?' the man said, his voice tinged with an emotion Michael could not quite place. 'I am Thomas Waterman, at your service. Please, let's go through to the drawing room.'

Michael followed him through to an ornate but old-fashioned room, and took a seat beside the fire. His clothes steamed slightly as the day's drizzle dried from them.

Waterman sat opposite, staring at him. For a while he said nothing, and Michael fidgeted, wondering how to start the conversation he needed to have. Eventually, Waterman broke the silence, his words surprising and confusing Michael. 'I've waited so long to meet you. I didn't know you were back in Ireland or I would have sent an invitation.'

'Sir? Are you mistaking me for someone else perhaps?' Michael frowned. That was the only explanation he could think of for Waterman's words.

'No, I don't think so. You are Kitty McCarthy's son, are you not?'

'I am.' Here was a way in to the conversation. 'In fact, that is why I am here. She lived in one of your cottages in Kildoolin. I am newly returned from

America and am trying to find out what has become of her. I left Ireland, you see, during the famine in 1849, and have not heard from her since.'

'I know exactly when you left Ireland, dear boy,' Waterman said, that strange mix of emotions clouding his speech – a tinge of joy, Michael thought, mixed with disbelief and anguish.

Michael frowned. How could he know, why would it have been of interest to him? It dawned on him that perhaps Waterman remembered when James O'Dowell left, and was somehow aware another local person had been on the same boat. 'Sir, do you have any news of my mother?'

Waterman shook his head. 'After you left, I instructed Smith not to demand any further rents from your mother. Smith died of the cholera not long afterwards anyway. I did not go up to Kildoolin for many years – your mother had made it clear she did not want to see me, or accept any help from me. There is no one left in Kildoolin now.'

'Forgive me, sir. I am confused. Did you speak to my mother, then?'

'I gave her food, and offered her a job with board and lodging. She turned me down. She was too proud to accept.' Waterman shook his head, sadly, then turned away from Michael to put more wood on the fire.

'You offered her a job?' Michael dimly remembered the food Kitty had brought home one night, just before he'd left. She'd said it had been given to her by James O'Dowell. He'd known then that was a lie, but had been too hungry to question her further about it.

'Yes. I knew she would be alone and starving after you left. I would have bought her passage to America too, if she'd asked, but she would only accept money for one ticket, for you.'

Michael stood and shook his head. 'No. My mother sold a piece of jewellery, a brooch shaped like a Celtic knot, to buy my ticket.'

Waterman smiled indulgently. 'She showed me the brooch. It was worthless.'

Michael stared at the older man, his mind working overtime. The brooch was worthless? How then had she come by the money?

'I first met your mother when she was just fifteen,' Waterman went on, a wistful look in his eye. 'She was a beauty back then, a real beauty. She was still beautiful, even when she was so painfully thin at the height of the famine.'

Michael felt a cold chill grip him from the inside. What was Waterman implying?

'Michael, son, look in the mirror. You can't believe you were Patrick McCarthy's son, surely? You so dark, where he was fair, and your mother flame haired?'

'No! She wouldn't!'

'Why do you think I paid for your ticket? Because you were my son, my only son, and I owed it to you to give you a chance!'

'No! She sold the brooch. She told me that. She never lied. Never!' Though she *had* lied to him, he'd known that even then, about the basket of food. Michael paced around the room. It wasn't true. Kitty had hated this man. She couldn't have lain with him. Not willingly . . . A terrible thought came to him. Perhaps she hadn't been willing. It would explain her hatred of Waterman.

'She sold me something. But not the brooch. She sold me something else,' Waterman said, quietly.

Michael stared at him and shuddered with revulsion. 'What do you mean?'

'Didn't your mother ever tell you? Didn't she say I'd offered to do all I could to help you, that you should turn to me if ever you needed assistance? Do you need that now? I can set you up with an allowance perhaps. You can live here, or, if you prefer your own space, I shall build a house for you in the grounds . . .' Waterman crossed the room towards Michael and reached out a hand to pat his shoulder.

Michael flinched as though burned by Waterman's touch. 'I am a rich and successful man now, Mr Waterman. I do not need your charity. I will of course repay you the cost of my ticket to New York. But I must ask once again, do you have any idea what became of my mother?'

'You don't need to repay me, son. And I am sorry, I have no news of Kitty. She told me to keep away from her and so I did. I expected her to call again and take up my offer of a job, whenever she felt desperate enough, but she never did. There was nothing more I could do.' He gazed out of the window, not meeting Michael's eyes. 'Have you checked with the priest? Perhaps there are records . . .'

'I have, and there are no records of her death or burial. But that means nothing, the way things were during those terrible years. I cannot believe she is gone though.'

'I am truly sorry. I wish you luck in your quest to find her. If you do, send her my . . . my regards.' Waterman hung his head for a moment, then looked up at Michael with sad, watery eyes before continuing. 'If there is anything I can do for you . . . you are my only son, my heir . . . I have no other . . . I will leave everything to you, if only you will acknowledge me as your father . . .'

Michael had moved towards the door to show himself out, but turned back at these last words. Waterman looked suddenly aged and diminished. Gone was the proud man who'd sat on his horse, surveying his lands and the peasants working for him. In his place was this broken, lonely man, the last of his line, with no one to share his life, no wife and no children.

'I need no assistance. And I have no desire to be your heir. I shall leave you in peace.' Michael opened the drawing room door. 'And sir, Patrick McCarthy was most certainly my father. The best father any man could have had.' With that, he strode across the hallway and let himself out through the front door without a backward glance. It was time to go up to Kildoolin.

He pondered what he had heard as he walked back to the road from Ballymor, along it a short way, and then turned left up the track to the village. It couldn't be true. Kitty had sold her brooch to raise the money, as she'd said. And Thomas Waterman could not be his father. He'd always known he'd been born before his parents married but that wasn't so uncommon. Kitty had always said Patrick was the only man for her, and that she'd known it from the moment they first met at the Ballymor fair. She must have been only fifteen when they met, and Patrick had swept her off her feet and got her pregnant, but was only able to marry her a few years later when he'd saved enough money to keep a wife and child. That was the story Michael had always believed, the story he would go on believing. That sad, broken man back there, for whom money had not bought happiness and whom his mother had hated, was nothing to him. Nothing.

Why then had Waterman been so excited to meet him, and was prepared to name him his heir? And why had he framed and hung a juvenile sketch by Michael in his hallway? He shook his head sharply as if to banish the thoughts from his mind. Waterman's years on his own must have addled his brain and given him fancies. He was deluded; there was no other explanation. Kitty would have said he'd been touched by the faeries.

The mist was closing in as he climbed the hill to the village. The track was clearly rarely used these days but was still obvious enough, although heather and gorse were encroaching from both sides. He'd thought he could remember every twist and turn, every new vista at each slight rise, but the mist made it all look different, otherworldly, unfamiliar. It was unnerving – approaching the place where he had grown up but finding it hidden from view by the swirling white fog – right until the moment when he crested the last hill, and the end cottage loomed out of the mist. He let out the breath he hadn't realised he was holding, and carried on along the row to Kitty's cottage.

It was all so different from his memory. Even though the village had been almost completely abandoned when he'd left, the cottages were still whole, in good enough condition that people could have moved straight back into them. Not now, though. Over a decade of neglect meant roofs had collapsed, saplings grew in doorways, shutters and doors were rotten and hanging off their hinges, birds nested in the remains of the thatch, sheep had sheltered in some, leaving their dung behind.

Kildoolin would never be inhabited again, that much was obvious.

At last he came to a halt outside the cottage he thought had been theirs. It was hard to be sure, with the entire row so dilapidated, but a quick count from the end of the row confirmed it, and the stream still crossed through the village beside it.

He stood outside for a moment, gazing at its frontage. It was smaller than he remembered, and in a worse state than many in the row. Kitty must have stopped living here many years before. The roof had partially fallen in, and the left end wall – where the chimney had been – had completely collapsed, leaving just a pile of stones. He entered the cottage, picking his way over the rubble that littered the floor. There was the old table – or what was left of it – two legs had rotted leaving it resembling a horse brought to its knees. The potato loft had collapsed – the area where Michael had slept now only a pile of rotting wood and more rubble. A blackened and dented cooking pot lay amongst the ruin of the chimney. He picked it up and gazed at it. How many meals had he eaten, cooked in this pot? How many potatoes had been boiled in it over the years? Something caught Michael's eye where he had lifted the pot, and he crouched in the gloom to investigate. Some rotting fabric, and another blackened piece of metal – this one small, to fit in the palm of his hand, shaped unmistakably like a Celtic knot. The brooch. The brooch she said she had sold, to buy his passage. Here, still, in her cottage.

So she had lied about that after all.

What had she sold to buy the ticket? Waterman's words came back to him. *She sold me something else.* No.

Whatever had happened between them in the past, she would not have lowered herself just to buy him his chance in life. He owed her so much, but surely, she would not have gone to such lengths for him? Would she?

The idea of his mother with Waterman made bile rise in his throat. He flung the brooch down into the pile of rubble and stumbled out of the cottage into the swirling mist, back down the track to Ballymor. Let the faeries have Kildoolin. There was nothing there for him.

CHAPTER 25

Maria

I gave a full statement to the police later in the morning after I'd found Sammy. He'd been taken by his parents back to their caravan for a good sleep. The Gardaí were convinced that Sammy was referring to me when he talked about a lady who'd kept him warm overnight with her cuddles, and they frowned when I said I'd found him just as it was getting light.

'I suppose the child is confused about the time,' said one, whose name badge read 'O'Connell', and the other – McAteer – nodded.

'Sure, that must be it. Poor little lad. It must all be running together in his mind.'

There didn't seem to be any reason to press the point or tell them about my dream. Sammy was safe and well, and that was all that really mattered.

Guard O'Connell was checking his notes. 'We need to get something done about that unsafe wall. Little boy had a lucky escape. Hey, Paulie, over here!' He waved Paulie over. The old man heaved himself off his bar stool – the first time I'd seen him leave it since the day I arrived when he went to fetch Aoife – and shuffled across the pub floor to join them. 'You free this afternoon? We've got a job for you and that tractor yoke of yours.'

They'd finished with me, so I went upstairs for a nap and to phone Dan. I felt a sudden need to talk to him and tell him all that had happened. God, if only he was here now – I knew I'd want to go straight to bed and sleep safely wrapped in his comforting arms for the rest of the day.

But the call went straight to voicemail. I checked my watch – it was midday, and he'd be at work, but he never switched his phone off. Even in meetings he'd just set it to vibrate. Very odd. I felt annoyed with him for not being there for me when I needed to talk. Maybe he'd pick up my message when he had his lunch, and would ring me back then. Perhaps his phone was playing up again.

I made myself a cup of tea and lay down on the bed for a nap, but sleep would not come. My mind was buzzing with all that had happened – reliving the moment I'd come across Sammy in the cottage when I'd thought for a heart-stopping moment that he might be dead, remembering the delicious feeling of him sleeping in my arms. My hand instinctively went to my bump, which seemed to have grown since yesterday. One day, that bump would be a young child like Sammy. It was hard to imagine, but was beginning to feel more real.

After an hour I gave up on sleep and went back down to the bar. It had emptied out. The Gardaí were gone, and Paulie was not on his usual bar stool.

'Hi, Maria. Did you sleep? Can I get you any lunch?' Aoife was busy loading the glass washer.

'No, I'm not hungry after that enormous breakfast earlier, thanks.'

'Ah, OK then. Shout if you need anything. I've my work cut out to clear up now. Paulie's gone off with the Guards to see about that dangerous wall. 'Tis a fine day, not like yesterday. Sharon and Dave should have waited till today for their walk, so they should.'

'Irish weather's so unpredictable. I suppose they thought it might clear up – I know that's what I thought when I set off yesterday.' I looked out of the window. Aoife was right – the promise of a good day that the dawn had held had come to pass. Might as well make the most of it. I decided to go back up to the village and see what Paulie was doing to that cottage.

I went back up to my room to put on my well-used boots and pack a few things in a rucksack – water, a fleece, some chocolate and my mac, because you never knew with Irish weather. It was when I was on my way out of the pub that a taxi pulled up and, to my enormous surprise, a tense-looking Dan climbed out of the back seat and stood peering up at the O'Sullivan's pub sign.

'Dan! What are you doing here?' I felt a surge of emotion run through me – love mixed with relief. I'd been through a lot in the last twenty-four hours and now here he was, my love, my protector. I no longer needed to face things by myself.

He visibly relaxed on seeing me. 'Looking for you. I've obviously found the right place then?'

'Yes, this is where I've been staying. It's lovely to see you, but I'm confused – why have you come? What's happened?'

He stepped forward and folded me into a welcome embrace. It felt as though I was home at last. 'It's me who needs to be asking what's happened,' he said. 'You sounded so distraught last night – all that stuff about a missing child, and your mother's email. I was worried. So I booked myself onto the first possible flight to Cork this morning. And here I am, gasping for a coffee.'

'Come in, Aoife will make you one,' I said, pulling him back towards the door. 'Where's your luggage?'

He pulled a toothbrush and toothpaste from one jacket pocket, and a pair of clean socks from the other. 'I travel light.'

'You certainly do.' I just stood and gazed at him, grinning, for a moment. It was so good to see him.

'You're not really showing yet, are you? How many weeks is it now?' I realised he was looking at my midriff.

'About sixteen. There's a bit of a bump. You'll see, later.'

He pulled me towards him again, in a huge hug. 'I've really missed you. We've got a lot to talk about.'

We went back inside, I introduced him to Aoife, and she hurried off at once to make him coffee and rustle up a sandwich. Dan had not eaten anything other than a banana since leaving home at five thirty.

'So,' he said, 'what's happened about that child?'

I loved that his first thoughts were for Sammy. I smiled. 'He was found, safe and well, early this morning. He's with his family, back in their caravan now.'

Aoife arrived with the coffee. 'You forgot to mention, Ms McCarthy, that it was you who found him. She's a real hero, so she is.' She grinned at Dan. 'You should be very proud of her.'

'Wow! I *am* proud of her. Come on, Maria, tell me the full story.'

While he ate, I told him everything that had happened since I'd phoned him last night, including my dream and little Sammy's insistence that a lady had been with him all night. 'You'll think I'm mad, but what if it was a ghost? The ghost of Kitty McCarthy, perhaps?'

He reached across the table and took my hand. 'You're right, I think you're a little mad. Wonderful, but mad. I expect he dreamed it. Sometimes children make things up, and even come to believe their stories themselves. Especially, I would think, in a situation like poor Sammy was in. What a horrible thing to happen to him. I'm so glad he's OK.' He squeezed my hand. 'And you. Thank goodness you're all right as well. You've been amazing.'

He stood up and came round to my side of the table, leaned over and wrapped his arms around me from behind. 'Imagine,' he whispered, 'if that was our child.'

I put a hand on my bump. 'Doesn't bear thinking about.'

'No.' He was silent for a moment, holding me, then straightened up and shook himself. 'You were off out somewhere when I arrived, weren't you?'

'Yes, I wanted to go back up to the ruined village. There's a very precarious-looking wall in the cottage where Sammy was found. They're going to bulldoze it. I . . . I don't know why, but I felt I should be there when it happens.'

'I'll go with you, if you still want to? I'd quite like to see the scene of your heroism. And we can talk on the way, about . . . the other stuff, your mum's email, how you are, all that.'

'My pregnancy you mean?'

'That's the one.'

I glanced at his shoes. Trainers – they'd be all right for the walk. 'Come on then, and we'll go.'

*

All this exercise, up and down the track to Kildoolin, could only be doing great things for the shape of my legs and my overall fitness. This afternoon's walk was the best yet – a perfect day with blue skies, sunshine and just enough of a breeze to keep me cool. And Dan's company. I realised how much I'd been missing him. We talked non-stop all the way up – well, to be honest, I talked and he listened. I needed to unburden. Declan had been a good friend and confidant, but there was nothing like being able to talk to someone you'd known for years, who knew you inside and out. Was it really only a few hours ago that I'd walked up here to search for little Sammy? So much had happened so quickly. I told Dan about the wave of fear I'd felt when I saw him sleeping in the cottage; the relief when he'd stirred at my touch; the feel of his warm little body in my arms as we waited for the Gardaí and his parents to arrive; Sharon's overwhelming relief when she enfolded her child in her arms after her night of agony.

Dan asked me all about the pregnancy – had I been sick? Could I feel it move yet? What was the due date? – so many questions!

'Boy or girl?' he said, as we stopped for a breather part-way up the track, and sat on a flat-topped rock.

'What? I've no idea. How should I know?'

'I wondered if you had any . . . I don't know . . . "boy" feelings, or "girl" feelings. Or prophetic dreams, other than the one that led to Sammy, of course.'

'No, I haven't.' If the truth were told, I'd spend so much effort trying to put the whole pregnancy out of my mind I hadn't considered whether it would be a girl or a boy. Till now it had been just an unspecific foetus in my mind. A collection of cells, not a person. I tried to think about it now. 'A girl would be nice. But then, Sammy's so sweet, and I wouldn't mind one like him . . .'

'Mmm. I'd like a boy. Or a girl. Either, really. What do you think of the name Charlie, if it's a boy? Or Andrew, after your dad.'

'Hmm. Maybe. Perhaps Grace if it's a girl.' One of the names from the McCarthy gravestone, I realised.

'That's nice.' Dan stood up and held out a hand to pull me upright. 'Shall we get going again?'

We walked in silence for a while. I could not believe I'd been happily discussing baby names, after so long trying to deny that I was pregnant. It all seemed so much easier to deal with now that Dan knew and was with me.

'I should have told you I was pregnant long before. I should have told you as soon as I knew myself. I'm so sorry, Dan.'

He stopped and folded me into his arms. 'It's all right. I know now.' We kissed, long and deep, and I knew that everything was all right between us. More than all right. Being in Ireland had proved to me that Dan was my future. And Kitty had shown me I could be a mother, a good and loving one.

We'd noticed the new tractor-tyre marks on the track leading up the hill, and could hear the noise of the work at the village long before we reached it. The sound of the tractor's engine, shouts, some laughter. Finally, we came over the little rise just before the village and could see what was going on.

'What a view!' exclaimed Dan, as he looked across the moors to the sea, just as I'd done on my first visit. But my attention was on the activity in the ruined village.

There were perhaps a half-dozen men, including the two Guards and Paulie sitting in the cab of his tractor. It had a kind of bulldozer bucket attachment on the front, and the Guards – O'Connell and McAteer – were directing Paulie to the precariously leaning wall beside the stream. As we watched he skilfully positioned the tractor on the other side of the stream and brought the tipped-over bucket attachment gradually down onto the wall, its leading edge tucked around the top of the broken wall. He eased it backwards, then drove the tractor back a little so that the wall was pulled down over the stream. There was a huge crash as the wall fell and the remainder of the cottage's roof also fell in. A cloud of dust rose up, and when it settled all that remained of the building were two walls and a pile of rubble.

The men cheered. I felt strangely bereft. That cottage had sheltered Sammy and before that had once been someone's home. Families would have lived there. The father digging his potato patch, tending to animals, the mother cooking potatoes in her pot while children played at her feet. Generations, perhaps, had been born and brought up here, in a life that was always hard but became impossible when the famine struck. They'd died or emigrated, but as Declan had explained to me the cottages were left standing in case someone ever came back to claim them. And although this particular one had been in ruins before, it was now beyond repair. I watched as Paulie knocked a few more parts of the wall down and levelled the piles of stones a little to ensure they were safe, until Guard O'Connell waved at him to stop. Paulie drove his tractor back onto the main track and switched off the engine, although he stayed sitting in the cab, taciturn as ever.

Guard O'Connell was touring the remaining walls, checking they were stable. As he picked his way over the pile of rubble, he suddenly stopped and crouched down, then waved to Guard McAteer to join him.

I ran over too, with Dan at my heels. 'What is it? What's happened?' Guard O'Connell was crouched near the spot where I'd found Sammy. He pointed into the rubble.

'Look, see? What's that look like to you, Pat?'

McAteer hunkered down and peered, then began shifting some of the stones. O'Connell joined in, while I stood in what had been the doorway of the cottage, watching.

'An animal, you reckon?' O'Connell said to McAteer.

The other guard shook his head. 'Sure and that's no animal. Look – there.' He shifted a few more stones then stood up, holding something. Dan caught hold of me and pulled me back, into his arms.

Guard McAteer was holding up a human skull.

CHAPTER 26

Kitty, 1849

It was four weeks since the *Columbus* had left the docks of Cork city. As Kitty made her weary way down the rutted track towards the town, and the day's hard labour ahead of her at the road-building site, she wondered whether Michael would have reached New York yet. What was it like there? Had he found food and shelter, a job, friends? As she'd done so many times over the last few weeks she lifted her eyes to gaze at the sliver of silver that lay across the moors, and stared as though if she looked hard enough she might catch a glimpse of the ship. It would be many more weeks until a letter from Michael reached her, she knew, if indeed it ever would. She realised that if the worst happened and Michael did not survive the crossing, or perished soon after landing in America, she might never hear from him, and would never know what had happened.

She turned onto the road and began the trudge through the town towards the worksite. As the road building progressed, the worksite moved further away from Ballymor and her walk became longer and longer each day. Her back and arms were sore from breaking rocks, her hands calloused and raw from wielding the lump-hammer, and her belly ached with the ever-present hunger. For the thousandth time she considered whether she should swallow her pride and go to Thomas Waterman, take up that housemaid's job he'd offered. Sweeping floors and blacking grates in a warm house with no food shortages would be so much easier than her current life.

But to accept help for herself from a man who'd raped her? No. She could never do that.

One day, about a fortnight after Michael had left, she had arrived home to discover a basket of food set upon the doorstep. Bread, cheese, potatoes, beetroots, some slices of cold beef wrapped in paper and a jar of pickled onions. There was no note with it, but the basket was similar to the one she had carried back from Ballymor Hall on the day Waterman had given her money for Michael's fare. It was from him, she knew, but, at the same time, she was starving with no food in the cottage and a few days yet before she could next expect to be paid. She told herself the basket could have come from anyone, the food would go to waste if she didn't eat it, and she feasted on its contents. It lasted until she was paid, and thus her death from starvation was put off for a while longer. For she was certain that was how it would end for her. She would collapse by the roadside one day, crawl into a ditch and sleep for ever. She had seen plenty of others do just that, their skeletal bodies lying uncovered for hours, sometimes days, before being removed and buried in a mass grave.

Sometimes she thought she should just stay at home, with a turf fire banked high, her blankets wrapped around her, and sleep the days away until she woke no more, and be reunited with Patrick and her babies. But the thought of a letter from Michael, telling her his news, reporting on his life across the ocean, would make her shake off these morbid, defeatist thoughts and she would rouse herself, eat what she could find and go to work.

Today the work wasn't so bad. It was raining heavily and, although that made it uncomfortable for her and the other labourers, it kept the overseer away. She was able to rest frequently, wield her hammer with less force, and generally conserve what little strength she had. She kept her mind occupied with dreams of Michael in his new life and the day passed relatively quickly, although the rain continued all day.

At last it was time to down tools and make her weary way home. She pulled her sodden shawl tighter around her shoulders and, head lowered, feet dragging, she forced herself to walk the five miles back to Kildoolin. There was some cornmeal awaiting her for dinner that she'd bought with her last wage. She did not allow herself to fantasise that another basket might have been delivered, although she had left the empty one outside the cottage door, in case someone came to collect it and drop off another . . .

The track up to the village was in a worse state than ever, rutted and muddy with a stream running down the middle of it. Kitty's feet were already soaked through so she just trudged through it all, careful to keep her balance in the gusting wind on the worst sections. The stream that flowed through the village had become a raging torrent since the morning. Kitty noticed it had split a little way uphill, with one new stream diverted directly towards her cottage, rushing down alongside her cottage wall before crossing the track and heading on down the hill. She had to wade across this to reach her door.

Inside, she pushed the door shut against the strengthening wind, stripped off her wet clothes and wrapped herself in a blanket, then set to work building a turf fire to warm herself up. She boiled water and cooked the cornmeal, washing it down with water, flavoured with a few mint leaves she'd gathered earlier in the week. There was nothing for her to eat in the morning.

She was so cold from being wet through all day. She gathered all the shawls and blankets she had and made a nest for herself on the floor beside the fire. Lying there, staring up at the chimney breast, she noticed an alarmingly wide crack in the stonework. The new part of the stream was just the other side of this wall, she realised. Was it washing away the foundations of the cottage? Well, there was nothing she could do about it, not now, at any rate. She supposed there was nothing to stop her moving into one of the other cottages in the village, now that they were all empty and Smith was no longer coming by each month demanding rent. Waterman had kept his word about that. She resolved to have a look at the other cottages in the morning, and perhaps move her few belongings into one. Her own, that she had lived in since marrying Patrick all those years ago, no longer seemed safe with that gaping crack in the stonework.

She lay before the fire, wrapped in her blankets, and stared into the flames, examining her feelings about leaving this cottage. Not long ago she'd have hated the idea. Her children were born here – all but Michael – she'd had happy days here when Patrick was still alive, before the Hunger. She'd never thought she would leave, even to move into another cottage in the village. But now – now she couldn't bring herself to care where she lived. The children were dead, Patrick was dead, Michael was gone across the ocean. She was only staying in the village out of habit and because she knew of nowhere else. But she might as well move into a more secure building. Tomorrow. She would do it tomorrow. For now, she needed to sleep, and rest her aching legs and back. Her aching belly she would just have to ignore. Thank goodness she had turf, and blankets, and was beginning to warm up while the storm raged outside. She was comfortable, at least. She would be all right. God would protect her and Mother Mary would watch over her as she slept.

*

It was in the darkest part of the night, when the fire was reduced to a few glowing embers, and when Kitty was in a deep, dreamless sleep, that the diverted stream undercut the cottage wall so much that it dislodged a stone in the base of the fireplace wall. The crack, already six inches wide, gaped wider still as stones in the wall shifted downwards to fill the gap left by the missing one. The wind, which had grown to gale force as the night wore on, gusted suddenly, its full might hitting the weakened wall. With a groan and a creak, the chimney breast fell inwards, into the cottage, and the rest of the end wall of the cottage followed it. Kitty, mercifully, was hit on the head by one of the first stones to fall, her skull smashed and her dreamless sleep switched instantly into black oblivion. The rest of the stones fell on her body, till there was almost nothing of her visible. A casual observer might have spotted a corner of blanket emerging from under a particularly large stone, and if they'd knelt down in the dirt and looked closely, perhaps moving one or two of the smaller stones, they would have spotted part of her left hip and, further along, perhaps some of her auburn hair.

But the village was empty. No one passed this way. Smith no longer came for rent, and Kitty had made it clear to Waterman that he was not welcome. The basket of food had been his last attempt at showing her what she was missing by not accepting his job offer. When she didn't follow it up by calling at the Hall to say thank you, he decided not to bother again. She'd come to him when she was starving, he was sure. He remembered her parting words to him: that he could do more for the people of Ballymor. He thought too about his groom's skeletal, starving parents. But he thought most of his son Michael, who might also have starved to death, before Waterman was even aware of his existence. Kitty may not want his help but others were grateful for it. His eyes had been opened, and he did what he could to ease the suffering of the local people. It was what Michael would want him to do. By the time he did take his next ride up to Kildoolin some months later, and discovered her cottage in ruins, the word around town was that she had left the area, gone to Cork perhaps, to try to raise money there to join her son in America. Waterman, wanting to stay within reach of her as his only means of hearing news of his son, went to Cork to search, but found no sign of her. She'd gone to Dublin perhaps, some folk said, or over the water to Liverpool, from where far more ships sailed for America. Waterman had sighed, and returned to his estate, hoping against hope that one day Michael would return to Ireland and seek out his true father.

CHAPTER 27

Maria

Funerals are held quickly in Ireland. Aoife had told me it was not uncommon for someone to be buried the day after they died. Even with ancient bones, such as those found in the ruined cottage, there was no waiting around. With the help of Paulie's tractor, carefully pushing away the larger stones and with the manpower of as many volunteers as could be found (including Dan, although he insisted I should not lift any heavy stones myself), the bones were gradually recovered over the rest of the afternoon. There was a complete skeleton, which had been buried when the chimney breast fell, long, long ago.

I'd thought that the police would want to date the remains, to investigate whether they belonged to any known missing person perhaps. But Guard O'Connell told me they would most certainly belong to someone who'd died at the time of the famine. Many people had died in their own cottages back then, and in the case of isolated cottages may not have been found for weeks, months or even years. It was apparently not the first time that famine-victim bones had been found in recent years. If the chimney breast had fallen on the body not long after death then it was easily possible that they would never have been noticed. Never, that is, until Paulie's work with his tractor dislodged some of the stones covering the remains.

'All we can say for certain is the bones are very old,' O'Connell said. 'These stones were covered in moss and had not moved for at least a century – we've old photos from the early 1900s showing that this cottage by the stream was partially collapsed even then. So the Gardaí have no interest in these remains. All we need to do is give them a decent Christian burial.'

Declan was called up to Kildoolin to supervise the removal of the bones, which were reverentially placed into a cardboard coffin, and carried down to Ballymor by four men, followed by Declan, Dan and me, and the other volunteers. The mood of everyone was quiet and subdued. This poor person must have suffered so much, and he or she had had to wait a hundred and seventy years to be decently and respectfully buried.

When the little procession reached town, the coffin was taken into the church and placed in a side chapel. Everyone followed, and Declan led the people in a few impromptu prayers. Tears sprung to my eyes as I watched the townspeople, all standing with their heads bowed, paying their last respects to someone they'd never known, who'd died so long ago. Dan squeezed my hand tightly throughout and I was glad of his company, and the strength he lent me. Declan announced that the remains would be buried the next day, in the same area of the churchyard as other famine victims. All would be welcome to attend.

At last we went back to O'Sullivan's. It had been quite a day, and I was exhausted. We spent the evening sitting quietly in my room – now *our* room – and I took the opportunity to read a little more of Michael McCarthy's biography, the book Declan had lent me.

Dan had brought his Kindle, and seemed happy to sit and read as well. I realised he too had had a very long day, starting with his early morning dash to the airport. Any other in-depth talks could wait until the next day.

But part-way through the biography I came across a passage that made me sit up and grab hold of Dan's arm. 'Listen to this!' I read a couple of paragraphs out loud to him.

There was an occasion in the 1880s when Michael McCarthy visited Ballymor, and your author was able to meet with him and talk about his early life. One fine spring day I persuaded him to walk with me up to the abandoned village of Kildoolin, where he had spent his earliest years. All its inhabitants had died, moved out or emigrated around the time of the Great Famine, and the cottages – originally built to house workers for the Watermans' copper mines – left to rot.

There is not much to see in the village now – just a row of tumbledown cottages such as can be seen anywhere in the west of Ireland. However, revisiting them seemed to move Mr McCarthy, and he talked at length about his pre-Famine memories of his mother, father and siblings. Their cottage, he recalled, was the one immediately downhill of where a stream crosses the track in front of the row. This one was in a particularly poor state of repair, with the chimney breast and part of the roof caved in, a mound of rubble where once the fireplace had been.

'Downhill of the stream? Is that the one where . . .' Dan began, his eyes wide.

'Where the bones were found. Yes! That's it! And the description of it matches the state of the cottage when I found little Sammy there, before Paulie got at it. So those bones . . .'

'Could belong to Michael's mother!' Dan was as excited by the idea as I was. 'You've found her, at last!'

'Bloody hell. I think I have! Got to tell Declan.' I opened the door to rush downstairs. Aoife would have his number.

'Why?'

'I think Kitty should be buried with her children,' I replied, and Dan nodded solemnly.

Thankfully, I wasn't too late. Declan confirmed the gravedigger had not begun – he was due to dig the grave in the morning, and, yes, he could dig beside the existing McCarthy memorial. Declan was as intrigued by it all as Dan and I were.

'It is always good to be able to lay someone to rest after all these years, but to be able to put her with her family under a named stone is even better,' he said. 'She will truly be able to rest in peace.'

*

There was a huge turnout the following afternoon for Kitty's laying to rest. She was, as Declan promised, put in the same plot as her family, with Michael's memorial stone at her head. Only Michael McCarthy was buried elsewhere – in Highgate Cemetery in London. Declan read some prayers and performed the funeral rites, as the cardboard coffin was lowered into the grave. I admit to shedding a tear or two, as I stood beside Dan, watching. We would never know exactly how she had died, but at last the mystery was solved and she was reunited with her family.

Sharon and Dave were at the church too, along with Kaz, Nathan and Sammy. They stood beside us, and I quickly introduced Dan to them. Sammy slipped his little hand into mine, to my delight and surprise. There was something rather lovely about the feel of a warm, trusting little hand in mine, and I felt honoured.

'Was that the lady who kept me warm?' Sammy asked me in a whisper, as the coffin was lowered.

'You know, I think it might be,' I whispered back.

*

It was Tuesday, and our last night in Ireland. Dan had booked himself onto the same flight home as me, from Dublin, although he'd flown into Cork. We were due to drive to Dublin in my hire car and fly home the next day. There was, of course, only one way to spend the evening and that was in the bar of O'Sullivan's, Dan drinking Guinness, me on sparkling elderflower, with Paulie in his usual place at the bar and a live band due to play later on. It was Sharon, Dave and their family's last night as well, as they were moving to a different campsite on the Dingle peninsula for the remainder of their fortnight, so they'd come for their dinner and to say goodbye to the community. Declan was in the pub too.

Sharon gave me a massive hug when the family got up to leave. 'We must stay in touch. Here—' she pulled out a piece of paper from her pocket '—my email and mobile number. At the very least you must let me know if it's a boy or a girl.'

'Of course I will,' I replied, scribbling my own contact details onto a napkin for her.

'I'm going to want to read your book as well, when it's published.'

I grinned. 'I've got a lot of work to do on that first!' Actually, I was beginning to wonder whether I would be able to finish it before the baby came. Well, I'd give it a shot, and I could always come back to it later, baby allowing.

'Staying for the band?' Dave said.

'Yes, I think we will,' I replied, and at that moment I felt it. A wriggle, a shuffle, a rolling over, inside my tummy. I put a hand on my bump and stood still, focusing inwardly, willing it to happen again.

Sharon put her hand on my arm. 'Did you just feel the baby move?'

I nodded, too stunned by this new sensation to speak.

She smiled. 'First time?'

'Yes.'

'I thought so. I recognised that look of wonder on your face. It's a truly magical feeling, isn't it?' She spoke quietly, so only I could hear, excluding Dave and the kids who were waiting for her nearby. I felt as though I was being welcomed into the motherhood club. There it was again, a fluttering, a fidgeting, someone making him or herself comfortable within my womb. I smiled. 'I guess this is something only us women can ever experience.'

'Yes. It's amazing. When I first felt Sammy move it was like I truly understood what it meant to be pregnant for the first time. That there was another life growing inside me, completely dependent on me, but my clever old body was able to provide everything needed to make a whole person, a separate individual, someone that could wriggle around inside me whenever he felt like it.'

'It's incredible, when you put it like that.' She was right. I realised it was only now that I truly understood it all. This wasn't just a collection of cells, a bump, a bit of fat. It was a brand-new human being, made by me and Dan. Someone who would have his or her own personality, their own likes and dislikes, their own opinions, their own life.

'And—' she grinned '—you wait till your baby gets hiccups.'

'Hiccups? In the womb?'

'Oh yes. Usually right when you're trying to get to sleep.' She rolled her eyes, and the two of us dissolved into giggles.

'What are you laughing at, Mummy?' Sammy asked.

'You, with hiccups,' Sharon told him.

'I haven't got hiccups.'

'You did have, about six years ago.'

He frowned. 'But I'm only five.'

And that set us off again, but this time Sharon scooped him up onto her hip and held him tight as she laughed.

So this was motherhood. I had a sudden, certain feeling that I was going to like being part of this club.

We hugged again, and the family left. I looked around for Dan, and spotted him sitting with Declan, deep in conversation. They were talking seriously, occasionally shaking their heads or laughing a little. I wondered what they were discussing. I imagined it might have something to do with our future, Dan's impending fatherhood, our marriage. Declan would be passing on words of comfort and wisdom to help Dan cope with the big changes ahead of us. I inched closer so I could earwig a little. Couldn't quite catch everything they were saying but I definitely heard the words 'Munster', 'European Championships' and 'Thomond Park' and realised they were merely talking about rugby. I rolled my eyes. Typical men.

'Maria!' Declan got up when he noticed me standing there. 'Your man's a rugby fan. I hadn't realised.'

'Rugby! There was me thinking you were talking about something important. Like advising him on how to be the best possible dad!'

'Ah now, Maria, the thing is, you're both good people. And that means you'll make good parents. No one has to be the best possible – everyone just needs to be good enough. Sure and it's a scary prospect to have a little one's wellbeing to think of, to put first for so many years, but you'll manage. Take each day as it comes. If you do everything for your child with love in your heart, you won't go far wrong.'

There it was – the wonderful Declan wisdom. I could manage that. I could do everything for my child with love in my heart. Kitty had shown me how. I had love already in my heart for this tiny, wriggly bundle. And if that's all I needed, I'd be fine as a mum. More than fine. I'd be a *good* mum. I smiled. 'Thanks, Declan.'

'No problem. Come on now, sit down with us. I'll get us all another drink. J2O is it, for you?'

'Thanks.'

He raised an eyebrow in Dan's direction, who nodded agreement to another pint, and went to the bar. I sat down next to Dan.

'Nice bloke, that priest.'

'Yes, he is.'

'He's a Munster supporter. But they won't have a chance against Quins this season.'

'Probably not.'

'Are you OK, Maria?' Dan gazed at me, worried by my short answers.

I smiled, remembering the feel of the baby's kick. 'Yes, Dan. I'm perfectly OK. More than OK. Everything's going to be just great.'

He grinned, and leaned over to kiss me. We broke apart only when Declan returned with the drinks, coughing discreetly to warn us he was back.

Declan stayed till the pub closed, unusually for him. By the time the national anthem was played, he and Dan were best mates, planning on meeting up at the Thomond Park rugby stadium in Limerick the next time Munster played Harlequins there. We swapped email addresses, and promised to keep in touch.

As he left the pub, Declan gave me a hug. '*Slán*, Maria. Goodbye. And remember what I said. You're a good person and I know you'll be a good mother. And, thinking of that email you had from your own mother, maybe that's her olive branch. Give her a chance, promise me?'

'I will. Thanks for everything. You've helped me so much.'

'Ah, I think it was the little fellow Sammy who helped you most, Maria.'

Yes, him and Kitty, my own great-great-great-grandmother, reaching out to me across the centuries, showing me how to do this motherhood thing, the most important job I'd ever have.

CHAPTER 28

Michael

The first thing Michael did when he got back to O'Sullivan's, after the disappointing and inconclusive visit to Kildoolin, was to take his artist's materials out of his trunk. The light was not perfect in his small room at the pub, but it would do for his purposes. He took out a small canvas and his pencils, and made a quick sketch – of a woman with long, flowing hair, sitting on the doorstep of a pretty thatched cottage, looking out across heather-clad moors towards a sliver of distant silver sea. He rummaged in his trunk for paints, brushes, a palette, jars of turpentine, caring not about the mess he made as he tossed clothes and books aside in his haste to find what he needed. He painted fast and furiously, filling in a glorious blue sky, purple heather, a whitewashed cottage, a gown of deepest green and hair of fiery auburn. Last, he painted a brooch, a delicate Celtic knot in gold, pinned on the woman's breast.

It was not the first time he had painted Kitty. In New York he had imagined her boating on the lake in Central Park, reclining on a chaise longue in a fashionable Manhattan apartment, and strolling past the shops on Fifth Avenue carrying a lacy parasol. He had painted all these scenes, and used them as both examples of his work and as a reminder of her when he needed comfort. He'd included the brooch in all these pictures – the brooch, the lucky talisman, he'd thought, that had paid his passage to America. The worthless brooch that had lain for years amongst the rubble in the ruined cottage, and would remain there for ever.

Painting, as usual, helped to calm him, helped him make sense of his conflicting emotions and runaway thoughts. By the time he stopped painting he had accepted, more or less, that he would quite possibly never know what had become of his mother. But he would continue to search for her. There were workhouse and soup-kitchen records. Perhaps she had died nearer some other parish in the neighbourhood and been buried there – he would check records in them all. Perhaps she had gone to Cork in search of work.

He formulated a plan. He would settle in Ireland, at least for a while, but would move from town to town starting here in the south-west. He would solicit commissions from the gentry, and between paintings he would continue the search to discover what had happened to her. If she had died, he wanted to be able to pay his respects at her last resting place. He owed her that much at least.

But before he left Ballymor, he would commission a gravestone to commemorate his brothers and sisters. The only question he had, was whether he should include Kitty's name on it or not. He decided, in the end, to leave it off. It would feel too final adding her name, when he had not yet done all he could to search for her.

*

The next few weeks, then months, passed in a whirlwind of activity for Michael. He seemed to be always on the move – following up leads that might lead to portrait commissions, or that might lead to his finding Kitty. When the word got around that a wealthy man was looking for a relative, all sorts of people came forward claiming that they could tell him (for a small remuneration) of a woman living alone in a distant cottage; of a girl in a workhouse who'd lost her memory; of someone who'd gone to Dublin but had the flaming red hair Michael was looking for. He followed up all these – even the least hopeful-sounding ones. He checked records at every workhouse in Cork and Kerry, in every town where a soup kitchen had opened, in as many churches as he could reach. All was in vain – he could find no clue what had happened to her.

'Some of those who died while employed on the public works,' a council clerk in the town of Skibbereen told him, 'were left where they fell, in the ditches beside the road, covered with the very rocks they'd been helping to break.' He looked at Michael with an expression of deep sympathy. Michael remembered with sadness the man on the road-building scheme, who'd died in just this way, whom he and Kitty had covered with stones. 'Our records are incomplete,' the clerk went on. 'So many people were buried with haste in mass graves. If that was the fate of your mother then we shall never know.'

Eventually, with a heavy heart, Michael returned to Ballymor and had Kitty's name added to the family memorial stone. It felt like an act of finality – an acceptance that he would never know the truth about what happened to her. He could only hope that she had not suffered too much in her final days.

During all this time, he managed to find plenty of commissions and began to make a name for himself as a portrait artist amongst the Irish aristocracy. He took an apartment and studio in Dublin to use as a base when painting, and travelled around the country in search of Kitty from there. Every now and then, he found a vista so beautiful he felt the need to paint Kitty again, with the view as the background. Maybe she had never travelled beyond the county of Cork, but in his paintings she travelled throughout the country, experiencing the best that Ireland had to offer.

In time, a commission took him to London, and once there he found a massive new market for his work. He gave up the lease on the Dublin apartment, and took up one in London, overlooking Regent's Park. The neatly mown lawns, manicured shrubs and ornamental trees were a world away from Kildoolin's wild golden gorse and purple heather.

Some months after moving to London he found himself painting the portrait of the younger daughter of an aristocratic but relatively poor family. Her name was Clarissa Byatt, her hair was as black as his own, her skin was clear as moonlight, and her mouth smiled in a teasing way as he painted her. He was grateful that his occupation gave him an excuse to gaze upon her sweet face for hours on end, and by the time the portrait was complete he had both fallen in love and decided he should have a new wife. Enough time had passed since poor Eleanor's demise. He asked her father for her hand at the same time as delivering the completed portrait, making it clear he expected no dowry and easily had the funds required to keep a wife.

There was some discussion about whether Clarissa, as a member of the Church of England, should convert to Catholicism or whether Michael should convert to the C of E, but in the end they found an Anglican vicar who was happy to marry them whatever their denomination. Michael got the necessary dispensations from the Catholic bishop to marry a non-Catholic in a non-Catholic church, and they were wed in a quiet ceremony in St Margaret's church beside Westminster Abbey. Kitty would have approved of her new daughter-in-law, he thought, although she would have been overwhelmed by the grandeur of the church and its enormous neighbour, and perhaps disappointed that the wedding was not taking place in the parish church of Ballymor, where she had married Patrick McCarthy.

The marriage was a happy one, and in time produced five children, all of whom reached adulthood strong and healthy. As he watched his children grow and blossom, every now and again Michael would allow himself a few minutes to consider how much Kitty would have loved her grandchildren. She lived on, he supposed, in them, and especially in one – their third child and eldest daughter, who had a pale complexion and bright red hair, and who, at Michael's suggestion, they had named Kitty.

CHAPTER 29

Maria

We had a pleasant and easy drive across Ireland to Dublin, around the M50 and into the airport. It was good to have Dan's company on this return leg. We talked non-stop about the events of the last couple of days, going over everything from the moment I'd met the frantic Sharon in the mist to the burial of Kitty's remains. It helped to assimilate it all. I knew I'd be reliving the moment I'd come across little Sammy in the ruined cottage for the rest of my life. And, I suspected, reliving the moment he'd crawled onto my lap for a cuddle and fallen asleep in my arms. I think something had clicked inside me right then, something that had made me finally begin to understand and accept what motherhood would mean, and to appreciate the joys it could bring.

We were at the airport in good time, had a snack lunch and boarded the plane. I was sad to be leaving Ireland. 'I'll be back soon,' I whispered, as the plane took off, circled, and I had a final glimpse of the island known as Ireland's Eye as we flew over the Irish Sea.

'What's that you said?' Dan asked.

'Just hoping we'll come back to Ireland soon,' I replied. As I spoke, the baby kicked inside me, as though in agreement. 'Give me your hand,' I said to Dan, and I placed it on my tummy.

He stared at me, and twisted in his seat so he could hold his hand there more comfortably. The baby moved again. 'There. Did you feel that?'

He grinned. 'Amazing! Makes it all seem so real, doesn't it?'

'It certainly does.' I was touched to see there were tears in his eyes, as he held still, hoping to feel our child move again. I had never seen him cry before, but these were good tears, tears of wonder, joy and hope for our future.

'Maria, I was wondering,' he said, softly, 'whether you've given any more thought to that question I asked you, before you went away? You know . . .'

'Whether I want to marry you?' I said, smiling.

'That's the one.'

I didn't reply immediately, because at that moment the pilot made an announcement to say we'd now reached our cruising altitude of fourteen thousand feet on this short flight, the weather was good in London and we could expect to arrive at Heathrow on time. He advised passengers to sit back and enjoy the flight.

I waited till he'd finished, then turned towards Dan. 'Dan Widefield, of course I would be *delighted* to marry you.'

'Oh my God!' he exclaimed. 'Thank you! I feel like I'm on top of the world!'

'We are!' I laughed. 'Well, at fourteen thousand feet at least. Only half the height of Everest, but high enough.'

He leaned over and hugged me, kissing my face until I gently pushed him away as people were staring. This was our private moment. We were engaged, at last, and I had never felt more happy. As if in approval, the baby wriggled again and I once more grabbed Dan's hand so that he could share. 'It feels like we're a proper family now,' he said. 'I'm sorry I don't have the ring on me – I left in such a hurry.'

'I know. With only a toothbrush and socks. And you are wearing three-day old underpants.' That made us both chuckle, eliciting further odd looks from fellow passengers.

It was a joyful journey. I spent the last part of it reading the rest of the biography of Michael McCarthy. I was becoming rather fond of my ancestor, who'd unwittingly been instrumental in bringing Dan and me back together. My trip to Ireland was supposed to help me forget my fears of the future; but instead it had forced me to face up to them, and realise that the future was good. Different, yes, and full of challenges, but something to look forward to, together with Dan, always.

The moment we arrived back home Dan rushed to his bedside drawer and brought out the ring he'd chosen for me. I slipped it onto my finger where it fitted perfectly, and felt blissfully complete.

*

It was while I was still unpacking that afternoon, plugging my laptop back in its usual place in the dining room, that I remembered I had never replied to Jackie's email, with all its soul-searching revelations. I hadn't even thanked her for the sizable cheque she'd sent yet. 'She must think I'm ignoring her,' I said to Dan. 'But I am still not sure whether I should reply by email, phone, or go to see her.'

'I think a face-to-face meeting would be best,' Dan replied. 'She's opened her heart to you. This could be the beginning of a new chapter in your relationship.' He looked at me tenderly. 'Give her a chance, Maria,' he said, echoing Declan's parting words.

'I will,' I promised him, and as I continued unpacking I tried imagining phoning her, inviting her out for coffee and a cake somewhere quiet where I could thank her for the money and where we could discuss her past, and what it might mean for our future relationship. I also needed to talk about how I'd behaved when Dad died and she'd needed me. Our distance since I'd been an adult was at least partially my fault. It would be a difficult meeting, but after her email it was up to me to make the next move.

I was just putting a pile of washing into the machine when the doorbell rang. Dan answered it, and I heard him usher someone into the sitting room. He came through to the kitchen where I was just switching on the washing machine. 'Maria, it's your mum. She's in the sitting room. Go on in to see her. I'll bring some tea and biscuits shortly.'

'Oh my God. Right. Thanks. Here we go, then.' For some reason I felt the need to pat my hair and smooth down my clothes. Ridiculous. This was my mother. I went through and found her perched at one end of the sofa, looking as nervous and uncomfortable as I felt. There was a small repetitive movement in her jaw, as though she was chewing the inside of her mouth. She did not stand when I entered, so there was no awkward dance wondering whether to air-kiss her or not.

'Hi, Jackie,' I said, and sat at the other end of the sofa. There was a wall of cushions between us. 'Thanks so much for the cheque. That was very generous; we really appreciate it.'

She dismissed my words with a wave of her perfectly manicured hand. 'Don't mention it. It's what people do, as I understand it.'

There was an awkward silence for a moment. The elephant in the room shifted uncomfortably. I cleared my throat. 'Thanks too, for your email. I'm sorry I haven't replied yet but . . .'

She looked away, staring at a photo of Dan and me that stood on the mantelpiece. 'I imagine you weren't quite sure how to respond.'

'No, I . . .'

I was about to tell her about the dramas in Ireland, that had taken my time and energy, but she turned back to me and continued speaking. 'It's all right – I wasn't expecting you to reply immediately. I just felt you should know all that stuff about me, now that you're going to be a mum yourself. I see you're getting quite a little bump there now.' She nodded at my midriff, and I found myself instinctively putting a protective hand over my bump. 'Have you felt it move yet?'

I nodded. 'Just these last couple of days, yes.'

'That's a very special feeling. I'm glad it is going well. If ever you have a day when there is no movement, please, go and get checked out. Just in case.' She pressed her lips together and tipped her head slightly to one side. She was referring, I realised, to my stillborn brother, Jonathan. It was still so strange for me to consider I'd had a brother and, before him, a sister, who was presumably still out there somewhere.

'I will, Jackie, I promise. I'm sorry about, you know, your baby. The one that died. And the other one that you had to give up.' Without realising what I was doing I reached out a hand to her, and she mirrored the gesture. Briefly, we touched hands on the cushion that lay between us. She looked stunned, a multitude of emotions crossing her face – discomfort at the unaccustomed closeness, but also I thought I could see a hint of expectation.

'Maria, I don't want . . . I mean, there's no need for us to discuss all that I told you in the email and agonise over what might have been. It's all in the past, and I don't want to have to go over the details or think about it too much. It's too painful for me. But I felt you should know about it. In case you were thinking – I don't know – that you might have inherited my bad-mother genes. It's not my genes, it's my background. If things had been different, who knows, I might have been quite a good mother. Not the best, but better than I was.' She took a deep breath and gazed at me, and I saw it again in her eyes – an expression of cautious optimism about what the future might bring for us. 'I can't believe I'm going to be a grandmother. It's a strange feeling. There's going to be a new little person who's partly made from me – if I hadn't existed neither would he or she – yet the baby won't be my responsibility the way you were. There'll be a natural distance. It's . . . well . . . I suppose it's quite exciting, really.'

I smiled. 'Yes, it is exciting.'

'Pregnancy was never exciting for me. Just worrying, terrifying really. Well, I suppose history doesn't have to repeat itself. You're like me, but perhaps you don't have to be the same as me. You can be a good mum, better than I was. And I can have a go at being a grandmother. Can't promise I'll be any use, though.'

'Mum, you'll be just fine.' If you do it with love in your heart, I thought, but decided saying that might be a step too far.

She stared at me. 'You called me Mum.'

'Yes, I did, didn't I? It kind of . . . slipped out. Sorry.'

'I'll let you off, just this once.' She smiled again.

Dan came in then, with a mug of tea for each of us and a plate of biscuits. He sat down to join us after Jackie patted the chair next to her. As we drank our tea, we moved on to safer topics of discussion. I told her all about our adventures in Ireland – my book, my research into Michael McCarthy, rescuing little Sammy, discovering the bones, then finding out they probably belonged to Kitty McCarthy.

'She's your ancestor, is she?'

'Yes, the woman in the portrait, that Dad had and now I have.'

Jackie looked thoughtful. 'It must be nice knowing your ancestry. I never had a family.'

'You've got me. And Dan. And this little one.' I patted my bump. I took a deep breath. She'd offered an apology of sorts for her maternal shortcomings. It was my turn now to give some ground. 'Jackie, I'm sorry I was such a rubbish daughter after Dad died. I should have supported you more, instead of running away. I should have stayed and helped you through that horrible time.'

'You were only a child.' She took a tissue from her bag, and surreptitiously dabbed at her eyes while pretending to blow her nose.

'I was seventeen. Old enough. But I was too wrapped up in my own grief to realise that we could have used that as a way of starting again.'

She stared at me. 'Do you really think we could have?'

I nodded and took her hand again. 'Or we could try to start again now.'

'Now that there's a new generation just beginning, yes, it seems like a good time to try. For the baby's sake.' She smiled, a warm one, unlike any I'd seen on her face since Dad died. 'He'd have been so proud of you, you know, and thrilled at the idea of becoming a granddad.'

We sat in silence for a moment, remembering Dad. That was one thing at least we had in common – our love for him. That, and the new generation growing now in my womb, could be the starting point for our new, closer, more understanding relationship.

Jackie shook her head slightly, as if to bring herself back to the present. 'That little boy you rescued, was he all right in the end?'

'Yes, he seemed none the worse for a night out in the open.' I didn't go into the detail of how he'd insisted a lady had kept him warm. It was too hard to explain, and anyway Jackie wasn't the kind of person to believe in anything supernatural.

'Well, that's good then. Well done for finding him.' She looked down at her lap. 'I'm proud of you, Maria.'

'Thank you.' I looked at Dan, who grinned at me. He was right – Jackie's email did look as though it'd be the beginning of a new closeness between us. Suddenly it dawned on me that it was our baby that had begun it all. Without my pregnancy she would never have written that email. This tiny, part-formed life inside me was building a family around itself.

'We've other news for you too,' Dan said. 'I'll let Maria tell you.'

I held out my left hand to show her my ring. 'We're getting married. Not yet sure when, but you'll be the first to know when we've set a date.'

'Oh, that is very good news! And about time.' She coughed slightly. 'A child needs two parents, in case one of them turns out to be rubbish.'

I couldn't help myself. I leaned across the sofa and pulled her to me in a huge bear hug. I even kissed the side of her head – I could not remember ever kissing her before.

She tolerated it for a moment and then gently pushed me away, picked up her bag and stood to leave. 'I must be going now. Thanks for the tea. Keep well, Maria.'

I stood too, and followed her out to the front door. As she opened it, she stopped and turned. For a moment I thought she was going to do something totally out of character and kiss me goodbye, but then she spoke. 'I know it's a way off yet but when your child is born, and begins to talk, I think I'd like him or her to call me Nana. Not Granny or Grandma – those make me sound so old. And Jackie wouldn't be right. I rather like the sound of Nana.'

And, with that, she turned and left without another word. I was left with the broadest grin on my face. My mother, who'd never let me call her Mum, wanted to be called Nana by her grandchild! She was definitely softening, and all because of my unborn baby. I felt so proud of our child – so much already accomplished and yet still in the womb!

*

The next day – Thursday – the sun was shining yet the air was cool, a perfect day for a walk. I had a mission to accomplish, and felt the need to do it alone. Dan had one more day off but was happy enough to stay at home and cook our dinner, while I set off by train and bus for Highgate Cemetery. I'd visited Michael McCarthy's grave once before while working on my university thesis, so I had a vague idea whereabouts in the cemetery it was. I entered the East Cemetery through its gate, and wandered along the shady winding paths, past crumbling gravestones and tombs festooned with ivy and moss, each one commemorating a life hopefully well lived. It was a beautiful, evocative place and I had to stop myself from peering at every grave to see who was buried there and imagining their lives. I turned off the main path and headed up hill, towards the area where I knew Michael was buried. I recognised some graves from previous visits – one with an angel reclining full length on a tomb; another with ornate carvings of weeping angels; one with Grecian columns set around a huge family tomb.

Finally, after checking the names on several gravestones, I found Michael's. His was a relatively simple headstone, surmounted with a Celtic cross as a nod to the land of his birth. The inscription was straightforward, too:

Here lies Michael McCarthy, painter and portrait artist.
Born 1831, died 1897.
A devoted son, husband and father. Rest in peace.

I knelt before the grave, and traced my fingers over the words.

'I found her, Michael,' I whispered. 'She was right where you'd left her, when you went to America. In her cottage, by the hearth, waiting for you. Protecting children who needed help. Teaching her descendants about love and motherhood.'

I put my hand into my pocket, and pulled out the blackened Celtic knot brooch. I'd considered cleaning it up, keeping it and wearing it, but the metal was bent, the pin was lost and it was only copper after all. More fitting that it should be buried with Michael, who'd included it in so many of his paintings. It must have meant something to him, for every 'Kitty' painting featured it somewhere. I dug a small hole in the dry earth with my fingers, right beside the gravestone, and pushed the brooch deep down into it.

'So you can feel close to her,' I told him. 'She never stopped loving you – her firstborn child. And you, in your search for her, produced some beautiful pictures. I will try to tell your story, and its resolution, as best I can. You, and she, will never be forgotten. Rest in peace, now. She is found.'

As I stood up again, stretching my legs, the baby kicked in that now familiar feeling. I smiled. I understood it now. That special, super-strong bond between parent and child.

I was so looking forward to meeting our baby. The future was calling.

AUTHOR'S NOTE

The famine (an Gorta Mór or Great Hunger) in Ireland lasted from 1845 to 1850, and is one of the defining events of Irish history. As Declan explains in my novel, the great tragedy is that although the potato crops failed for several successive seasons, Ireland was producing enough food to feed its people, but that food was being exported, mostly to England. While some English landowners were aware of the starvation of their workers and did what they could to help, many were either not aware or didn't care. To absentee landlords, the plight of the Irish people was something distant that they did not want to be concerned with.

The UK government and local authorities did, eventually, step in to help. Corn was imported and distributed, public works schemes were started, poorhouses built and soup kitchens set up. But in far too many cases it was too little, too late.

It is estimated that a million people died during the famine either directly as a result of starvation, or due to disease, exacerbated by weakness from lack of food. As the starving people thronged closely together in the workhouses and soup kitchens, disease spread rapidly. In addition, a further one and a half million emigrated during this period, mostly to the United States or Canada. In the following years, Ireland's population reduced still further by emigration – in total it fell from approximately eight million before the famine to a low point of around three million in 1900. The population has never fully recovered.

In this novel I have taken a novelist's liberty with the geography, and moved the hills, moors and copper mines of the west Cork peninsulas to within a couple of hours' horse-and-cart journey of Cork city. Ballymor and Kildoolin are both fictional, although inspired by real places. Anyone who has visited Achill Island in County Mayo may have recognised the abandoned village of Slievemore in my descriptions of Kildoolin. And Ballymor is based on small towns such as Clonakilty and Skibbereen in County Cork.

For those wanting to learn more about the Irish famine, I can recommend a visit to the Skibbereen Heritage Centre, which is a hugely informative if rather haunting experience.

ACKNOWLEDGEMENTS

Huge thanks to my editor, Victoria Oundjian, for recognising the potential of this story and pushing me to get the best from it. I think this is my favourite to date, although it was possibly the most difficult to research. Thanks also to the eagle-eyed Sandra Silcox whose attention to detail allowed me to get the dates and timelines right, eventually.

Thanks are due also to my son Fionn McGurl, who was this book's first reader, and whose feedback on the first draft was, as always, very helpful and encouraging.

My husband is Irish, and it's through him that I've come to know Ireland, its people and its ways. I adore the country, especially those remote peninsulas of west Cork. Thanks to my Irish in-laws for helping me develop an ear for the speech patterns, and an understanding of the Irish ways of looking at the world. I hope I've got them right in this book.

While working on this novel I spent a fortnight touring Cork and Kerry, and was much inspired by the towns, countryside, museums and people there. The Heritage Centre at Skibbereen deserves a special mention for its informative displays about the famine. Also useful was the Cobh (formerly known as Queenstown) Heritage Centre.

And finally, thanks to my husband Ignatius who gave me a very informative if rather dry book about the Irish famine when he first heard about my idea for this novel. Thanks too, of course, for his continued support and patience while I spend all my time writing and little of it with him. It'll all be worth it in the end!

HQ
One Place. Many Stories

The home of bold, innovative
and empowering publishing.

Follow us online

 @HQStories

 @HQStories

HQStories

HQ Stories

HQMusic